"I thought you swore you'd never **come back,"** Jillian whispered, her eyes glittering with emotion.

"And a promise is a promise, Jeremy."

"And some promises," he countered in a husky rasp, "are made to be broken."

"Yeah, that's one thing everyone knows about you, so I guess I shouldn't be surprised." Then, as if there was nothing out of the ordinary going on, she turned to walk away.

Just. Like. That.

Oh, no. No bloody way. She was out of her everloving mind if she thought she was getting away that easily. Gripping her shoulder, Jeremy spun her around.

The anger was crashing through him now, faster than he could control it. Like a fault line ready to explode, his anger had seethed beneath his easygoing surface. Every time he saw her—and couldn't touch her—it had grown.

"I'm going to say this once, Burns. Do. Not. Touch. Me."

Not touch her? Not likely.

Books by Rhyannon Byrd

Silhouette Nocturne

Last Wolf Standing #35
Last Wolf Hunting #38

*Bloodrunners

RHYANNON BYRD

fell in love with a Brit whose accent was just too sexy to resist. Lucky for her, he turned out to be a keeper, so she married him and they now have two precocious children, who constantly keep her on her toes. Living in the Southwest, Rhyannon spends her days creating provocative romances with her favorite kinds of heroes—intense alpha males who cherish their women. When not writing, she loves to travel, lose herself in books and watch as much football as humanly possible with her loud, fun-loving family.

For information on Rhyannon's books and the latest news, you can visit her Web site at www.rhyannonbyrd.com.

LAST WOLF HUNTING

RHYANNON BYRD

Silhouette Books

n●cturne™

SILHOUETTE BOOKS

ISBN-13: 978-0-373-61785-2
ISBN-10:   0-373-61785-2

LAST WOLF HUNTING

Copyright © 2008 by Tabitha Bird

www.silhouettenocturne.com

Printed in U.S.A.

Dear Reader,

The world of the Bloodrunners is a complex blend of fate and free will, of passion and prejudice…of beauty and betrayal. A world that finds the half human, half werewolf Runners separated from their Lycan birth-pack because their bloodlines are considered less than "pure."

In *Last Wolf Hunting,* the second installment of the trilogy, two people who are drawn together by destiny within this unjust society find themselves torn apart by circumstance. The gorgeous, irreverent Bloodrunner Jeremy Burns, and the pack's Spirit Walker, Jillian Murphy, have spent ten long years feeling as if a part of them was missing. And though their hearts are battered and bitter, they still crave that which they've lost. Until, after a decade of separation, fate brings them together once again….

Jeremy and Jillian's story is a provocative, emotional tale of second chances—of a perfect moment, once thought forever lost, finally recaptured. I hope their journey will touch your heart, and that you'll pull for them along the way.

All the best!

Rhyannon

To my mother-in-law, Chris,
for your endless support and treasured friendship.
With much love,
Rhyannon

THE BLOODRUNNERS LAW

When offspring are born of a union between human and Lycan, the resulting creations may only gain acceptance within their rightful pack by the act of Bloodrunning: the hunting and extermination of rogue Lycans who have taken a desire for human flesh. Thus they prove not only their strength, but their willingness to kill for those they will swear to protect to the death.

The League of Elders will predetermine the Bloodrunner's required number of kills.

Once said number of kills are efficiently accomplished, only then may the Bloodrunner assume a place among their kin, complete with full rights and privileges.

Chapter 1

A bitter mountain breeze wrapped around his long frame, whipping his shaggy hair against the furrowed ridges of his brow as Jeremy Burns hiked through the Maryland forest. Like a wrathful banshee, the relentless autumn winds howled with fury, while his fellow Bloodrunner, Cian Hennessey, quietly kept pace at his side.

They'd been working their way through the woods for a good fifteen minutes now, each step taking Jeremy closer to the last place on earth that he wanted to be. His muscles were hard with tension, biceps bulging against the seams of his shirt, his skin fever-hot despite the chill of the air. Blood pumped through his veins in a powerful, heavy rhythm, his heart hammering like a drum, senses honed to a razor's edge, sharp and precise.

And it was all because of a girl. All because of a woman. That was the relentless, infuriating thought burning its way through his tired mind as he hiked, the silvery moonlight glinting against the ravaged limbs of the trees, making them look like gnarled monsters in the shadowed darkness. But monsters didn't scare him. Hell, he *was* one of the monsters, complete with fangs and fur and a deadly appetite that could get him into trouble should he fail to exercise fierce control—which was why he always kept a white-knuckled grip on the animal side of his nature. For a Bloodrunner, losing control was never an option, but then neither was fear. And Jeremy had done a damn good job of mastering both—until it came to *her.*

He hated to admit it, but he was terrified by the growing knot of anticipation inside of him. The one that kept sniffing at the nighttime air, eager for a whiff of that lone, perfect fragrance that never failed to drive him out of his mind. Honeyed and womanly warm. Earthy and rich. It'd been woven into the very fabric of his soul, imprinted upon his senses like a tattoo needled into his skin. Just the thought of that mouthwatering scent made him hard and aching, not to mention irritable as hell.

"Do you think she'll be there?" he muttered in a gritty rasp, slanting a look toward the man at his side.

"Who?" Cian pulled a pack of cigarettes from his jacket pocket and flicked a sharp glance toward Jeremy, his pale gray eyes shadowed beneath the thick veil of his lashes. "The Murphy witch?"

"Who else?" he grunted impatiently. Jillian Murphy was the *only* woman on his mind—and the Irishman damn well knew it.

Taking a long drag from his now smoldering cigarette, Cian lifted his right brow in a cynical arch. "What? I'm psychic now, as well as irresistible?"

"Trust me, I have no problem resisting you," Jeremy quietly snarled, narrowing his eyes on the grinning bastard. Normally he enjoyed trading barbs with the Irishman, but not tonight. Tonight he was too tense, too bitter to have a sense of humor.

As if impervious to the thread of warning in his words, Cian barked a rich, husky laugh. "Aw, there it is. I knew your inner smart-ass was hiding in there somewhere, Burns. And to answer your question, yes, I think she'll be there. Why else do you think I decided to tag along?" His white teeth flashed in a taunting smile. "I'm here for moral support, you know."

"Moral support my ass. More like you're here so that you can run back to the Alley with some juicy gossip for the others." Jeremy knew his partner, Mason Dillinger, and the other Bloodrunners would be champing at the bit to hear the details of his first night back. "Face it, Hennessey. I'm on…to…you."

The soft words trailed off as the mountain winds suddenly surged from a new direction, swelling with power. Jeremy inhaled with a sharp, deep breath, and his head immediately shot back as if he'd been clipped under the chin.

Oh, god. There it was. Like a messenger in the night, the shivering breeze carried the fertile scents of the forest…and something more. Something lush and achingly familiar. Something that goddamn belonged to him.

With no choice but to follow the primal, ruthless dictates of his beast—*of his wolf*—Jeremy found himself staring up at the starry canopy of the bruise-colored sky. His feet were no longer moving, his entire being focused on taking in more of that decadent, head-spinning scent, so richly spiced that he could actually *taste* it.

That is so damn good, he thought with a low growl, wanting to roll the evocative flavor around on his tongue, savoring it like some strange, illicit pleasure. All it took was that instant flash of recognition, and the sweetly addictive scent melted into his skin, into his bones and blood and the violent, erratic pounding of his heart.

Jesus, he was so screwed. He had to be stronger than this, dammit.

Shaking his head to clear it, Jeremy silently cursed himself for being so easily seduced. He pushed his shaking hands back through the windblown strands of his hair, then shoved them deep in the pockets of his weathered jeans and forced himself to keep hiking.

It still amazed him that this was actually happening. That he was on his way back to the pack of werewolves who looked on his half-human heritage as a stain, an aberration—something that made him less than worthy. Because of his past, he knew it was a mistake to tempt fate by going back to the mountaintop town of Shadow Peak, the place the Silvercrest called home. But he didn't have a choice. He'd drawn the shortest straw among the Runners, making it his mission to catch the traitor who was tempting Lycans to turn rogue, to hunt innocent humans as prey, and teaching them how to dayshift. Rogues were dangerous enough bastards on the best of days, but show them how to take the shape of their beasts beneath the heat of the sun and they became that much more difficult to hunt down…not to mention kill. Jeremy figured he should know, considering his scars were still healing from his last run in with a group of them.

And now he could sense that Jillian was near. The woman who was meant to be his lifemate. The woman who was meant to make him complete.

As if, he silently snarled. Instead, this dark, seething need for her only made him feel hollow and raw, as if a part of him had been peeled away and amputated. He wanted so badly to ignore her existence, to forget, but it was impossible. And god only knew that he'd tried. For a long time, he'd mistakenly thought he could bury his memories and anger and bitterness in a warm, willing body. But no matter how eager or solicitous his bed partners were, he'd never been able to move past the fact that they weren't *the one* he truly wanted.

Pathetic. And now look at him, practically panting as he tried to breathe Jillian into his system like a drowning man gulping at air.

Maybe he'd have been able to handle it better if he'd had more time to prepare, but the chain of events that set this night in motion had come hard and fast. A mere seven days ago, Mason had defeated the rogue werewolf Anthony Simmons in a challenge to the death. The Bloodrunners had gathered that next evening at Mason's cabin and drawn straws to determine who would return to the pack to track down the traitor—the one who had been controlling Simmons. Like a bad joke, Jeremy's straw had been the shortest, and in a nightmarish daze, he'd found himself going before the Silvercrest's governing body, the League of Elders. He'd submitted his rogue kills, claiming his right to rejoin the pack as a full-fledged member, then served as best man at Mason's wedding. That had been two days ago—and here he was, on his way home. He'd barely had time to pack and settle things at his cabin, much less get his head in order.

Rubbing one hand against the back of his neck, Jeremy shuddered as a soft current of air suddenly slithered across his skin, leaving a spray of goose bumps in its wake. The cool eastern breeze snaked its way through the swaying trees, ruffling his hair as the wind caressed his face and arms with another eerie stroke of warning. *Go back*, it seemed to whisper within his ear. *Go back, while you still can.*

Pine needles crackled beneath his booted feet as he shook off the unsettling sensation and navigated his way through the last thick fringes of the forest. They were getting close. Up ahead, his keen eyesight allowed him to make out the hazy glow of the torch-lit clearing where the Silvercrest werewolves conducted business better suited to the wild than the civilized atmosphere of their secluded town, built on private land a few miles up the mountain.

A half minute later, the sounds from the clearing reached their ears. It was obviously a Challenge Night, just as Dylan Riggs, the youngest Silvercrest Elder and unlikely friend to the Runners, had informed them that afternoon.

"We're almost at the clearing," Cian muttered at his side, lighting another cigarette by pressing the end to the glowing orange tip of the first. "I'm not ashamed to say that I always hated this place when I was younger. It gives me the creeps."

"Yeah, I know what you mean." Jeremy lifted his head and sniffed the air. It was thick and heavy with tension, all but cloying against his skin. Tonight's fight must be an unusual one, he thought with a wondering frown. Male agitation rose sharply on the wind, but with the women it was sizzling and swift, like a burning fuse.

It was imperative that he stay alert and concentrate, but Jillian's scent grew more intense the higher they hiked, revealing her explosive emotions at the same time it messed with his head. She was scared tonight, on edge, filled with an overwhelming sense of dread, but Jeremy knew she'd be putting on a brave face for the pack she considered hers, though she was witch, not wolf.

The women of her bloodline had served the Silvercrest werewolves for centuries, gifting them with their powers. When her mother, Constance, stepped down from her place as Spirit Walker, Jillian had assumed the vital role of healer and spiritual leader of the pack. He knew they loved her, respected her and looked up to her, though she was still a young woman of twenty-eight. And why shouldn't they? She'd given her entire life to them. Hell, she'd even turned her back on him for the sake of her precious pack of werewolves.

"That sounds like one hell of a fight," Cian murmured.

He grunted in agreement, his sense of foreboding growing stronger, edgier.

Low grumblings from the onlookers now provided a steady background of sound, layered beneath the harsh breaths of the opponents as they battled against one another, the occasional howl belted out by the crowd scraping across the calming sounds of the forest like sharp blasts of a weapon.

"Give up, bitch," a woman's guttural voice sneered, "and I just might let you die easy, instead of ripping you apart, piece by piece."

Jeremy's eyes went wide at the realization that the opponents were female. It wasn't unheard of for one woman to challenge another, but then it wasn't exactly common, either.

"What a delightful-sounding shrew," Cian snickered, his lips twisting into a wry smile as he pretended to shudder. "Reminds me why I've vowed to remain eternally single."

A high-pitched cry rent the air in the next instant, echoing through the forest, and that same voice snarled, "Oh, yeah, you're mine now."

He bit back a curse, thinking that voice sounded suspiciously familiar. "It's Danna Gibson," he stated flatly.

Cian sent him a comical look of disbelief, then chuckled softly under his breath. "Christ, your luck just can't get any worse."

Jeremy had to agree. This night was going to be awkward enough without running in to one of his old girlfriends, especially Danna. Not that he and the Lycan had ever had anything serious. He'd dated her a handful of times when he was younger, before Jillian had come home from school and he'd felt the call of a lifemate for the little witch. After that, Jillian had been the only woman he was interested in. But his reputation as a young man who enjoyed his sexual variety had been hard to shake. The girls he'd had flings with in the past, like Danna, had been jealous of his sudden, possessive interest in Jillian, and her parents had simply hated his guts. Rumors about his so-called continued sexual conquests had kept the gossipmongers busy, but he'd tried to ignore them, focusing all his attention on getting the shy Jillian to give him a chance.

Instead, it'd all blown up in his face, and in the end, it'd been Danna who Jillian had accused him of fooling around with the same day he and the little witch had shared their first and *only* kiss. The same day Jillian had told him she was finally ready to give a relationship between them a chance, after having fought what was between them for months.

Months that had felt like goddamn years, Jeremy had wanted her so badly.

After he'd left the pack, he'd heard that Danna had gone on to marry a small-brained, chauvinistic jerk, and been miserable ever since. Tonight wasn't the first time she'd challenged another female—and if her husband's track record was anything to go by, it wouldn't be the last. Magnus Gibson was like a dog in heat, slobbering after anything with a pulse.

Jeremy shook his head in disgust. If it was a true match based on love, the males of his kind were never tempted to stray from the loyalty pledged to their wives…but when couples were married without belonging to one another both in heart and soul, well, the rules of nature changed. Sad, but all too true.

"I wonder what the hell's going on up there." He cut Cian a questioning look from the corner of his eye, but the Irishman lifted one shoulder in a hell-if-I-know gesture, his attention warily focused on the warm glow of light up ahead.

"Whatever it is, I've got a bad feeling about it," the Runner grunted, a deep crease seated between his ebony brows.

"Yeah. Me, too."

When a new voice, soft and smoky and lilting, rang out through the night, Jeremy nearly tripped over the gnarled root of a sprawling oak tree. "For the last time, Danna, I did *not* touch your mate."

Oh, hell. The voice behind those words knocked the air from his lungs like a vicious kick to the chest. Jeremy slammed to a jarring stop, while senses already sharpened to precision revved into overdrive. His mind didn't want to accept it, but his body knew the truth.

It was her.

Jillian.

He was close enough to scent the damning details now, everything narrowing into a concentrated focus that had him pulling in angry gulps of air, greedy for every drop he could take in. The sensory intake was shocking and almost painful in its intensity, the heat of her lush little body, all hot and angry from battle, nearly doubling him over, while panic suddenly had him exploding into action.

He shoved a low-hanging branch out of his way, wondering what the hell she'd gotten herself into this time. Even though Jillian had the blood of a wolf flowing through her veins, the fact she was witch made it impossible for her to shape-shift. Danna was twice Jillian's size and as vicious as a pit bull, not to mention underhanded—no doubt the Lycan was cheating like hell.

And what in god's name was Jillian doing fighting one of her own wolves?

Vaguely aware of Cian at his side, Jeremy's booted feet moved faster with the speed of his thoughts, until he finally broke through the last yards of the forest at a full run, erupting onto the edge of the clearing in a blur of movement. Then he nearly staggered to his knees, his legs all but crumpling beneath him as he took in the scene playing out before him like some kind of macabre nightmare.

Jillian Murphy stood in the center of the Challenge Circle—beautiful, brave and bleeding.

And she was about to die.

Chapter 2

Jillian glanced his way for a startled second, before jerking her attention back to Danna. Jeremy realized that although shock had dried up his ability for speech—leaving a gaping hole of cold, jarring disbelief in its place—he'd made a sound. A dry, choking kind of noise, like a wounded animal. It didn't matter that she was covered in dirt and sweat, her temple bloodied and her left cheek scraped raw. She was perfect and sexy and a part of him. Hate. Hurt. Pain. In that moment, none of the injustices of the past mattered.

My mate, he thought with a possessive snarl, realizing that he was growling low in his throat, drawing curious stares from the members of the pack who had gathered to watch. "Did you know about this?" he growled, cutting an accusing look at Cian. "Did you know Jillian was fighting?"

The Irishman arched one dark brow. "Do you think I'd have been late getting to the Alley and almost missed seeing something like this if I did?" the Runner drawled with a slow smile. "Not bloody likely, boyo."

"Just keep your damn eyes off her. I don't want you looking at her."

"And how do you plan on stopping me?" Cian laughed, clearly goading him.

"Don't push me," he warned in a deadly rasp, working his jaw. "Not tonight, Hennessey."

No, tonight he had no control. It'd just been stripped away by the sight of Jillian Murphy engaged in mortal combat with a Lycan.

It was painfully obvious he was going to lose her—but he couldn't grasp the concept, like something slippery and slick that kept wriggling through his fingers. He struggled to get his mind around it, but he might as well have tried to grasp an ethereal trail of smoke, or the puffy white confection of a cumulus summer cloud set within the deep rich blue of the sky.

None of this was right! Had everyone in the pack lost their goddamn minds? Spirit Walkers did *not* fight their own wolves. To challenge a witch was one of the greatest taboos throughout all of Lycan culture, right up there along with eating your neighbors and shape-shifting in the middle of Time's Square on New Year's Eve. If the wolves were expected to survive in the modern world, rules had to be followed. If they weren't, their way of life would come crashing down around them faster than a house of cards.

No, Lycans didn't challenge their own Spirit Walkers. Jillian might be wolf in spirit, but her body was all too vulnerable when it came to physical demands. Even in her human shape, Danna towered over Jillian's lithe five-five frame. And Jeremy had no doubt that Danna would press her physical advantage.

As if spurred by his thoughts, the Lycan's hands shed their human shape, transforming into lethal, claw-tipped weapons. Danna pulled back one powerful arm, then lurched forward, her claws cutting through the air like a scythe, aiming straight for the vulnerable flesh of Jillian's pale throat. Jeremy felt his heart drop, a primal shout of outrage trapped in his chest as he waited for the fatal blow he was helpless to stop. But the death strike never came. At the last second, Jillian dropped to the ground and rolled, avoiding the vicious slash of Danna's long, deadly claws.

Danna quickly lunged, leaping for Jillian before she could scramble to her feet. Again, Jeremy expected to see her ripped by the Lycan's claws, but Jillian threw up her arms, palms out, as if to hold off her attacker…and Danna's body slammed to a jarring halt. The air between the two women sparked with a pale blue electrical charge that sizzled, crackling like oil in a pan, while the air filled with the scent of burnt ozone.

Feeling as if he'd been cracked across the forehead with a two-by-four, Jeremy stared, stunned to witness how Jillian's powers had grown since she was a girl of eighteen.

"Well, now. She looks like a right handful," Cian murmured, slapping him on the shoulder, his wide mouth curled in a devil's smile. "I almost envy you," he added, the words softened by the Irishman's low, lyrical laughter.

"Piss off," Jeremy grunted, which only made the Runner laugh harder.

In the circle, Danna flexed her claws at her sides, shoulders hunched, her tangled hair all but standing on end in her rage. "Using your powers is cheating!" she snarled.

"And shifting your hands isn't?" Jillian panted, rolling to her feet, her wary gaze fixed on the woman determined to kill her. Danna made a low, chuffing noise and stepped slowly to the side, her movements mirrored by Jillian, who Jeremy noticed was carefully keeping the Lycan in front of her.

She couldn't afford to let Danna catch her unawares. Already, blood trickled down her left arm from an ugly gash that slashed across her bicep. Impatiently, Jillian wiped at the wound, smearing the crimson color over her pale skin. From there, Jeremy's gaze traveled over her body, lingering on the sexy strip of glistening bare abdomen revealed between the low waistband of her shorts and the hem of her black sports bra.

Despite being in the midst of a fight for survival, she looked…incredible. The tight workout shorts fit her firm backside like a glove, making his mouth water even though his throat remained dry with fear. And he didn't even trust himself to take a longer look at her chest. Seeing her firm breasts squeezed into that skintight top would only be asking for trouble he didn't need, seeing as how he was already hard and anxious and hurting.

His gaze lifted against his will, proving he had the willpower of a gnat.

Nice going, Burns.

When he was a young man of twenty-two, Jillian's breasts had never failed to fascinate him. High. Round. Firm and fine and just shy of being too much for her slight frame, they'd driven him out of his mind with lust. And now that she was grown, her sleek little body pulled him like a lodestone…too tempting to resist. There was no choice but to let his gaze roam, eyes hot with appreciation as he took in the smooth texture of her skin, all damp and warm from exertion. She was so sweet and pale and feminine…and yet, so strong, so powerful.

The human half of him knew it was a primitive reaction, but he couldn't ignore the animal part of his nature that *liked* her like that: sexy and sweaty, with the intimate scent of blood on her skin. He wanted to nuzzle against the scratches on her arm and take her taste into his body, before trailing his mouth down the damp perfection of her flesh, greedy for the warmth and textures, until he got to what he wanted most. And once he spread those sleek, muscular thighs, opening her like a secret that'd been meant for no one but him, he'd lean forward, his breath held hot in his chest, muscles rigid with anticipation and the sharpest edge of excitement he'd ever known, and he'd touch her with his tongue.

He knew what would happen then. The pleasure of it—of her—would be so intense, it'd crash through him harder than anything he'd ever experienced, like a shockwave that shook him to his core. Something reverent and spiritual and sexual all at once. Something that changed him. That ripped him apart and then put him back together again. On the outside, he'd look the same—but on the inside, he'd be…different. Changed.

And you're veering off course again, you idiot. Focus!

Right. He needed to find someone who could give him some answers. Jeremy quickly scanned the crowd, half of whom were staring at him with avid interest, the other half glued to the sight of Danna prowling around Jillian's body as the witch stood her ground, keeping a wary eye on her opponent.

A few yards away, Jeremy spotted Magnus Gibson. The tall, rangy Lycan slumped against the weathered trunk of a towering pine, complexion waxen as he watched his wife stalk his…*lover?* The word stuck in Jeremy's throat like a stone, nearly choking him.

Hell. He so didn't want to board that repulsive train of thought right now. The idea of Magnus slipping into Jillian's firm little body made him nauseous. Gritting his teeth, while keeping one eye on Jillian and Danna, he moved toward the Lycan and fisted his hand in Magnus's sweaty, beer-stained T-shirt, then jerked the drunken ass to his feet, shaking him to get his attention.

He had to do something, because the inability to take immediate action burned in his gut like acid. He hated the restrictions that kept him from doing what he wanted, on his own terms, which would be to charge into the clearing, grab Jillian up and take her to immediate safety.

Unfortunately, it wasn't that simple.

By accepting Danna's challenge, Jillian had entered a sacred Challenge Circle. No one could enter, not without being slammed onto their backs with a metaphysical sledgehammer, their head left ringing with a migraine reported to last for days. The circle served as a nonlethal means of keeping fights even and fair, but right now, it stood between him and the woman who had been created as his other half. Didn't matter that they couldn't stand one another—he wanted to save her, *needed to,* and it pissed him off that he couldn't.

He also needed to pound something, dammit, and Magnus seemed as good a place to start as any. Lifting the heavy jerk off of his feet, Jeremy smacked him against the trunk of the pine. "Why the hell can't you control your woman, Gibson?"

"Control Danna?" the hulking Lycan slurred, his pale blue eyes blurry and bloodshot. "You've gotta be outta your mind."

Jeremy ground his teeth together so hard, it amazed him they didn't turn to chalk in his mouth. "Then why not try keeping your pants zipped for a change?"

Magnus's eyes went round, making him look like an owl. "I didn't touch the bloody little witch! You think I want this? Do I look crazy to you? If anything happens to that woman," he sneered, jerking his shaggy head of coal-colored hair toward the clearing and the two opponents, "do you know what kind of curse those crazy Murphy bitches might bring down on my head?"

Stepping closer, Jeremy fought the urge to gag when the stench of stale whiskey and sweat smacked him in the face.

"If you didn't want trouble," he ground out through his teeth, "then you shouldn't have cheated with the pack's Spirit Walker to begin with."

"I just told you that I didn't!" the Lycan sputtered. "Are you deaf? I've never laid a hand on Jillian. I was having some fun with Carrie, the new little waitress who works over at the coffee shop."

"Jesus," Jeremy muttered with disgust. "You ever thought of being faithful?"

"To that shrew?" Magnus's color shifted to a sickly shade of green. "I repeat, do I look crazy to you?"

Jeremy was clearly talking to a brick wall—and he stubbornly refused to look too closely at the relief he felt at knowing Jillian hadn't let Magnus touch her. Not that he should care, but dammit, he did.

Still, something wasn't adding up here.

"If you've never touched Jillian, then why is Danna trying to kill her?"

Magnus made a gruff, snorting sound of disgust. "Danna found one of Carrie's pale blond hairs on my shorts and assumed it was one of Jillian's."

Jeremy's hand clenched, and the collar of the foul-smelling shirt pulled tight enough to make Magnus gasp. "And why would she think Jillian Murphy would be interested in you?"

The Lycan looked at him as if he were daft. "To get back at Danna for what happened with you!" he wheezed, trying to suck enough air into his lungs. "Geez, man, you're not as sharp as you look, are you? Danna has always worried about Jillian, because of her...uh, *complicity* in your breakup."

Jeremy stared, unable to believe such a word had just slipped from Magnus Gibson's mouth. "Complicity?" he snorted, shaking his head in disbelief. "Since when did you start using words like *complicity?*"

"Word of the day calendar," Magnus muttered, his tone daring Jeremy to make fun of him.

But he wasn't in a teasing mood. Instead, he snarled, "Well, you can inform your bloodthirsty wife that her *complicity* is a moot point."

He wanted to argue that you couldn't break up a relationship that had never started, but bit his tongue. Jillian hadn't dumped him because of rumors—that had only been an excuse. No, he'd always suspected the real reason was her fear of the Elders, or more importantly, of disappointing them. Not that he was explaining any of it to Magnus. It wasn't any of the bastard's business.

Ever mindful of the battle taking place just a few yards away, Jeremy kept one eye on Jillian, watching as she maneuvered to avoid Danna's strikes. The witch was quick on her feet, he'd give her that. Danna might have the advantage of size and strength, not to mention razor-sharp claws, but she was no match for Jillian's speed.

Jeremy set Magnus back down on his feet, but kept a firm grip on his shirt. "You're going to have to explain this one to me, Gibson. Why the hell would Danna's challenge have anything to do with what happened ten years ago?"

Magnus rubbed at his throat. "You really don't get it, do you? I never knew you were such a thickheaded ass."

"Keep pushing him," Cian murmured from behind Jeremy's left shoulder, obviously listening in, "and you're not going to like where it leads. Trust me."

The Lycan glared a quick look at Hennessey, swallowed so hard that his Adam's apple bobbed in his throat like a buoy and quickly shifted his bleary gaze back to Jeremy. "Danna's not the only one, but she worries the most, because she's the one you were rumored to be with that night. But ever since all that crap went down between you and Jillian, a lot of your old girlfriends have been waiting for her to take her revenge."

"How? By stealing their men? You're joking, right?"

Magnus shrugged. "Not exactly Jillian's style, I know, but who knows how a woman's mind works. All I know is that the witch has been fighting off challengers for longer than I can remember, and every damn one of them has been a woman you dated back before you left."

Aw, hell. If that were true, Jillian would have been fighting off more than a few. God only knew he'd been reckless back then, bedding the members of the pack as a way to thumb his nose at the laws that kept him excluded from its inner workings. That is, until the summer when Jillian had come home from boarding school and he'd finally met the girl who would one day become the pack's Spirit Walker. After that, Jeremy had never touched a pack female again—not that Jillian had ever believed him.

He didn't want to believe what Magnus claimed. "It's a nice story, but I'm not buying it, Gibson."

"Well, you should," someone drawled from the thick shadows darkening the edge of the forest, "because it's the truth."

The husky words came from the tall, built-like-a-brick-house female walking slowly toward them, her red hair gleaming a vivid copper in the hazy light of the torches as she came to stand at his side. Elise Drake, daughter of the man at the top of the Bloodrunners' list of possible suspects. *Son of a bitch.*

Part of the reason Jeremy had returned to Shadow Peak was so he could keep a close eye on Stefan Drake, the pack's most notorious Elder. If things worked out, he'd be able to uncover the proof the Bloodrunners needed to nail Drake's sadistic ass, putting an end to his plans. But it wouldn't be easy. If he *was* the traitor, there was no way in hell Drake would go down easy.

"You really have no idea what her life's been like, do

you?" Elise smirked at him, the look in her dark blue eyes saying she knew something he didn't—but that he should—and it pissed him off. Not that he wasn't already angry. Hell, at this rate he was going to choke on rage before the night ended.

"What the hell's that supposed to mean?"

The redhead's gaze flickered briefly to Cian, who had propped his shoulder against a nearby tree. The Irishman stood with his arms crossed, a small grin playing at the corner of his mouth, as if he found the unfolding drama fascinating entertainment and had decided to just step back and watch. He winked at Elise, earning him an angry sneer, and she quickly turned her attention back to Jeremy.

"It means that she's lived with what went down between the two of you for ten years, while you got to leave and pretend it never happened. More than a few of your old girlfriends have challenged Jillian over the years, thinking she'll go after their men because she wants to get back at them for having had you, when she never got the chance herself. As if she'd be driven by envy or jealousy or some kind of twisted revenge. They seem to think she's still tearing her heart out over losing you."

Her lip curled, blue eyes moving slowly over his body, from the top of his blond head down to the scuffed toes of his hiking boots. "God only knows why they'd think she cared. You never brought her anything but trouble."

Ten years ago, Elise had been a stuck-up snob who made it her business to act like the prima donna pack bitch. Her attitude had always matched her appearance, fiery and cool all at once. When had she become friendly with Jillian? The two women were as different as night and day.

"I still think this is bullshit," he muttered.

"Don't believe me, ask around." She shrugged, as if to say

she didn't care what he decided to do. "The League gave her no choice. Though she refuses to kill any of them, if it weren't for her powers, she'd have died by the hand of one of your exes long ago. I suppose the Elders feel it's just punishment for the fact she ever allowed you to get close to her, when they'd warned her repeatedly to stay away from you."

The coolness of her tone told him she was speaking the truth, and he scowled as the implications sank in.

All this time, she'd been fighting in life-and-death situations…and he hadn't even known. Despite the fact Bloodrunner Alley and Shadow Peak were separated by mere miles, the powerful racial conflict that existed between the half-breeds and the Lycans was what truly created distance between the two. Located south of the town, on the mountain, within a secluded glade, the Alley provided Jeremy and his friends with the privacy and isolation they preferred. Since they weren't members of the pack, they didn't travel into the Silvercrest town of Shadow Peak…and the Lycans stayed clear of the Alley. In fact, the name itself had come from a derogatory slur made by one Lycan years ago, who had referred to the Runners as half-breeds who were no better than "back-alley mongrels."

And suddenly Jeremy felt like the outsider he'd been his entire life—even when he'd lived in Shadow Peak. He hadn't known about the challenges Jillian had fought over the years, simply because he wasn't pack. Because he and the Runners weren't part of their social structure. She could have died, and he wouldn't have been there…wouldn't have even known it was happening. Rage at the entire situation poured through him in a fierce, steady flow, but there was pain, as well. A churning bitterness at the social chasm that existed between his world and hers.

"If she was ordered to fight a Lycan, why doesn't she have

a weapon?" he asked, determined to get what answers he could.

A slow smile spread across Elise's mouth, her dark eyes gleaming with what he could have sworn was pride. "Says it isn't honorable."

Yeah, that sounded like Jillian. Stubborn to a fault. "She had to have known Danna would cheat by shifting."

"Oh, she knew," Elise murmured, turning to watch the fight. "The rules of the Challenge Circle say no weapons. That's all that matters to her. Our Jillian is too set on doing what she believes in, too freaking honest for her own good."

Not your *Jillian.* My *Jillian.*

Jeremy had to bite back the telling words before they slipped off his tongue, like something that was his right to say. But they were there, crowding into the corners of his mouth, making him sick and angry and riding the hard edge of explosive.

Within the Challenge Circle, Danna charged, swiping at Jillian, catching her in the side with a vicious strike that would have proven mortal, if Jillian hadn't been quick enough to avoid the brunt of the blow. As it was, five thin streams of blood appeared on her skin, just over her ribs.

"You can slip in now, Jilly," Elise called out suddenly from his side. "She's wearing herself down."

"Slip in?" Jeremy echoed, cutting her a sharp look.

Elise flashed him a sly smile. "Shh…just watch."

In the circle, Jillian nodded, the only acknowledgment she made to Elise, but the next time Danna made a move for her, she closed her eyes, lifted her arms again and this time she pushed them forward with a hard, thick shoving motion. The fey lines of her face became etched with strain, while her skin flushed a deep, brilliant rose, and her hair whipped around her face, as if caught in a violent breeze. Danna slammed to a halt, howling with fury as she gripped her head between her claws, screaming…and then she hit the ground. Hard.

And once she fell, she stayed down, knocked out cold.

A roar went up from the pack—long, curling howls breaking the heavy silence that had held everyone in its grip during the fight's final moments.

Looking around, Jeremy spotted Cian at the edge of the crowd. The Irishman saluted him with two fingers against his temple, before he slipped into the shadows, heading back the same way they'd come.

Jeremy wasn't surprised to see the Runner leaving. Hell, he knew Cian would be hightailing it back to the Alley, eager to tell everyone about his reaction to Jillian's fight. Mason wouldn't ever let him live it down, considering he'd spent the past decade swearing that he couldn't care less about the little witch.

When he looked back toward the circle, Jillian was checking the unconscious Lycan for a pulse. Apparently satisfied that Danna was merely metaphysically coldcocked, and not seriously injured, she stepped from the circle, heading straight toward Jeremy as someone from the crowd of bystanders handed her a small towel.

His blood surged, palms damp and heart hammering as he watched her walk toward him, blotting her face with the towel, her body silhouetted against the glowing light of the moon. It hung there in the sky like a pearl, iridescent and bright, leaving her expression in shadow until she stood only a few feet away. "I thought you swore you'd never come back," she whispered, her eyes glittering with emotion. "And a promise is a promise, Jeremy."

He mentally bit his tongue, not wanting to have this argument with her here, for everyone's ears. "And some promises," he countered in a husky rasp, remembering to let go of Magnus, who remained propped precariously against the trunk, "are made to be broken."

"Yeah, that's one thing everyone knows about you, so I guess I shouldn't be surprised." Then, as if there was nothing out of the ordinary going on, she said, "I'll talk to you later, Elise," and turned to walk away.

Just. Like. That.

Oh, no. No bloody way. She was out of her ever-loving mind if she thought she was getting away that easily. Gripping her shoulder, Jeremy spun her around, the movement throwing her off balance and slamming the front of her body into his.

The anger was crashing through him now faster than he could control it. For too long he'd been the easygoing womanizer, going through life without a care in the world, nothing more important than tracking down the next rogue and sending him back to hell. Only now was Jeremy starting to realize just how much of an act it'd all been—like a fault line under pressure, full of tension, ready to explode, his anger had seethed beneath his surface. And every time he'd seen her—and couldn't touch her—it had grown.

The bookish-looking girl had blossomed into a woman who, if not classically beautiful, was the most attractive thing he'd ever set eyes on. Flaxen hair that nearly shone white in the sunlight, so bright it hurt your eyes. Bee-stung lips and an impish nose decorated with a jaunty spray of pale freckles. She was so… Christ, he didn't even know how to describe it. Everything she did, whether it was talking, walking or just taking a bloody breath, held an innate sensuality that made his body hurt like a toothache, pulsing and raw and angry—certain *parts* significantly more than others.

The problem was that no matter what he'd sworn or vowed

or claimed, no matter how irritated or furious she made him, touching Jillian Murphy was something he wanted…and wanted badly.

Jeremy wrapped one arm around her lower back, the other lifting to fist in the silken mass of her hair, and lowered his face. He was so close, he could see the intensity of his expression reflected in the clear black depths of her pupils, her velvety brown eyes gone big and round as she stared up at him in shock. Their breath mingled, panting and soft, and then suddenly the tiny hairs on the back of his neck stood up in warning. At the same time, Jillian stiffened in his arms, while a low, menacing growl sounded behind him.

Releasing Jillian, he whipped around, watching as Danna Gibson slowly pulled herself to her feet within the circle. She threw back her head and howled at the moon while the change washed over her, cloth shredding as fur rippled over her expanding body, transforming into the shape of her beast: a six-foot, slathering werewolf covered in golden brown fur. Danna lowered her wolf-shaped head, her fangs shining silvery white in the moonlight, and smiled at him.

"She going to hide behind you now?" the werewolf sneered, swaying on her feet.

"I'm not hiding," Jillian rasped, her face ashen as she stepped to Jeremy's side. Danna watched her for a moment, then charged, moving at full speed as she fell to all fours and leapt from the circle, launching an illegal attack.

Jeremy shoved Jillian behind him, shielding her with his tall body. He was prepared to take the werewolf out, when Magnus leapt on his wife, taking her to the ground. They rolled across the damp grass of the clearing, struggling for dominance, until Magnus finally pinned her beneath him, pressing her face-first into the ground.

"Dammit, Danna! Enough!" her husband shouted. "If you

kill her outside the circle, you'll be put to death! What are you even thinking?"

"I want her blood," the Lycan snarled, bucking against her husband's weight, but for once it seemed Magnus was intent on doing what was right. He held her tightly, even as she howled like a demon, her long claws digging into the damp, giving earth. "I'm tired of you making me look like a fool!"

"Get her out of here," Magnus grunted, jerking his head toward Jillian.

Jeremy stared down at the wrestling pair, the crowd riveted as they watched the bizarre events that resembled some kind of twisted soap opera. "Learn to control your woman," he said softly, the low words firm with conviction, "or I'll do it for you. If she comes within a foot of Jillian again, I'll consider it a threat."

An odd, choking sound of outrage rattled in Jillian's throat. "What do you think you're doing?" she demanded. "This isn't your fight, Jeremy, and I'm *not* your responsibility. I'm not your anything!"

As if she hadn't even spoken, Jeremy kept his stare on Danna. Her eyes were black, bottomless pools, and he realized that whatever spirit she'd possessed when younger had been slowly eaten away by hatred. Hatred for her life, her husband, her choices.

Quietly, he said, "Don't make me kill you, Danna, because if I so much as see you looking in Jillian's direction, I'll do it."

Then he turned, nudging Jillian ahead of him as he headed for the line of trees. He hadn't taken two steps before she whipped around so fast that her long tangle of hair fanned out around her shoulders, looking beautiful and silky and warm in the pale moonlight. He wanted to sink his fingers into the golden strands, wanted to feel them against his skin, his face, his body.

"I'm going to say this once, Burns. Do. Not. Touch. Me."

Not touch her? Not likely. In a flash of movement, Jeremy had her arms secured behind her, holding her immobile as he pressed his hard body into the lush softness of her own, keeping her trapped there against him. Lowering his head, he whispered his words into the delicate shell of her ear. "Stop fighting it, Jillian. I don't like it any more than you do, but it seems that this little war is over."

"Like hell it is," she hissed, beginning to struggle, only to stop when she realized she was merely wasting her strength. "Danna isn't just going to stop because *you* told her to!"

"I was talking about *our* war, Jillian. The one between you and me. But you might as well know that I won't have you fighting."

She made a rude sound, telling him what she thought of his arrogance. "And that matters how?"

He moved closer, nuzzling his nose against the silken skin at the side of her throat. "It should matter to you, little witch. Unlike the other pack males, I don't cower before your authority. If I have to drag you kicking and screaming from this clearing, I'll do it."

Her body vibrated against his. "Why?" she whispered, her voice nearly soundless with disbelief. "What is it to you if she beats me to death?"

So many answers sat on his tongue, lying in wait, but there was only so much Jeremy was willing to admit—even to himself. "I'm pack now, which means I have a respect for the lives within it."

"Even mine?" she scoffed, and he could feel her battle to hold herself rigid in his arms. "You've grown soft in your old age, Jeremy."

A low, gruff laugh rumbled in his chest. "You know what your problem is, Jillian?"

"Which one? I have several," she huffed. "And one of

them is sticking his nose into things that are none of his concern."

"You've always been my concern," he admitted in a husky rasp—but he certainly didn't sound happy about it.

"Don't," she warned softly, glaring up at him. "Let me go, Jeremy. I need to deal with Danna. I don't have time to play games with you."

"Like I was saying. Your problem," he drawled, enjoying the shiver that trembled through her when he nudged his rigid, denim-covered erection against her bare belly, "is that you just never know when to quit fighting."

He could almost hear her teeth grinding. "If you think I actually want to fight her, then that just goes to show how little you know me. I don't have a death wish, and I don't need you stepping in and acting as if I'm your responsibility. I've managed to survive the last ten years without you, and I'm not about to beg you for help now. I can take care of myself."

"Not hardly," he muttered. She jerked away from him, unsteady on her feet, and he suddenly realized that she was close to collapsing. "Jillian?"

She blinked at the odd, husky note of concern in his voice. "I'm okay," she said thickly, as he resettled his hands at her waist, his palms rough against the softness of her skin.

"Like hell you are."

She pushed back the wisps of hair that had fallen over her brow, wiped the back of one delicate wrist across her upper lip. "Really, I'm fine. It's just that using the power takes a lot out of me."

He didn't like hearing that, knowing that she'd have only been able to hold Danna off for *so long*.

"You can let me go now," she said quietly, breaking the heavy silence that had settled between them.

Jeremy shook his head at her stubbornness. "I don't think so. You look ready to fall on your face."

She gave a soft, tired laugh. "Such a charmer, Burns."

"I'm not interested in charming you," he muttered under his breath.

"If I didn't know better—" she sighed "—I'd think you sound as if you actually care. But we both know that isn't true, don't we, Jeremy?"

He grunted, and in the next instant she was off her feet, landing with a soft whoosh against his shoulder.

Stalking into the forest with a purposeful stride, Jeremy allowed his mouth to curl with a slow, wicked smile of satisfaction. He still didn't trust her, and no way on god's green earth was he going allow himself to feel anything for her. But he was tired of denying himself the thing he wanted most in this world. For whatever time he was back, he planned on having her. *She* belonged to him, and after tonight, his wicked little witch was going to know it.

Chapter 3

Jillian had the uncomfortable feeling her world had just been shifted off its axis, and it wasn't only because she was hanging upside down over the shoulder of a gorgeous Neanderthal. No, it was the emotional meltdown going on inside of her, rioting and out of control. The farther Jeremy carried her into the moonlit woods, where the shadows thickened and the intoxicating, purely masculine scent of his body surrounded her, the more urgent that feeling became, until she was panting harder than she had during the challenge.

You are so in trouble, Jillian.

She shouted and threatened and seethed the entire way up the mountain, but it didn't make any difference. The bastard just kept going, ignoring her as if she weren't even there, hanging over his broad shoulder like a sack of flour. She knew she could use her power to trip him or knock him on his arrogant backside, but she couldn't guarantee she wouldn't brain herself in the process. Nor did she relish the idea of rolling around on the ground with him. Resisting her body's instinctual impulse to get as close as possible to him was hard enough—she didn't want to test her willpower by finding herself sprawled over him...or under him.

A telling shiver slipped through her system, and it wasn't from the cold.

"What did you do, walk here?" she finally snapped, sounding waspish, hating herself for the fact that she'd have rather been running her palms over the hard, sleek muscles down his back, instead of pounding them with her fists. She could feel his heavy obliques shift as he moved, her mouth watering at the prospect of having so much raw power and strength beneath her hands.

"Partly," he grunted, shifting his hold on her legs, one of those big, rough hands too close to her bottom. Too close, yet not close enough. A part of her wanted to wiggle a bit to the side, until she got it right where she wanted it. And man, did she resent that part.

"Partly? What does that mean?" Jillian tried to make her tone as annoying as possible, thinking that if she could just keep fighting with him, she wouldn't have time to pay attention to those *other thoughts* swimming through her head. Naughty, provocative thoughts complete with writhing bodies, keening cries and warm, sweat-slick skin. Thoughts too dangerous for her peace of mind on the best of days, but when she was alone with this particular Bloodrunner in a remote part of the mountains, surrounded by the primal forest and not a hell of a lot else, they were damn near lethal.

The pack was at least a half mile behind them now, Jeremy's long legs making quick work of the sloping terrain, taking them farther into seclusion with every second that passed by—each moment taking her deeper into treacherous emotional territory that could too easily crush her. Trying to ignore that unsettling bit of knowledge, Jillian pulled her mind back to what she'd been saying. "I don't get it, Jeremy. How can you 'partly' walk somewhere?"

They entered a small glade surrounded by eight majestic pines interspersed with fledgling red and white oaks, and Jeremy stopped, moving in a slow circle as he surveyed their surroundings. When he seemed satisfied with what he found, he set her on her feet as easily as he'd lifted her.

"I'm going to need my truck in Shadow Peak, but I felt like walking tonight, so I parked down below the rise and hiked with Cian the rest of the way to the clearing, instead of going into town first. Dylan called earlier to let me know there would be a challenge tonight," he explained, slanting her a dark look, "but he didn't mention who'd be fighting."

She arched one brow, determined to ignore the frustrating way the silvery moonlight glinted so perfectly off the burnished gold of his hair, making her want to reach out and bury her fingers in the warm, silken threads. "He probably thought you wouldn't care."

"Right." He snuffled a soft laugh under his breath, as if she'd said something funny, and Jillian struggled not to flinch from the provocative heat of his stare. His eyes had always been too mesmerizing for his own good—not to mention hers. The one time she'd allowed herself to be conned by those hazy swirls of green surrounded by thick, amber-colored lashes, she'd paid the price of a broken heart. But now she knew better. Knew better than to trust the promises swimming in their glowing depths.

He stepped closer, grinning a little when she took a hasty step back, as if he knew what it cost her to be near him. The way he moved should have been outlawed. All long muscles and masculine grace, like a predator—like something on the hunt for its prey. His head tilted the tiniest fraction as he watched her, and it was a heady sensation, standing at the focus of all that blistering male intensity. For a brief moment, Jillian wondered just how close his wolf was to the surface, how close to the edge he'd been pushed.

"Do I make you nervous?"

She crossed her arms over her chest, acutely aware of just how little clothing she was wearing. "Why would you make me nervous?" she drawled sarcastically, arching her brows. "It's not like you've brought me here against my will or anything."

A slow, crooked kind of smile lifted the corner of his mouth. "You can keep trying to taunt me, but it won't matter." He blew out a slow breath, looking like a wicked, golden god of a man as he just stood there, staring down at her. "I hadn't planned on any of this, but tonight seems to have knocked some sense into me. Now that I'm back, we've got to deal with what's between us." He paused, rubbing one hand over his stubbled jaw, the gently rasping sound easily heard against the soft quiet of the forest. "We're not leaving here until we've talked this out, Jillian. But first, I want to know why you agreed to fight those challenges."

She hated that she had to control the urge to stomp her foot like a frustrated child. "Why? Because I didn't have a choice. I've never wanted to fight the stupid things, but your never-ending list of past lovers just pushed and pushed, until the Elders ordered me to accept!"

"So it's true then, that the League made you fight. Elise thinks they're punishing you."

Her gaze skittered away. "Maybe."

"Because of one kiss?" he asked, his tone skeptical.

"It seems they knew me well enough to know what that kiss signified." She jerked her gaze back to his face, hoping he could see just how angry he made her. "They knew I'd decided to put my trust in you, despite their warnings and threats. And it took all but a few hours for you to go running off with Danna, proving just how stupid I'd been to believe in you!"

"So they make you accept those ridiculous challenges, risking your life." She watched him work to master his emotions. After a moment, he quietly said, "That's some punishment, Jillian. I'm surprised you just lie down and take it, or are you still terrified of disappointing them?"

"I have no choice in the matter. Whenever I try to refuse, they consider it a show of weakness." She sighed, still rankled over the League's insistence that she meet the challenges. "And we can't have any weak links in the chain of power, Jeremy."

"God forbid you actually stand up to them," he said with soft menace.

Her chin lifted a notch higher. "Unlike you, I have respect for the League."

He brushed that frustrating topic to the side with the sweep of his hand, and chose another argument. "Why do you suppose no one ever told me you were fighting? I can understand the pack's silence, since I avoid them like the plague and they probably wouldn't waste their breath talking to me, but what about Dylan? What about my parents?"

Jillian shook her head, wondering why he didn't get it. "There's no conspiracy, Jeremy. Your parents have spent so much time away, I doubt they even know. And like I said, Dylan probably didn't say anything because he knows you couldn't care less about what happens to me."

His jaw locked, and a cutting flash of frustration ripped across his rugged features, before quickly disappearing, as if he'd thrown the emotion into some mental vault and slammed the door. "This argument is going nowhere," he rasped, looking away to stare up at the star-studded sky.

A moment of silence deepened between them as he gazed at the stars, his expression intent, as if looking for answers in their shimmering lights, and Jillian seized the opportunity to study him, to soak in all the breathtaking details that made her tremble with physical awareness. In the decade since he'd left Shadow Peak, he'd grown from someone with boyish charm and golden good looks, to a man who overshadowed everyone around him. He was *that* dynamic, his aura blinding and burning with intensity. A man who drew your eye and trapped it, with that blond, sun-bleached hair, dark golden skin and those smoky hazel eyes, his body battle-hardened and beautiful, the chiseled features of his face too masculine to be called anything but rugged. She even loved the strong column of his throat, with its fading scars, and the blond stubble on his cheeks and chin.

"We should have hashed this out between us before I came back, Jillian."

The deep, provocative timbre of his voice hit her as heavily as the breathtaking power of his scent, making her burn from the inside out, as if she'd swallowed a smoldering ball of fire that now glowed in her belly, shooting like incandescent sparks through her fingers and her toes. Lighting her up. Turning her on.

She swallowed, struggling for her voice. "And just when were we supposed to do that?" she asked, mentally wincing at the husky sound of lust rounding out the edges of her speech.

His gaze lowered, those enigmatic eyes going dark, filled with thickening shadows. "We could have done it at the reception."

Jillian knew he was referring to his partner's wedding, which had taken place just days before—and where his return to the pack had first been announced. They'd spent the entire night avoiding one another, though she'd snuck glances at him as often as possible, unable to help herself. And it still irritated her that no one in the League had thought to inform her of what was coming that night, leaving her to learn of his return in a crowd of people, all of whom had watched her with avid interest when the news was announced. "Yeah, that would have been swell, but I really thought I'd had enough good news that day," she replied with a small, tight laugh, terrified at the knowledge that every moment she spent with him was breaking her down, weakening her resolve. He was like Kryptonite to her Superman, that one fatal weakness that could change her life forever by systemically stripping her defenses.

"Jillian…" he sighed, sounding as if she was trying his patience "…whether we want it or not, I'm back. I'm here and we have to face the facts."

"Somehow," she muttered, "I don't think my facts are the same as yours."

He shook his head as he studied her. "You know, you always were stubborn, but I don't remember you enjoying a fight this much before."

"I don't want to fight you, Jeremy." She lifted one shoulder and blew a wisp of hair out of her eyes—casual gestures meant to disguise the dizzying confusion going on inside of her. "I just want you to leave me alone."

"Won't happen. Not today. And not tomorrow. I've come to a decision tonight, little witch. One that's been a helluva long time coming." His eyes went hotter, the sexy, smoky green swirling with a primitive violence and hunger that made heat crawl its way up her spine, melting over her skin like liquid fire, leaving her seething in a need too sharp to contain. Any moment now, the dam would burst—and god help her when it did. "I mean to have you, Jillian."

Her eyes went wide. "Wow. Just like that? Jeremy says he

wants me and *poof,* I'm his?" she drawled, desperately clinging to an illusion of indifference. "I hate to rain on the parade here, but I just don't feel the same way anymore."

"Like hell you don't." He laughed, daring to flash her an arrogant, predatory smile. She had the feeling he could see right through her, as if by looking into her eyes, he could see into her very soul and the dangerous truths that she'd buried there. "You're lying, and we both know it."

"And you read minds now?" She snorted, hoping he didn't know how he affected her, but it was a stupid wish. All he had to do was breathe, and he could tell just how hungry she was for him.

He arched one tawny brow. "I don't have to read your mind," he said lightly. "Not when I can scent your body."

Jillian opened her mouth, but nothing came out, as if the denial had simply dissolved on her tongue.

"Kinda intimate, isn't it?" he whispered, the words silky, seductive, scratchy and a little raw. "Knowing that I can smell the need, the hunger, growing in you. That it affects me more strongly than any other male, whether he's human or as bloody purebred Lycan as they come. That you were made for me. That you're *mine.*"

Jillian took another step backward, ready to flee, even though she knew she couldn't outrun him. "I was never yours," she argued, breathless as she swallowed the lump of panic caught in her throat. "Thankfully I got smart and opened my eyes to what you really are before it was too late."

"You didn't open your eyes to jack," he shot back in a soft growl. "And you sure didn't trust me."

"With good reason!"

"You gave up your future, your destiny, for a title," he sneered, his contempt for the pack and what it stood for evident in his tone. "You jumped on the first excuse you could

find to get rid of me, because deep down inside, you were terrified of having to choose between a life with me and your
precious wolves."

"I didn't give up my destiny!" she shouted. "The pack *is* my
destiny, Jeremy. I was born for this, but I've no doubt you
would have expected me to just up and walk away from it all,
because of your hatred. That is, if the League didn't strip me
of my position first, for making what they considered an 'irre-
sponsible choice,' whether nature meant for us to be together
or not!"

They were both breathing hard, their bodies tremoring
with anger as emotion tore through them. "And does your
job make for a lonely bed partner at night, Jillian? Does it
stay faithful to you?" His voice lowered, becoming more
intimate…more dangerous. "Does it keep you satisfied?
Make you happy?"

His husky words cut straight to her core, as if he knew just
how to wound her, the way a fighter knows instinctively
where to place his next blow. "My position calls for sacrifice,"
she said softly. "It's not anything I'd expect you to understand."

"You have no idea what sacrifices I would have been willing
to make for you." Shoving his hands in his pockets, Jeremy
hardened his jaw. "You never even gave me a chance to prove
myself, so forgive me if I still seem a little pissed about it."

"You didn't leave me any choice," she whispered, her
throat shaking.

"Like hell. I couldn't do anything about my reputation before you came home from school, but from the day I realized
what was between us, I never, *never,* gave you any reason to
distrust me."

Jillian stared at him, stunned. "You still deny you were
with Danna that night, after our first…our *only* kiss? After I

told you that I was ready to give a relationship between us a chance?"

His nostrils flared as he drew in a deep breath, the arc of his cheekbones flushed the dull red of anger. "If you had ever taken the time to ask me yourself, I could have told you that I didn't lay a hand on Danna Gibson that night. I hadn't touched anyone but you since you came home from school," he growled, his voice like gravel. "And after you threatened to sic your mother and your precious League on me if I ever came near you again, I was too furious to even think about sex. It took me months before I cooled down enough to go around another woman, Jillian, much less take her to bed."

"That's—"

"Pathetic? Sad? Embarrassing?" he sneered, cutting her off. "Yeah, I know. But like I said, I was crazy about you. I'd have given you anything you wanted, but it wasn't good enough for you. No, you were just waiting for me to screw up," he continued, his anger mounting again like a great, swelling wave skimming the surface of the blackest ocean. "The second someone came running to you with some bull-shit story about me, you jumped at the chance to believe them. And we both know why that was. You were afraid of more than just trusting me to be faithful, Jillian. You were ter-rified of what you knew we could have, of how powerful it could be. You ran from that like a frightened little girl, be-cause you were scared that it'd mean you would have to make that choice between our relationship and your position. But that would have been a choice forced on you by *them*, not me."

Despite his conviction, she didn't truly believe him. It was one thing for him to make such a claim now, when a relation-ship between them was impossible, but back then, Jillian knew he wouldn't have been so accepting of the path her life was meant to follow. No, he'd have never been willing to live in Shadow Peak or understand her loyalty to the League. And living in the Alley would have presented its own problems. He would have resented the time she spent in town, with people he despised, and the pack would have been furious at the idea of their Spirit Walker living with the Runners. She had no doubt they would have demanded her resignation.

"What do you want from me, Jeremy?" she asked in confusion, fighting not to fall apart as all the pain from the past decade crashed down on her, smothering and dark. "I know you no longer want to bond with me, so then what are you after?"

He made a rough, sarcastic sound in the back of his throat. "You're right. No one said a damn thing about bonding, and I'm no longer a starry-eyed kid who hopes for things he's never going to have."

"You were *never* starry-eyed."

His voice went lower, barely human beneath the seething emotion in his words. "Where you were concerned, I always had my head in the clouds. You let me down, Jillian. Changed me."

"Don't you dare turn this back on me!"

"I'll do whatever I want to you, because *this*—" his feral gaze moved slowly down her body, affecting her like a physical touch "—belongs to me. It's *mine*." The husky words were rough with lust...and something deeper. Something so dark and emotional that she had no frame of reference for it. "You want to know what I want? I want you *under* me. Pure and simple."

The way he looked at her made Jillian feel as if he could see right into her, all her secrets exposed before him, laid out in a shocking display of intimacy. He was waiting. Waiting for a sign, for the briefest glimpse of weakness or a crack in her armor. Slips she couldn't afford to make, not when her very soul was on the line.

She knew she needed to keep her focus…but it was happening again. She couldn't think when too close to this man, not when she kept getting tripped up in the details. Everything about him pulled her in, controlled her like the most hypnotic of drugs. Like smooth, thick syrup, he invaded her mind, slowing down time, until she was caught. Trapped. Held prisoner by a need to reach out and learn, firsthand, if he was as warm and hard as he looked. As silken and rugged and coarse.

"You want me, Jillian. Lie about everything else, but don't try to lie to me about this. I can feel it," he argued in a gritty whisper, his voice hitting her like the warm spill of fine wine into her blood, making her limbs feel heavy, her heartbeat swift and deep and pounding. "I can see it written on your face. See it in the pulse of your throat. The tight little tips of your breasts. I can tell by the warm, sweet scent of need pouring off you."

"Why? Why are you doing this?" She hated that her voice sounded desperate even to her own ears. "You don't really want me. You despise me, Jeremy."

"Sure I do." He laughed, the warm sound dark and wicked and rich, and he smiled just a little at her. "I've been angry at you for years, Jillian, but it doesn't seem to matter. I still want to rip your clothes off and go at you right here." He slammed one wide palm against the thick trunk behind her. "Just press your back against this pine, hold your sweet little ass in my hands and get a taste of what you were always too afraid to let me near before."

Her chin trembled as she said, "I was never afraid of you," even while her conscience screamed, *Liar!* She'd been afraid of making herself vulnerable to him—of discovering that he didn't love her the way she'd loved him. Afraid of him breaking her heart. Afraid of choosing him over what was expected of her. Afraid of standing up to her parents and the League and making her own decisions, controlling her own destiny.

"Do us both a favor and stop wasting our time with lies," he said sharply, "because you never were any good at it. You're even worse now."

She opened her mouth, but didn't know what to say, the words lodging in her throat until it felt as if she'd choke on them.

Jeremy pressed closer, a dark, dangerous force that made something hot and tight and achy unfurl in her belly, a warm glow of sensation slowly spreading like liquid heat through her veins. "Just out of curiosity, who was it that came to you with that story about me and Danna? One of your so-called friends? The same ones who used to hit on me every time you weren't looking? I never touched them, but that didn't stop them from offering what I didn't want."

"No. It wasn't—"

"Forget it," he muttered, moving away from her. "What the hell does it matter now? What's done is done. I don't need your trust anymore. Don't need it, and don't want it. But I'll take what I didn't get before."

She wrapped her arms tighter around her body, struggling to hold herself together. "You're out of your mind, Jeremy."

He laughed, just staring at her, the look in his hazel eyes too piercing and beautiful to hold. Even in a rage, he called to her, that brutal, intense energy reaching out, grabbing at her. "So Mason is always telling me."

"Then maybe you should listen to him!"

"Maybe I should," he murmured, staring intently at her mouth, a provocative glint in his smoky eyes that made her shiver.

"At any rate—" he sighed, sounding drained but focused "—I'm home and I'm here for a reason. You know that, Jillian. I know you want what's best for your wolves, and you're too connected with the Silvercrest not to realize that something bad is coming. The pack is going to crumble from within if the one responsible isn't stopped. I can help you."

"I don't need your help," she argued in a trembling rush, knowing very well it was a lie. She loved her wolves, but she also accepted that a select few were capable of bringing down the entire pack, their narrow, close-minded, inherently hateful view of the world threatening to choke off life for the rest, like a blood clot slowly working its way to the brain. Once it struck, the effects would be terminal…and the Silvercrest would be lost.

She knew Jeremy's words rang of truth, but self-preservation demanded she argue. It was the only sane thing to do! She couldn't work beside him, no matter how tempting it would be to have his broad shoulder to lean on and his keen intellect to offer guidance. Facts were facts, and she knew her limitations. If she were forced to be near him, she would give in, fall victim to the wild, raging rush of pleasure that called their bodies to one another…and in doing so, hand him the power to destroy her.

It was times like this when she actually hated being a witch, hated the limitations it put on her life. "I appreciate the offer, but I can handle this on my own."

"Like hell you can."

Her chin lifted, driven high by pride. "The League can offer me guidance."

His eyes darkened as he moved back into her personal space, the brackets around his mouth tight with frustration, his voice low, full of gravel and bite. "If we're going to make this work, we have to get past our history and try to trust one another. Your precious League isn't going to be able to help with this one, which is why I'm going to tell you something that no one but the Runners and Dylan know. The rogues who were following Simmons knew how to dayshift."

Jillian blinked, swallowing against the lump of surprise in her throat. "Th-that's impossible. I heard rumors, but I thought it was just panic talking."

His right hand lifted, rubbing at the pale scars on the side of his throat, gifts from a run-in with the rogue wolves. "Trust me, it's true. Simmons taught them how…and someone taught him. We learned from Robert that it's a power held by—"

"Those who serve on the League of Elders," she cut in, her voice hollow with fear. Anthony Simmons was the rogue Lycan that Jeremy's partner, Mason, had defeated in a fight to the death just days before. Obviously Robert Dillinger, Mason's father and a Lycan who had been denounced from the League itself when he took a human wife, had shared what he knew with the Runners—that only those who served on the League possessed the ability to teach another how to dayshift.

"I know about it," she admitted in a hoarse whisper. "I was told about dayshifting when I formally accepted my position, after my mother stepped down. It's a defense mechanism—a weapon of war, meant to be used in the event our way of life is threatened. To teach it to a rogue would be punishable by death, their only intent to make it easy for the rogues to kill humans. And their own kind. It even masks their scent, so that they're impossible to track."

Jeremy nodded, his expression bleak. "Yeah. You getting the picture?"

She shook her head, unable to get her mind around it. "You think we have a traitor on the Silvercrest League? That one of the Elders has turned and…what? That they want to turn our wolves rogue and set them free on the humans and the Bloodrunners? For what purpose?"

"We're still working on that," he murmured, and she could

tell there was more he wasn't telling her. Apparently his exchange of trust only went so far. "But no matter what their motive, you're in over your head here and you need me. I'm not going to let anything happen to you."

"Why?" she asked, her confusion genuine, not coy.

"Why? Why? Why?" Jeremy laughed, the rough sound lacking any real humor. "Can't you ever say anything else, woman?"

"I just don't understand why you want to help me. I really think it'd be best for both of us if you just…kept your distance and stayed away from me."

"That's going to be pretty hard to manage," he said with another one of those slow, easy smiles, "considering I'm going to be *inside* of you."

Panic clawed at her now, biting and sharp, her mind too aware of the fact that her body wanted nothing more than to take him. All of him. Every hot, hard, incredibly thick inch— and never let him go. Her voice shivered when she spoke. "Not in a million years, Jeremy."

"Don't," he rasped softly, lifting his hand to touch his thumb to the corner of her mouth. Her lips trembled from the light, calloused touch, making her want to turn away at the same time she wanted to turn her head and nuzzle the warmth of his palm. "Don't say something that's going to embarrass you later on, after I prove you wrong."

His words slapped her in the face like a dousing of ice water. "You arrogant bastard," she choked out, jerking her mouth away from his touch. "It's amazing one man can have such a high opinion of himself. I wouldn't tou—"

"Stop," he grunted, cutting her off. His eyes narrowed, holding her, making it impossible to look away. "We have a connection, Jillian. You can pretend all you want that it doesn't exist, but it isn't going to just disappear."

"No. You're wrong, Jeremy. There is no connection. What-ever we had," she said coldly, "you killed it a long time ago. I'm not a naive little girl anymore. I've learned how to take care of myself. I don't need you. Not now. Not ever."

He leaned close, curling his rough hands over her shoul-ders, and she turned her face away…but he merely whispered into the sensitive shell of her ear, as if he was telling a secret. "You just keep saying it enough times, and maybe you'll start believing it. But we both know the truth. I'll hunt you down if I have to, Jillian, but we both know how badly you'll want me to catch you in the end."

"You can hunt me," she gasped, struggling to jerk out of his hold, away from the dangerous, evocative heat of his mouth, "but you'll have to chase me to hell and back before you ever catch me."

With the touch of his calloused fingertips upon her chin, Jeremy slowly pulled her face back to him, staring down at her through thick, honey-colored lashes. The intensity of his gaze made her heart lurch, his hazel eyes dark and heavy with possession, as if he owned her.

"I know what hell's like," he told her, the huskiness of his voice like an intimate caress, shivering across her skin. "The threat of it won't scare me off."

His soft breath felt warm and sweet and wonderful against her trembling mouth, teasing her with the heady, erotic prom-ise of a kiss that Jillian knew she shouldn't want—but did. Badly. And the slow, crooked grin kicking up the corner of his mouth said he knew it, knew just how sharply the keen edge of anticipation was cutting into her.

"So I'm afraid you'll have to do better than that."

"Do better than what? What are you talking about?" she asked thickly. She was stalling, because she knew very well where he was going with his seduction routine.

"You're gonna have to convince me, little witch." Jeremy laughed softly, kissing the corner of one eye, trailing the rough-silk texture of his lips across her cheek, before nipping playfully at her tender lobe.

"C-convince you of wh-what?" she stammered. "That you're crazy?"

"Feels like it. Feels like I've been crazy since the day I set eyes on you." He shifted a fraction closer, overwhelming her with his heat, his scent—with the intense, rugged masculinity that was so much a part of him. "You're going to have to convince me of the one thing that we both know you don't have a damn chance in hell of doing."

She breathed in too sharply, trapped by the possessive power of his gaze.

"You're going to have to convince me that you don't crave me the same way that I crave you—and you're going to have to make it good, Jillian, because I can promise that I won't make it easy on you."

She shivered. He smiled in response. And before she could draw her next breath, his mouth claimed hard, deliberate possession of her own.

Chapter 4

The seeking touch of his lips against hers was a provocative answer to the churning want that had raged through Jillian's body for so long. Through so many sleepless nights, and so many frustratingly empty days, when she'd found herself surrounded by people...and yet, utterly alone.

"Jeremy, please," she whispered, tearing her mouth away. "Don't do this."

He kissed the fragile skin beneath her eye, the sharp edge of her jaw. "Do what?"

"I won't give in," she gasped, feeling him nip the sensitive tendon at the side of her throat. *"I can't."* She could hear the desperation in her voice, and knew he could, as well.

His lips moved in a soft, deliciously erotic caress against her skin as he spoke. "You're letting your fear control you, Jillian."

"What do you know about fear?" she demanded, her voice cracking, bleak with emotion.

"I know it scares the hell out of me," he confessed in a gritty rasp, his breath warm and damp, "thinking that I might have lost you during one of those challenges."

"Damn you, Jeremy." She tried to stumble back, but was caged in by the thick trunk of the tree, his hard body pressed against her front. He was a dark, raging presence before her, trapping her.

"I'm going to make it hard as hell for you to deny me," he warned in a ragged tumble of words. Then his mouth claimed hers again, angry and hot and hungry.

Sweet Jesus. She couldn't breathe. Couldn't think. But who cared? He made it so much more than a mere kiss. It felt too intimate, too carnal, like the decadent, provocative things he did to her in her dreams.

Jillian knew she should push him away, but more than that, she wanted to pull him closer. The details, so shocking and electric, overwhelmed her. The sexy, slightly rough texture of his lips. The silken stroke of his talented tongue. She could taste his hunger, his heat, and it was like going under...falling into him. Everything pulsed through her with a sharp, shattering awareness. And yet, she was lost, floating, her head fuzzy with the rioting sensations as his tongue claimed her mouth more deeply, the kiss slow and eating and deliciously sweet, like warm, melting honey.

She moaned, giving up, rubbing her tongue against his, and everything changed.

With a low, hoarse curse, Jeremy crushed her breasts with the muscular wall of his chest, while taking deeper possession of her mouth. It was something decadent, hungry and invasive, the way he penetrated her, shoving past any resistance, smashing it beneath his dark, persuasive need... Only, she wasn't resisting. Not anymore.

Jillian trembled, gasping. He growled low in his throat,

moving against her, and she could feel the hard proof of his erection, long and thick enough to make her breath catch. Her hands lifted, the cool tips of her fingers touching in a butterfly caress against the scorching heat of his cheekbones, and she flinched from the warmth of his skin.

"Touch me," Jeremy groaned against the corner of her mouth, nipping at her bottom lip, then diving back into the kiss with a breathtaking intensity that made her toes curl. "Put your goddamn hands on me, Jillian."

The shaken, guttural words slipped through her system like a dizzying rush of pleasure, all but making her purr. God, yes, she wanted to. Wanted to put her hands on the hard, lean lines of his magnificent body and learn him by touch, taking him in the way someone who'd lost their sight could lose themselves in another world through Braille. He was an unknown landscape she wanted to explore until she was privy to all its secrets, until it was so much a part of her she knew it better than she knew herself.

Jillian slipped her tongue past his lips, lost in the dark, honeyed sweetness of his taste, and took the aggressive sound he made into her mouth at the same time she pressed the flat of her palms against his ribs, fingers splayed, wanting to touch as much of him as possible. His body communicated its hunger through his skin, burning her, even with the barrier of his shirt between them. But she wanted flesh. Wanted to feel the silken texture of his skin, the blond whirl of hair that circled his navel, then trailed in a daring arrow toward the blatant, rigid proof of his lust.

Moaning deep in her throat, Jillian slipped her hands under the hem of his shirt and clasped his hot skin at his sides, just above the waistband of his jeans. His breath shuddered in his chest and he panted against her lips as he pulled away from the kiss, pressing his forehead against hers. The hunger and chaotic mix of emotion Jillian had always carried for this one man surged through her, filling her up, giving her the courage to do what she'd never done before.

Now, she didn't have a choice. Her body wouldn't let her fight what her heart knew was going to hurt her in the end. Biting her lower lip, she trailed her fingertips to the waistband of his jeans, then slowly stroked them inward. Any second now she was going to touch that intimate, powerful part of him that she'd never explored when younger. A fine sheen of sweat coated his skin, his flesh burning hotter. His lips pulled back over his teeth and he stopped breathing.

Her fingers pulled closer…closer…and then she heard her name being called out over the eerie silence of the forest.

"Jillian? Are you out there?"

She wrenched her hands away and shoved against his chest. "Sayre?" she tried to shout, breathless, wondering how she'd let herself get into this situation. She lifted her wide gaze and almost jumped from the searing look of lust darkening his eyes. His jaw locked, and he finally reacted to her pushing hands, taking a step away, the front of her body left chilled at the loss of his incredible heat.

It terrified her, how badly she wanted to pull him back to her.

Taking her hands from the firm muscles of his chest, Jillian pressed them to her sides, and tried to find a measure of calm, even while her heart hammered out a vicious tempo beneath her ribs. "Sayre?" she called out again. "Where are you?"

"Right here," her sister answered, the last word trailing off as the young woman stepped into the small glade and caught sight of them. "Oops," she whispered, blushing, her blue-gray eyes wide with surprise. The ends of her curly, strawberry-blond hair just grazed her jaw, completing the fey look created by her unique features. Her nose was delicate, her chin sharp, jawline almost fragile. Her skin was as luminous as a pearl, the arc of her cheekbones always flushed with a wild color of rose because Sayre could never move at a normal pace. She was boundless energy and exuberance, like a hummingbird always flitting from one spot to another. But she was wise beyond her years, her big eyes steady and calm within the thick fringe of her lashes. She was a wild spirit with a pure heart who never let others down, and she was the closest friend Jillian had ever had.

"Um, sorry," Sayre murmured, her curious gaze moving from one to the other. Jillian tried to avoid blushing, but knew her face was crimson. "I was so focused on finding you, I didn't pick up on the fact that you aren't alone."

"It's okay," Jillian said firmly, stepping out from between the tree and Jeremy's body, needing the space to breathe. "Jeremy and I were just—"

Before she could finish the thought, Jeremy took a step toward her sister, his green eyes full of startled surprise. "Sayre?" he whispered, while a slow grin curved his mouth. "I don't believe it. Is that really you?"

A wry smile curled across Sayre's mouth, and she ducked her head shyly. "Hi, Jeremy."

"You were just a scrawny little runt the last time I saw you."

Sayre's musical laughter filled the glade, and it made Jillian's heart hurt to think of how her sister had always followed Jeremy around when she was little, as worshipful as an adoring puppy. Sayre had been crushed when he'd left Shadow Peak, and it'd been so hard to explain to the little girl why he wasn't coming back. "Yeah, well, that was a long time ago," she said with an easy grace, obviously trying to put them at ease. "Not that I've ever managed to outgrow the scrawny thing. I may be taller, but I still look like a toothpick."

"Naw. You've grown into a beautiful young woman. I bet you have all the boys chasing after you."

"Hardly." She laughed. "But it's sweet of you to say so."

"Is everything okay?" Jillian asked, irritated with herself for the tiny flair of jealousy she felt at their easy camaraderie. "You know I don't like you leaving Shadow Peak on Challenge Nights. It isn't safe."

Sayre nodded. "Yeah, I know. But I had to make sure you were okay."

"I'm fine. How did you find me?"

Sayre's cheeks flushed, and she ducked her chin. "It wasn't hard, Jilly. You were broadcasting pretty loudly."

Jeremy arched a questioning brow in Jillian's direction. "Sayre's still growing into her powers," she explained quietly, "but they're already very strong."

"Obviously," he murmured, staring, and Jillian knew he was wondering just how strong her own powers had grown in the past decade.

"I didn't mean to interrupt," Sayre said cautiously, flicking a nervous glance toward Jeremy, "but I wanted to let you know that Eric was waiting at your house. He heard about what happened at the clearing and wanted to come looking for you. It wasn't easy, but I, um, convinced him to head home and let me check on things. I told him you'd call him later."

"Eric who?" Jeremy questioned, at the same time Jillian whispered, "Hell."

"Eric who?" he repeated, the words sharper this time.

"Um, Eric Drake," Sayre said too brightly, wincing when she caught sight of Jillian's glare.

Jeremy's eyes narrowed to slits. "Why would Drake be waiting at your house for you?"

Jillian opened her mouth, then snapped it shut. "Not to sound rude, but that really isn't any of your business."

"Wrong answer," he said silkily. "I'm making it my business."

"I'm not doing this in front of Sayre," she warned him in a quiet voice.

"All I want is an answer to my question." Jillian could hear the silent *for now* tacked onto the end of his statement.

"We're...friends."

"You and Drake?" he rasped, his tone full of disbelief and the hard, biting edge of anger. "Since when?"

"A few months now," she explained awkwardly, alarmed at the way he stumbled back a step, his expression little more than a hard mask, giving nothing away. But his eyes were like a window into his soul, and she knew the idea of her with Eric caused him pain. For years, she'd thought she'd take satisfaction in seeing him hurt, but she'd been wrong. Instead, his pain cut at her like a knife, jabbing and sharp, while shame pooled thickly in her belly.

"Why?" He didn't need to say more. She knew exactly what he meant.

Her hands fluttered nervously at her sides, and she wished she was wearing jeans so that she could hide them in her pockets. "We started working together on a few of the new reform committees for education and housing. We ended up spending so much time together that we've become...close—"

"If you two are so close," he interrupted, taking a step forward, hands planted on his hips, "why wasn't he there tonight?" His lip curled in cruel sneer, but she could see the burn of a darker emotion in the deep, smoky green of his eyes. Jealousy burned harder than anger or fear or arrogance, blurring the edges so that only the source flared through, sizzling and sharp.

Jillian lifted her chin. "I asked him not to come. And he respects my wishes."

"I'll bet he does," he snorted, the rude sound making her teeth grind.

She shot a meaningful look at her little sister. "Maybe it would be better if we finished this argument some other time, Jeremy."

"Yeah." He grunted under his breath and started to move away, then paused, his expression intent as he stepped closer and leaned down to whisper in her ear. Then he pulled away, gave Sayre a friendly nod of goodbye, and headed back into the forest.

Sayre walked quietly by Jillian's side as they made their way back to Shadow Peak, until the silence finally became unbearable. "You want to say something?" Jillian huffed, too on edge to be reasonable. "If so, please just spit it out and get it over with."

Her sister's slender shoulders lifted in a shrug. "Not really."

"Come on," Jillian groaned. "I can feel it, Sayre. After the night I've had, I don't have the energy to drag it out of you."

"I just… You're fighting it, aren't you?" Sayre turned her head, staring at her with solemn eyes that saw too much for a seventeen-year-old. "You love him, Jilly, but you don't want to. I think you want to give him another chance, but you're too afraid."

"It doesn't matter what I want. There's too much history between me and Jeremy. A future between us would be impossible, so it's best if we just stay away from each other." Though avoiding him was going to be hard to do, considering it looked as if they were going to be working together, but she kept that thought to herself.

"But he's your mate," Sayre murmured, lifting one delicate hand to drag softly through the changing leaves on the low-hanging branches, sending them tumbling from their perches.

They fell a short distance, before being swept up in the chilly wind and carried away…and Jillian wished her troubles could be dealt with so easily. Just brushed off and swept away, floating out of existence like a cloud. "That means you're meant to be together," Sayre added. "Nothing good can come of fighting it."

"And one of the things you'll learn as you get older is that things don't always turn out the way they're meant to."

Sayre made a soft sound of frustration under her breath. "Maybe they would, if we were brave enough to fight for what we wanted."

Despite the headache pounding through her skull, Jillian grinned. "You sound like an idealist, Sayre. I hope you never grow out of it."

It took her a moment to realize that her sister was no longer keeping pace at her side. When she stopped and turned around, she found Sayre standing beneath an ethereal beam of moonlight, her slender frame vibrating with tension. Her usual easygoing smile had been replaced by a pinched look of temper that had Jillian blinking in surprise.

"Stop talking to me as if I'm a child, because I'm not one anymore. I know you don't want to admit it, but I'm growing up, Jillian. I'm growing up and I have a brain that's fully capable of functioning. I can form my own opinions and beliefs, and I can see *more* than others. I can see what's really happening between you and Jeremy, even if you won't admit it. And I know why. I—I know about mother."

A soft breath jerked out of her lungs, and Jillian shook her head as if to clear it. "What?"

"Mother told me, when I turned sixteen. She wanted me to understand what had happened to her so that I would know to be careful."

"What did she tell you?" Jillian asked, wondering what

strange cosmic event had occurred in the universe tonight to throw her world into such chaos. She'd been on a steady, even keel for so long, allowing herself to feel so little—and now she felt battered by emotional waves, struggling to stay afloat in an endless, surging sea of commotion.

"All of it, Jillian. About the Lycan she fell in love with while away at school, about giving her virginity to him and about how he turned away from her even though he *knew* she loved him. Even though he knew how she felt, he used her and then abandoned her, because he'd only been looking to have some fun. He *didn't* love her in return. She told me that he was your father, and that after he left, she didn't think she'd ever love again. And then she came back to the pack and set eyes on Dad, and that was all it took. She not only found her lifemate, but a man who returned her love and one who was more than happy to accept you and love you like his own daughter. She told me…everything."

The center of Jillian's chest hurt as if she'd been kicked, and her hand pressed against it in an instinctual move to hold in the rapid pounding of her heart. "I didn't know that you knew," she whispered, wincing at the scratchy sound of her voice. "You never said anything."

"Mother asked me not to tell you that she'd told me, but I think it's something that needs to be discussed."

"Why?" she asked bitterly. "What good is going to come from it?"

"Because it's affecting your life, Jillian." Sayre tilted her head to the side, her blue-gray eyes luminous and bright in the silvery moonlight. "I think you're taking Mother's warnings to heart, aren't you? Because of what happened to her, you're afraid of following your heart. You've always been afraid."

She frowned, knowing it wasn't that simple. "There's more

to it than that, Sayre. I have my responsibility to the pack, which isn't one to take lightly. The League has never made any secret about their feelings on the subject, and I have to agree with them. Jeremy isn't the type to make a sacrifice for others. He would have demanded I stay away from Shadow Peak and abandon those who rely on me. And you know what kind of reputation he has. Any woman foolish enough to trust him is just that. A fool."

Sayre gave her a sad smile. "You don't believe in the power of love? In its strength?"

"You sound like a romantic," she muttered, feeling too old and worn-out, as if her youth had been dried up in heartbreak and bitterness.

"I am, Jillian. I've seen love. I've seen commitment and fidelity and a metaphysical union of the souls." Sayre gave a little grin. "However you want to describe it, it *does* exist. All you have to do is look at Mother and Father to see th—"

"He's not my father."

For the first time in her life, Jillian watched her sister's face flush with anger. "Don't ever let me hear you say that again, because it makes you sound like an idiot. He loves you like his own. Anyone can see that."

"I'm sorry," she breathed out, the shaky timbre of the words betraying her real emotions. "You're right. He does love me. I know that. I'm just…upset tonight, Sayre. This really isn't a good time for me."

"Jillian, the one who protects her heart from fear of loss ends up with no heart at all. Just an empty chest, because she has nothing to lose. I love you too much to see that happen to you. Look inside yourself. Jeremy may be bold and arrogant, but he's a good person. I think you've let the warnings and fears of the League bleed into your heart and have judged him unfairly. How could you know what he's willing to sacrifice for you, when you've never given him the chance? And you're already in pain from being near him and not having him. What could be worse?"

"What could be worse?" Jillian repeated, wiping angrily at the hot, stinging wash of tears she could feel gathering at the corners of her eyes. "How about loving him and discovering that he doesn't love me the same way?"

Sayre shook her head sadly, while the wind caught at her pale curls and tousled them around her fey face. "I've always thought you were the bravest person I know," she said sadly, "but you sound like a coward, Jillian."

Her mouth twisted into a wry expression that felt more like a grimace than a smile. "You're probably right." She took a deep breath, then jerked her head toward the direction of home. "Now, come on and let me walk you back. Mother is going to freak if you stay out past your curfew."

When they reached their parents' house, Sayre unlatched the gate, walked through and then closed it behind her. "He wants you, Jillian. And he doesn't seem like the kind of guy to give up once he sets his mind on something."

"I know," she murmured, recalling his earlier words. He wanted her for sex—nothing more. And he'd reminded her of the fact he meant to have her with those last whispered words in her ear.

Taking a deep breath, Jillian lifted her face to stare at the moon, as had become her habit over the years. She could lose herself in its soothing light, imagine she was some other woman…in some other life…with a heart that didn't belong to a man she could never have. "That's what I'm afraid of."

"No, it's not," Sayre said softly. "What you're afraid of is that you won't be able to resist him forever."

Jillian closed her eyes as the truth of those words spread

through her. By the time she opened them, she stood alone under the milky glow of the moon, the only sound that of the front door closing softly behind her sister.

Chapter 5

*H*ome.

Jeremy pulled his truck in to the familiar gravel driveway, the sight of the two-story house nestled among the autumn-colored trees sending him into a reeling tumble of memories. The massive weeping willow that he'd played in as a child still swayed like a giant swamp monster at the back corner, its long, leafy arms twisting wildly in the breeze. Even the fall of the curtains in the windows looked the same, the cedar facade as well kept as the day he'd left. The place hadn't changed at all in the past decade, as if time had stood still. Maybe it had. Damn, the wounds that had been inflicted here still felt as fresh as if it had all happened yesterday.

Without a doubt, his pride still stung.

Amazing now to think that he hadn't been back since things had gone south with Jillian, when he'd finally accepted the fact that she'd never choose him over her beloved pack…

that she'd never trust him with her heart and her happiness.
That night he'd moved his things to the Alley, and he'd never
set foot in Shadow Peak again. Not until he'd gone before the
League and submitted his Bloodrunning numbers. It had been
late then, just like now, and the town had looked eerily the
same after a decade, any changes softened by the concealing
shadows of night.

Time to go inside, he thought, and yet, he didn't move.

He swallowed the shaky feeling in his throat, and rested
his hands on the steering wheel, amused at himself for being
so emotional. He was a Bloodrunner, a hunter of killers, for
god's sake. He couldn't afford to be sentimental and nostal-
gic, but damn if his chest didn't feel tight at the thought of
setting foot in the house again after all these years. His parents
were at their beach property down in Florida, where they'd
spent more and more time over the past decade, visiting with
Jeremy at the Alley whenever they were home. When it'd
been decided that he would be the one returning to the pack,
he'd wanted to rent a cabin on the outskirts of town, but his
mother wouldn't hear of it. She'd wanted him home, in his
own room, where she said he belonged, and refused to take
no for an answer.

They'd always had faith in him, unlike some people, and
for that Jeremy knew he was unquestionably lucky. But even
after everything that had gone down, he didn't hate Jillian.
He'd wanted to, and he'd given it a hell of an effort—but the
part of him that belonged to her, that linked them together,
wouldn't let him.

Instead, his hatred had latched on to the pack itself, on to
the archaic laws that set the Runners apart because they
weren't what the others considered "perfect." That created the
social divide between the Alley and Shadow Peak, one based
on racism and hatred, bitterness and distrust. A timeless, en-

during fury surged through his veins, swift and brutal and vivid in its intensity, just like it had the day his father had first explained to him why he was considered "different" from the other children he knew. Why he and his small group of friends were picked on and called names by the residents of the Lycan town that was supposed to be their home…their family…their rock and their strength.

Purist bastards.

No, he'd never planned on coming back.

Instead, he'd planned to keep hunting, satisfied that his life held a purpose, proud of his choices, determined to ignore the little voice in his head that continually reminded him something was missing. Something vital and important. Something meaningful. Something he *needed*. And it wasn't the pack or a place that his life lacked, but a woman. *One* woman. One who at this very moment was probably snuggling up in front of a roaring fire with Eric Drake.

Son of a bitch.

From the moment she'd come home from school, Jeremy had known Jillian was meant to be his. But she'd stubbornly refused to let a relationship develop between them, until that one afternoon when she'd finally given in and allowed him to kiss her. Despite its innocence when compared to his sexual history, that kiss had floored him, affecting him more powerfully than anything he'd ever experienced. He could still remember the way she'd felt against him, in his arms, and how badly he'd wanted to take her out into the fields, lay her down into the soft green grass, strip her clothes from her body and make love to her until neither one of them could move. He could remember how her skin had felt beneath his hands as he'd touched her sun-warmed shoulders, the petal-soft sweetness of her mouth, the mind-drugging scent of her body.

"Kiss me again," she'd whispered when he'd finally

walked her to her door, so she wouldn't be late for dinner. He remembered the way his hands had shaken when he'd held her face and pressed his mouth to hers. Could still hear his own fractured groan when he'd lost control and driven the chaste kiss into something dark and hungry and lust-flavored. Wild with craving, he'd been ready to press her against the door and claim her then and there, but the sudden brightness of the porch light being flipped on had wrenched them both back to sanity. As it was, he'd had to cover his erection with his jacket when her mother had opened the door...and she'd known. He'd never been able to get anything past Constance Murphy.

Considering the warnings her mother had probably delivered about his character, Jeremy could have forgiven Jillian for being wary. Damn, he knew what his reputation had been, what it still was. But what he couldn't forgive was that she'd never even given him the chance. If she had, she'd have known how ridiculous it was to worry about him straying. He hadn't wanted other women—he'd only wanted Jillian.

Christ, he still did. He always had. Like his crooked bottom tooth, this insatiable hunger for her was always there...always with him.

And every woman he'd had since that kiss—since leaving the pack—had paled in comparison. That was why he was always left hungry, never satisfied. He could grasp at temporary relief, but true satisfaction—true peace—always hovered just beyond his reach.

Of course, the question of his fidelity had only been part of the problem. Even if he'd gained her trust, the pack would have still stood between them.

The pack, it seemed, would always stand between them.

His fingers tightened on the steering wheel to the point that it groaned, a fraction away from cracking, and Jeremy forced himself to release it, flexing his fingers one by one.

"God, you just need to get her out of your system." He thrust his hands back through his hair, shoving the thick mass off his forehead, then reached for the door and climbed out of the truck. Deciding he needed to walk out his tension, he left his bags in the cab and headed down the sidewalk, the night silent but for his heavy footfalls.

He made a left, then took a right at the next cross street, heading toward the softly glowing lights on Main Street.

He could hear the twang of country music coming from the pub that sat on the upcoming corner, and he debated whether or not to go in and have a drink. He could have used the steadying burn of whiskey in his gut at the moment, but it was a given that he wouldn't be welcomed as a customer there. Not that he cared.

As he neared the entrance to the pub, the front door swung open, letting out a stream of smoke and the grinding blare of music. A tall, broad man stepped onto the sidewalk, leaning down to light the cigarette hanging from his lips, his hands cupped around the fragile flame. The tip of the cigarette sparked, glowing a dark orange, and he shifted under the streetlamp as he tucked a silver lighter into his back pocket. The milky glow of light illuminated the distinguished angles of his face and short, dark brown hair clipped close to his head…and Jeremy's wolf stirred beneath his skin. The blast of energy from his animal drew the man's gaze as he lifted his head, his dark gray eyes glowing with a preternatural fire in the shadowed darkness.

Eric Drake. Just the bastard he wanted to see.

Jealousy crept up in him like a huge, ugly beast, hungry for confrontation. Wearing a feral smile, he braced his feet and planted himself right in the Lycan's path.

Drawing a deep drag off his smoke, Eric inclined his head toward the shadowy stretch of sidewalk at Jeremy's back. "You're in my way, Burns."

Jeremy arched one brow, his voice a silken, rasping taunt. "And here I thought maybe you were in mine."

A slow smile curled the other man's mouth. "Are we talking about the sidewalk…or a woman?"

Jeremy cocked his head. "I know everyone around here thinks you're the golden boy of Shadow Peak, but I'm not buying it, Drake. Apples never fall far from the tree, and your old man's as rotten as they come."

"Now see, that's where you're wrong." He paused, taking another slow, satisfying drag. "If that were the case, you'd be like your old man. Reliable. Worthy. Devoted. And instead, look how you treated the woman nature created for you."

"What's between Jillian and me is none of your business," he snarled, aware that his fangs were burning in his gums, just waiting to slip free.

"Wrong again. Jillian's my friend—"

"And she's *my* mate."

"And I care about her," Drake grunted, his metallic gray eyes narrowed. "I'd hate to see her get hurt because of some arrogant jackass who doesn't know how to leave well enough alone."

Jeremy took a step forward, vibrating with a low-frequency rage as he spread his arms wide. "You got a problem with me, help yourself."

Eric eyed him from beneath his lashes, then took another slow, deliberate drag on his cigarette. "Ya know, if I didn't know better," he drawled, grinning as he exhaled an ethereal stream of smoke, "I'd say you stink of jealousy, Burns."

"And if I didn't know better," he growled, taking a step closer, "I'd say you were just begging to get your ass kicked."

Shaking his head, Drake laughed softly under his breath. "God, this is going to be fun, having you back in town," he murmured, and the cell phone on his hip started buzzing. After taking a quick look at the number, he sent Jeremy a hard smile. "As fun as this has been, I'm afraid we'll have to finish it later."

Then he answered the phone with a low, "Hey, you okay?" and set off down the street in the other direction. Jeremy stared after him, unable to get the sick feeling out of his gut that Drake was talking to Jillian.

Goddamn it. Had she called the bastard for comfort? To tell him she was okay? Or for something more?

With that infuriating thought eating its way through his mind, Jeremy stalked off into the shadows, nothing more than the possessive burn of jealousy keeping him company along the way.

After a restless night's sleep, the morning sun was still a distant promise on the horizon when Jeremy reached the house leased by Dylan Riggs. The thirty-nine-year-old Elder lived in a single story cedar cabin, his small front yard immaculately landscaped, blooming with a cascade of colorful, vivid blooms despite the fact that it was fall. Jeremy jumped onto the front porch, knocked, waited, then knocked again. He heard shuffling from inside, and then a bleary-eyed Dylan opened up, wearing nothing but a pair of boxer shorts. His light brown hair hung over his forehead, upper lip curled in a snarl until his eyes focused on Jeremy.

"Morning, sunshine. Late night?" Propping his shoulder against the door frame, Jeremy crossed his arms and arched one brow as he took in Dylan's haggard appearance. Normally looking like something that had stepped off the cover of *GQ*, it was a shock to see him like this. "I'm not interrupting anything, am I?"

"Only my sleep," Dylan muttered. He pushed his hair back with one hand and scratched at his chest with the other. "Come on in. I need coffee."

Jeremy smothered a soft laugh as he walked inside, shutting the door behind him while his gaze scanned the room, taking everything in. It was strange to see how Dylan lived, after knowing him all these years. The house was surprisingly clean for a bachelor. Either Dylan was severely domesticated, in which case he planned to rib him mercilessly like any good pal would, or the guy had a bevy of women looking after him. He was leaning toward the latter. "So who was she?"

Dylan went still for a beat of three seconds, then sent him a sharp look over his shoulder. "Who was who?"

"The woman who kept you up all night."

"Like I'd tell your sorry ass," Dylan snorted.

"Come on." Jeremy sighed, hooking a chair with his foot and plopping down at the round kitchen table. "You know you can trust me."

"Yeah, right." Dylan's drawl was wry, his tone light, but there was something around the Elder's eyes that caught Jeremy's attention.

Shaking off the uncomfortable sensation, thinking this whole town was just screwing with his head, he watched Dylan open a cupboard and pull down a fresh bag of coffee beans. "So I know why I look like hell," the Elder grunted, "but why do you?"

"Didn't sleep much last night," he said, slowly releasing the air from his lungs, willing his tension to flow out just as easily, like water slipping smoothly down a drain.

"Which means I can't, either?" Dylan grouched, flipping the coffeepot on and turning around, bracing himself against the counter. He scratched at his chest again, then at the dark shadows on his cheeks and chin.

Jeremy gave a gritty laugh. "The rock being hurled through my mom's front window had me up at dawn. I'm not surprised I look like death warmed over, since I feel like it, too."

"Son of a bitch." Dylan's posture went rigid, while the coffeepot sputtered and steamed at his side, filling the air with the rich, smoky scent of fresh-brewed French roast. "You already have rocks being thrown at you? What'll be next? I knew this was a shitty plan, just like I told you before. Things are too unstable right now, and you're walking right into the middle of it."

Jeremy shrugged one shoulder. "Has to be done, Dylan."

"Why? You know I'm here to help—"

"We know that." He sighed. "But you've got to be careful or you're going to find yourself out of a job. If anyone on the League suspects you're trying to finger one of them as a traitor, your ass will be banished in a heartbeat. None of the Runners want to see that happen. You're one of the last voices of sanity left in this place."

"I still think this is too dangerous," the Elder muttered, his dark eyes hooded beneath a frustrated scowl that reminded Jeremy of when they were younger. Dylan's mother had come from a werewolf pack in upstate Virginia, and after his parents' separation, he and his sister had split their time between the two packs. Despite the fact that his father was an Elder, Dylan had been treated as an outsider by the Silvercrest, which had precipitated his friendship with the Runners. When his father passed away, Dylan had claimed the hereditary right of succession to take his father's place. There were many within the pack who had believed he was too soft to serve in a leadership role, until he'd proven them wrong by defeating a string of challengers.

To this day, he remained a friend, as well as a supporter, of the Bloodrunners.

"I know you want to help us," Jeremy told him, "but you're already walking a fine enough line as it is, Dylan. Be careful or Stefan Drake will demand your removal. And if not him, then one of the others. They already think you're too radical in your beliefs."

Dylan cursed under his breath and poured the coffee, then handed a mug to Jeremy and took a seat at the table. After a few blissful sips of the rich brew that fed the caffeine addiction his friends continuously ribbed him about, Jeremy got to the point of his visit. "I need some answers about Jillian."

Dylan took one look at his expression over the rim of his mug, and knew exactly what was coming. Blowing out a rough breath, he took a quick sip, then set his coffee on the table. Pushing both hands back through his hair, he said, "Hell, I knew this was gonna happen."

"You should have told me," Jeremy said in an even tone, curling his fingers around the thick handle of his mug, careful not to squeeze too hard lest he shatter it. "I had a right to know."

"She asked me not to." The Elder sighed.

He'd suspected as much, but it still pissed him off to hear it. His fingers tightened, and he forced himself to loosen his hold. "You should have told me anyway."

Dylan sent him an impatient look. "Jillian's my friend, Jeremy, same as you. Do you want me spilling all of *your* secrets?"

He spread his arms wide, while his mouth curled into a cocky smirk. "Hey, I've got nothing to hide. I'm an open book."

"Oh, yeah?" Dylan slouched in the kitchen chair, brows lifting in a skeptical arch. "Then you won't mind if I tell her you only date brown-eyed, petite blondes who look a helluva lot like her...and only for one night? You won't mind her knowing that I've never seen you with the same woman twice? That you're known for having a ruthless sex drive, but end your involvement there, never letting any of them get close to you, almost as if you were saving yourself for someone? As if your heart already belonged to another?"

There were times when Jeremy really wanted to tell Dylan Riggs to go to hell, friends or not. This was one of them. "Your point?" he challenged, his voice reminding him of the crushed glass he'd cleaned up just that morning.

"My point," Dylan shot back, a sharp sound of frustration in his throat, "is that you had better think long and hard before you decide on the rules here. Fair is fair. If I go spilling Jillian's secrets, yours are gonna get spilled, as well."

Irritation had him surging to his feet, pacing the cozy kitchen from one end to the other. "Don't give me that *fair is fair* bullshit," he growled. "Gossiping about my sex life and Jillian's fighting are two completely different things. She could have been killed, Dylan. She could have goddamn died in one of those fights! You should have told me what was happening."

Slumping back in his chair, Dylan eyed him with a fascinated mixture of surprise and humor. "And how was I supposed to know you even cared, Jeremy?"

He ground his jaw, refusing to touch that one. There was nothing he could say that wouldn't incriminate him—and the bastard knew it.

Dylan sighed, scrubbing his hands down his face…and that strange look was in his eyes again, as if he were somehow in pain. He rubbed the heels of his palms into his eyes, then dropped them into his lap, his gaze focused on the window, some distant point in the early morning sky. "Look, I'm sorry. I know it's hell on you, the way things turned out. I guess that's one of the reasons I've kept things to myself. Whether you like it or not, Jillian has had to deal with a lot of fallout from her involvement with you, and that isn't going to change. Not unless you're ready to make your return here permanent and claim her as your own. And somehow I don't think that's what you've got in mind."

Jeremy rolled his shoulders and shoved his hands deep into the front pockets of his jeans. "Why do I suddenly get the feeling there's a lecture on the way here?"

"Seriously, man. Jillian's been through a lot because of you—"

"Uh-uh," he muttered, shaking his head. "I'll take responsibility for my screwups, but I'm innocent in this one. She threw any chance we would have had away because she chose to believe one of her jealous little friends over me. Because she was too afraid to stand up to the League. Any hell she's had to live with was her own creation. I'm not taking the rap for it." He paused, focusing on getting his breathing back to normal, aware that he was losing his control. "Not that it makes any difference. You'll all believe what you want to believe. You always have."

"Cut the crap," Dylan rasped, glaring at him. "We've never talked about it before, but if you say you never strayed, then I believe you. But what I believe isn't important. Jillian's the one you need to convince."

"And why would I want to go and do that?" he grunted, working his jaw.

Dylan threw back his head and let out a deep, rumbling crack of laughter. Standing up, he walked to Jeremy and clapped him on the shoulder, a wry grin tilting the curve of his mouth. "You're my friend and I admire you, Jeremy. I really do. But if you think how you feel about Jillian Murphy isn't written all over your face, then you really are a dumb-ass."

"Gee, thanks." He grimaced, hating that Dylan was right.

"I'm not the only one who'll notice. You need to be careful."

"Yeah," he drawled with a heavy dose of sarcasm. "I'll be sure to keep my eye out for the bogeyman hiding under my bed at night."

Dylan's eyes narrowed as they stared each other down. "That's the problem with you Runners," he muttered in a quiet rasp, shaking his head. "You all think you're so goddamn invincible. I'm serious, man. Don't laugh this off. It's dangerous, you being back here. Whoever's behind this knows you're closing in. That's going to make them act."

Something in the guy's tone caught Jeremy's attention, making the hairs on the back of his neck stand up. "What are you saying?"

"You're here to do a job, Jeremy. Don't draw Jillian into the middle of it."

The line of his mouth went hard, and his brows pulled together in a dark scowl. "I'm not looking to get her hurt. You should know me better than that."

"I know you lose your head where she's concerned," Dylan argued. "I know you're so on edge at the idea of being near her again that you're all but buzzing with the vibes."

"You getting metaphysical on me?" he snorted, wondering when he's become so transparent. It was on the tip of his tongue to ask Dylan about Jillian's relationship with Eric Drake, but the idea of hearing anything he might have to say put a sour feeling in the pit of his stomach.

"Fine, be a smart-ass." Dylan sighed, propping his hip against the kitchen counter. "But I'm giving you good advice, Jeremy. Watch your back, trust no one and, for god's sake, watch Jillian's. She's too trusting by far, and the one you're after won't hesitate to hurt her to get to you."

"If I could do this without involving her, I would," he said after a heavy pause. "But you know I need her help. She knows the Silvercrest better than anyone, even better than you."

Dylan scowled. "Like I said, just don't trust anyone."

"You been watching old *X-Files* episodes again?" He laughed roughly. "You sound as paranoid as Mulder."

"That's because I *am* paranoid. We're hanging together by a thread here, man. Pull things too far in one direction, screw with the tension and the whole damn thing is going to snap."

"Warning taken," he said easily, heading for the door. "And I promise to be the soul of discretion. I won't step on any toes or tweak any noses. I'll be a goddamn Boy Scout."

"You don't even know the meaning," Dylan grumbled to his back.

He pulled the front door open, but turned back before heading out. "One more thing."

"Yeah?"

A wry smile curved his mouth. "Where does she live?"

Dylan shook his head, his expression heavy. "In the white cottage over on Lassiter Avenue."

He nodded. "Thanks. I'll keep in touch. "

"You do that. And be careful," Dylan called out as Jeremy headed down the porch steps.

"You know me," Jeremy answered over his shoulder. "Careful's practically my middle name."

Chapter 6

Jillian blinked against the brilliant shafts of early morning sunlight burning at Jeremy's back, setting his big body alight, as if he were glowing. God, she needed more sleep if she was expected to deal with him this early in the day. She hadn't even had her first cup of coffee or a shower yet.

But Jeremy looked as if he'd been up for hours. Scarred brown hiking boots covered his big feet, and she worked her way up from there. He wore jeans and an untucked white Irish linen shirt with thin green stripes, its sleeves rolled back on his dark forearms, the masculine tracery of thick veins and ropey sinew visible beneath his golden, hair-dusted skin. His throat was muscled and tanned, his jaw strong, chin firm…and the curve of his mouth warned her that he was going to be a handful. The warm glow in his hazel eyes only confirmed it.

"You shouldn't be here," she said huskily, surprised at

how thick her voice sounded. "If you needed to see me, you could have called and I would have met up with you somewhere."

"What's the problem?" he asked, trying to pull off a look of innocence, while his aura was all but buzzing with sharp-edged, predatory energy. He was on the hunt. And she felt like the prey.

Jillian only wished she didn't like the feeling quite as much as she did.

"I didn't say there was a problem. But—"

"Then what are we doing that's so wrong?" he asked with an easygoing smile, looking too sexy for his own good. "We're just two people who are going to work together to try and solve a mystery, find a bad guy, save the day. Heroic stuff. So where's the harm in that? Unless your loverboy doesn't like the idea of you spending time with me," he added silkily.

She clenched her teeth, then forced herself to relax. If she let him, he'd have her wound up in so many knots, she'd never unwind again. "Eric has nothing to do with me and you."

"Is that so?" he asked lightly, arching one tawny brow. Wearing a crooked grin, he looked her over, making her shiver despite the thick terrycloth robe she'd pulled on over her panties and tank top. "You and Eric Drake," he murmured thoughtfully, staring at the base of her throat, where she knew her pulse was fluttering wildly, revealing her reaction to him. And she *was* reacting. Jillian couldn't be near him, assaulted by that warm, crisp male scent and gorgeous body without suffering a meltdown. "Is he still here?"

Looking over her head, his dark eyes raked the shadowed interior of her home, sharp and suspicious. She knew, without even asking, what he was thinking. "No, he isn't hiding, Jeremy."

His gaze reconnected with hers, and she sucked in a

startled breath at the blatant burn of possession glittering in his eyes. "Then now's as good a time as any for you to explain what's going on between the two of you," he rasped, stepping closer, until she could feel the heat of his body. His scent was everywhere, surrounding her, seeping into her pores until she felt light-headed. "No little sisters, no jealous boyfriends lurking around the corner. Come on, Jillian, and enlighten me. I'm all ears."

Blowing out a deep breath, she suddenly didn't have the energy to keep butting heads with him on something he was going to learn for himself before long, anyway. "Listen, I think you got the wrong idea last night. Eric and I aren't a couple. Not like you're thinking. We really are just friends."

"Right," he drawled.

"It's true. But I'm in a complicated situation right now, and our parents…"

Her voice trailed off uncomfortably, and he filled in the rest. "Oh, yeah, I can see that," he supplied in a bitter tone, rocking back on his heels, hands shoved deep in his front pockets. "I bet your parents would cream over having his pure-blooded offspring perched on the branches of their family tree, even if his father is a sadistic bastard."

"It isn't like that, Jeremy. Eric has been helping me buy some time with the League," she explained gruffly. "It's nothing more than that."

His green eyes narrowed, as bright and intense as rain-splashed leaves in the spring. "What the hell does that mean?"

A sound caught her attention, and Jillian glanced to her right, seeing her elderly neighbor, Gloria, dressed in a floral housecoat and galoshes, getting ready to water her front yard. The old woman pretended absorption in her task, but Jillian knew Gloria would be struggling to hear their every word.

"Look, we really shouldn't be having this conversation outside for all the world to hear. I like to protect my privacy."

"Then invite me in," he offered silkily...tempting her to trust the devil.

Jillian rolled her lips together, and shook her head. "That wouldn't be smart."

A low, husky laugh rumbled up from his chest, the provocative sound making her toes curl. "Since when has anything we've ever done been smart?" he drawled, the corner of his sensuous mouth lifting the tiniest fraction. "Come on, I promise I won't bite."

Rolling her eyes, she stepped aside to let him in. "I bet you say that to all the girls."

"Only because it's the truth." The heat of his big body brushed hers as he moved past, making her muscles clench, while deep pulses of sexual tension invaded her system like a drug. God, it made her dizzy, the constant push and pull when they were together. "There's only ever been one woman I've wanted to sink my teeth into," he added in a seductive murmur.

"Poor woman," she snorted, trying to keep things light, when inside she was nothing but a chaotic jumble of destructive needs and dreams and desires.

His deep laughter made her grin, even while her belly fluttered at the sight of his head tilted back, the muscular line of his throat begging for the press of her lips. Giving herself a mental kick in the backside, Jillian struggled to pull herself out of the sensual haze engulfing her, and searched for something mundane to say as she shut her front door. "So, um, how's your first morning back in town been?"

A wry grin twisted his mouth, green eyes glittering with humor as he glanced her way. "Peachy. The welcoming committee around here is just swell."

"Don't tell me you're already causing trouble," she said with a frown, while her fingers fiddled with the knotted belt at her waist. He prowled the room at a slow, casual pace, but Jillian could feel the tension he kept under wraps. It reminded her of a rattler coiling its long body around…and around… and around, waiting for the moment to strike.

"Hey, it's not like I started it." His shoulders lifted in a careless shrug. "Haven't thrown a rock at a single window, I swear."

He stopped by her DVD shelf, running his finger over the various titles, and flashed her a boyish smile that made her go *still*. Everywhere. Inside and out. One smile, and Jillian was completely frozen, simply because of how much it reminded her of the twenty-two-year-old Jeremy she used to know. Swallowing, she struggled for her voice. "S-someone threw a rock at your parents' house?" she asked hoarsely.

"Yep." He moved on to study one of her many bookshelves that lined the walls. "Shattered the front window in the living room. Mom's gonna be pissed."

"God, this is a nightmare," she groaned, shoving her tangled hair off her forehead. "I have to grab a shower and get dressed. Have a seat or whatever. I'll be right back."

"Take your time," Jeremy murmured, wanting a few minutes to himself so that he could study her house without the distraction of her presence. Jillian headed down the hallway, leaving him alone in the living room. Whistling an old Metallica song under his breath, he stood in the center of the floor, his hands itching at his sides. He wanted to run them over the surface of her belongings, as if he could take in a part of her— *learn her*—simply by touching her things. A plush sofa in full-grain leather sat against the far wall, its rich chestnut color enhanced by the eggshell hue of the wall at its back, with a black-and-white Ansel Adams print hanging above it. In front sat a low coffee table in dark mahogany, and on the opposite wall stood an armoire with expanding shelves that were packed with books, its center doors pulled shut so that the TV couldn't be seen.

The corners of his eyes crinkled with a grin as he remembered how much Jillian hated television. She'd always preferred a good book to watching TV. Still whistling, he headed down the hallway, walking past the door to the bathroom, the muffled sound of Jillian's shower making him sweat. Needing a distraction from the thought of her naked body standing beneath the warm spray of water, he kept going until he found her bedroom at the end of the hall. Propping his shoulder against the door frame, Jeremy looked around, soaking up the intimate details like a flower soaking in sunlight and rain. They nurtured his soul in the same way, filling the empty hollows that had been starved for the details of her life.

Shadows painted the rich gray of the back wall as watery morning sunlight crept past the sheer white drapes covering the windows. A classic iron bed with footboard and headboard sat catty-corner, facing the door, its white sheets sleep-rumpled, probably still warm from her body, and in another lifetime, he would have wanted to go and roll around in them, soaking in her scent. Would have wanted to lie on those soft sheets and open his eyes to the early morning rays of light spilling onto the warm nickel finish of the bed, watching it wash over the delicate features of the woman lying wrapped in his arms, her expression relaxed in sleep, a satisfied smile on her lips, the provocative mark of his teeth on her throat.

"But you're smarter than that now," he huffed under his breath, hoping like hell it was true. Now, he just wanted to get as much of her as he could, for as long as he was there. Then he'd leave and get the hell on with his life. He'd find a way to—

"Jeremy?"

He jerked at the sound of her voice behind him, and felt his ears go hot, a muffled curse on his lips as she waited for him to turn around. The little daydream had left him rigid with arousal, and there was no way she'd fail to notice. Wearing a crooked grin, Jeremy turned and repositioned his shoulder against the frame, his long arms crossed over his chest.

"You caught me," he confessed in a husky rasp, the corner of his mouth twitching as he stared down at her. "I saw that bed and the moment got away from me."

She shivered, and he reached out and caught a drop of water that clung to an eyelash, careful not to hurt her. She was wrapped up in her grannie robe again, but underneath he knew she was warm and soft and naked, her skin still damp from the shower. He wanted to take her down to the floor so badly that he shook, his insides tremoring like a ground-breaking quake. "So," he said softly, wondering if his smile looked as wolfish as he felt, "you wanna go to bed with me?"

Did she want to go to bed with him?

Jillian placed one hand over her heart, the other across her lower abdomen, as if to protect herself, though she didn't fear him physically. No, that had never been the problem. But there was something infinitely fragile inside of her, something breakable, that only he could destroy. In truth, she feared the things he could do to her. Things he could make her feel, make her crave. The way he could shatter her into pieces and leave her broken. And he could.

Her heart was so very vulnerable to him, just like a slip of green breaking through the rugged ground to seek sustenance from the sun and rain, blooming with the heat and vitality of life, so fragile and easily ground into dust if not treated with care.

But she was her own worst enemy—because everything deep inside of her, all those secret places and organs and churning depths of desire, they all burned for him, eager and willing to sacrifice the sense and rightness of protecting herself. They wanted to lunge forward and lay down in offering at his feet. Wanted to spread her thighs and beg to take him into her, make him a part of her, whether he destroyed her or not. Just to have him close. The musky, male scent of his skin, its heat and silken texture stretched hard over powerful muscles that could so easily break her if he forgot to be careful. All of it leading to the ultimate moment when her walls were lowered and he would discover one of the most closely guarded secrets of being a Spirit Walker. A secret that had kept her from acting on her powerful desires all those years ago—one that would quite simply reveal her heart to Jeremy in the most intimate way.

No, she couldn't risk it. She *wouldn't* risk it.

"You think we should hop into bed together, just like that?" She tried to keep her tone light, though it was virtually impossible.

The heat in his eyes deepened, turning them a darker green, the skin stretched over his cheekbones flushed with color. "Yeah, just like that. The offer may sound casual, but I promise that once I get you there, there won't be anything casual about it."

"God, Jeremy." Her eyes closed, tears that she couldn't hold in leaking from the corners. They were hot with emotion, with starved desires that were so tired of being hungry. Of being denied. "Why do you have to be so provoking?"

"I haven't even started." He laughed softly under his breath, the sound rigid and strained, like his body. She felt his heat shift closer, and opened her eyes as she took a quick step back, needing to keep whatever distance between them she could.

His dark gaze smoldered, a kaleidoscope of questions shifting through their depths, as he stared down at her. "Dammit, Jillian, stop doing that."

"Doing what?"

"Scurrying away like a frightened little mouse whenever I get near you." He stepped even closer, until she could feel the physical heat of his body, the warmth of his breath...salty sweet, like his taste. So close she could see the golden shadow of stubble on his chin, the sexy crinkles at the corners of his hazel eyes. "I know I don't scare you. Not physically. Not like that."

"You're right," she conceded. Her skin felt damp in intimate places, and she knew it wasn't from her shower. She wet her bottom lip with her tongue, aware that her breath was coming faster, panting. "This is called self-preservation."

"You don't want to let yourself get too close to me, and I can't help but wonder why that is." His voice lowered, deepened, while the look in his eyes went darker, his lids heavy as he held her stare, daring her to look away. "You don't have to protect yourself from me, Jillian."

She found herself swaying toward him, when the memory of his words from the night before slammed into her, cutting through the haze of lust clouding her judgment. It hit with the jarring impact of a lightning strike, jolting her back to reality. He wanted her for sex—only for the moment, not forever. And if she gave in, when he left he would take a part of her with him. A part of her she could never get back.

"No. I won't do this," she whispered, reaching up to press against his chest.

"Do what?" he demanded, covering her hands with his own, the touch of his palms rough, warm. He flattened her hands against his chest, until she could feel the heavy, thundering beat of his heart. "What won't you do? Sex? Me?" He gave a low, sinful laugh. "If ever there was a time to be specific, Jillian, it's now."

"This…us…" she panted, trembling. "It isn't going to happen."

One of his hands settled at her waist, the other curling around the back of her neck, supporting her head as she stared up at him. His lips parted slightly, eyes glowing with the visceral hunger of his wolf, the intense need carved into his hard expression making her breathless. When he spoke, the velvet-rough timbre of his voice was mesmerizing, deliciously seductive. "Do you know how hard I've tried to forget you?"

She tried to respond, but couldn't get the words past the tightness of her throat.

Sensing his advantage, Jeremy moved closer still, and she found herself caught, trapped between his hard muscled length and the unyielding wall at her back. His chest pressed against the hard tips of her breasts, the shockingly thick bulge behind his fly lodged intimately against the hollow of her stomach, emotions churning in her belly like birds that had just been frightened into flight. "But every day your memory's just grown stronger, sharper," he murmured, that evocative voice deep and rich and rumbling…making her liquid and soft. "I've dreamed about you so many nights. Imagined having you under me. More times than I can count."

A choked sound vibrated in her throat, her eyes damp… hot. "God, Jeremy, don't do this to me."

"It's not me, it's you. You're the one who won't stop tormenting me. Who won't leave me in peace." He lifted his hand from her waist, running the back of his knuckles along the curve of her cheek, stroking her skin with a tender, reverent touch that made her chest hurt, her heart pound. "I've seen it happen so many times in my dreams. Watched your eyes go hazy, these smooth cheeks flush with color. Heard your breath catch in the back of your throat. Felt you spill over my hand, around my fingers, while your screams filled my head. Felt your body take me in, squeezing me, so tight and hot and sweet I thought I'd go out of my mind."

She drew an unsteady breath. "It isn't going to happen."

A sexy, irresistible smile played at his lips. "Yes, it will. As many times as I want it to. However many ways you can take it. I want them all, Jillian. Every goddamn one of them."

"Are you deaf," she said shakily, "or just stubborn?"

He leaned in close, and his lips touched her ear as he said, "I'm a realist, honey. It *will* happen, because it's what we both want—what we both need. And when I'm buried deep inside you—heavy, hot, thick—you're going to break so hard that you'll scream. So hard that I'll be able to taste your cries in my mouth. You can believe that, Jillian, even if you won't believe anything else."

"Who do you think you are?" she whispered, hating the way her voice trembled…and not with anger. Oh, no. It was like some kind of switch had been flipped in her head…and now she was being sucked in…all her struggles surging against an ever-growing current that rendered them useless, destroyed. "You think I don't know how good you are in bed? Ha! You think women haven't relished shoving your reputation in my face over the years, every chance they got? I'm sure you can make a woman scream just by looking at her, Jeremy, but it isn't going to work on me."

He didn't get angry, didn't smile. He just stared down at her, his expression hard, rigid with lust. "You're panicking."

"I'm not—"

"You're panicking because of what's happening here between us, and instead of giving it a chance, you want to run," he went on, clearly warming to his theory. He pressed closer, bracing his left forearm against the wall, his other hand settling like a hot, heavy brand against her hip. "You can tell yourself you want Eric, but it'll never happen... never stick. For one simple reason, Jillian. He. Isn't. Me."

A sharp, hoarse sound jerked from her throat. "Do you even know how arrog—"

"I know what I'm talking about," he rasped, cutting her off in a dark, provocative drawl, long fingers squeezing her hip, caressing her through the fabric of her robe as he watched her beneath heavy lashes. "Do you think I haven't tried to find a woman who could make me forget you?" He laughed, and the sound was scratchy, coarse...somehow damaged.

"But they were never enough," he added in a husky whisper, trailing his rough palm up her side, until it curved around the outer swell of her breast, his thumb sweeping out to stroke over her tight, sensitive nipple. "So you can keep telling yourself that it won't happen, but you know it's a lie. You want me, Jillian. You want what we have between us. You want to get it out of your system as badly as I do."

She closed her eyes, letting her head fall back until it banged against the wall. "God, Jeremy," she pleaded. "Please. Please don't do this to me."

The seconds stretched out as he stood staring down at her, holding her there, and then he slowly stepped away. "Okay," he rumbled in a dark, graveled voice, running one hand back through his hair, hunger all but pulsing off him in harsh, potent waves. "If you're going to insist on avoiding the inevitable—"

"It isn't—"

He went on as if she'd never interrupted. "Then let's get the hell out of here. This whole place smells like you and it's screwing with my head."

She blinked up at him, wondering if he would forever throw her off balance. "You want to leave? Now?"

"You go throw some clothes on, and then we can take a walk through town together. I was serious about us working together. I need to take a look around and get a feel for this place."

The change in focus was so sudden, Jillian felt dizzy. And looking at him now, she couldn't help but wonder if he hadn't planned it that way all along. It would be just like him. Because now the seed had been planted. No matter what she did, she wouldn't be able to *not* think about what had happened, about the deliciously wicked things he'd said to her, and how badly she wanted them.

Chapter 7

While Jeremy waited in the living room, Jillian rushed to get dressed. Her hands shook, heart racing as she searched for something to wear. Finally, after throwing on some jeans and a sweater, then ripping her brush through her hair, she was ready to go.

She met Jeremy in the living room, and ten minutes later, they were walking down the sidewalk together, side-by-side, enjoying the morning sunshine as it struggled to burn its way through the storm clouds that had settled like a shroud over the skyline.

When they turned at the end of the street, heading north, he spoke for the first time since leaving her house. "That little trick with Danna last night was pretty cool. How did you take her down like that?"

"When I heal someone, their natural shields are low and I'm able to ease their pain and promote healing by slipping into their minds and enlisting the help of their bodies. It saved my life when I discovered that the same theory applies to fighting. So long as I'm able to dodge their attack long enough that they grow tired, like Danna had, I can slip in and order their body to stop fighting, slamming a mental brake on their rage."

"But it comes with a price." At her look of surprise, he said, "You nearly collapsed on me after the fight, remember?"

Tearing her gaze away from the tender concern in his eyes, Jillian explained. "Using that kind of power takes a lot out of me, whether I'm using it to stop an opponent or healing an injury."

"That makes sense." He slanted her a curious look, and the corner of his mouth twitched with a boyish grin. "So what else can you do now that you're all grown up?"

"Just so you know, my powers are *not* sexual," she drawled, chuckling under her breath at his hopeful tone. At least not that she knew of. But how could she tell him how her powers affected her sexuality, when she didn't even know herself? In that regard, they were as yet untapped, like doors in a house that had never been opened. Until they were unlocked—until someone had possession of the key—there was no way of knowing what waited inside.

Jeremy rubbed his palm against his whiskered jaw. "Not sexual? Dunno about that." He shook his hand out as if he'd touched something hot and been burned. "That kiss last night damn near fried my circuits."

Jillian shot him an *as if* look and gave a feminine snort. "I would think something as simple as a kiss would be pretty boring for a man of your reputation, Burns."

A deep chuckle rumbled up from his chest, but there was an intense heat smoldering in his eyes as he said, "Normally, I'd agree. But that was before I got reminded that kissing you *isn't* like kissing other women."

"Time to change the subject," she murmured, forcing herself to look away from him.

"All right," he said after they passed an elderly couple out taking their morning stroll. "So where *is* Eric?"

"I have no idea." She sighed. "I hardly keep him on a leash, Jeremy."

He rolled his shoulder in that way that men do when they didn't want to look as if they cared one way or the other, but the look he cut her from beneath his lashes smoldered with intensity. "He isn't acting the way he should, you know."

"Oh, yeah? And just how should he be acting?"

He rolled his shoulder again, flashing her a crooked smile. "It's simple. If he really wanted you, he should have planted his fist in my face the second I got within two feet of you. It's what any reasonable guy would have done," he delivered, so deadpan, she couldn't help but laugh.

Jillian was still grinning when they turned the next corner, but her smile fell the second she set eyes on the group ahead of them. A ragtag gang of teenagers lounged in front of Harris's convenience store, their expressions dramatically indolent, full of angst and anger. Coal-black eyeliner rimmed their bloodshot eyes, and their scraggly heads were wreathed in clouds of smoke from the hand-rolled cigarettes they clenched between their stained fingers. She was trying to lead Jeremy across the street, when one of the boys turned their way and he caught sight of the words emblazoned across the front of the kid's T-shirt.

"Son of a bitch. Look at that."

"'Simmons Rules,'" she read aloud. Feeling desperate, knowing a confrontation was inevitable, Jillian tugged on his bicep, trying to pull him in the other direction. "Come on, Jeremy. There's no need to go looking for trouble."

"Sorry," he murmured, staring intently at the group, "but trouble's exactly what I've come looking for."

"Jer—"

"Just wait here for me," he rasped, pulling away from her. "All I want to do is say hello."

"Right," Jillian muttered under her breath, watching as he headed back toward the teenagers. Whether his actions were borne from bravery or stupidity, she couldn't decide. When he stood a few yards away, the group separated, revealing a Lycan in his early twenties. Jillian recognized him instantly as Dustin Sheffield. She didn't know the young man well, but she knew *of* him. His father, Cooper Sheffield, was considered Drake's right-hand man here in town, handling the Elder's dirty work. Ironically, Sheffield also held the title of security chief for the pack. Like his father, Dustin was tall and dark, with golden eyes continually shadowed by a thin veil of hate. He was also brawnier than his group of friends, and clearly considered the alpha of their ragtag gang.

Jerking his chin toward where she stood, Dustin flashed Jeremy a cocky grin and drawled, "That's a pretty piece you have waiting on you there, Runner. She's always seemed kinda shy to me, but today…" His voice trailed off and he lifted one shoulder in a casual gesture, while his golden eyes moved down her body in a slow, sexual caress that made her stomach turn. "I dunno, there's something about her. She just has that look that says she'd like to get f—"

Jeremy's sharp growl cut him off. "Don't even think about it," he warned in a lethal tone that had the younger Lycans stiffening with aggression as they spread out behind their leader.

Dustin's smile flashed, sharp and bright and brittle. "Aw, come on, man. You can't blame a guy for following his instincts."

Jillian watched as Jeremy took an aggressive step forward. "Your instincts are going to land you in something you can't handle."

* * *

"You have no idea what I'm capable of handling," the Lycan drawled, tempting Jeremy to knock the cocky look off his face then and there. "And you can't touch me. In case you aren't aware, seeing as how this is your first day back home and all, I'll be nice and explain the situation," he added with a challenging smirk, and at that moment, Jeremy would've bet his favorite body parts that the young man had already gone rogue. "My name is Dustin Sheffield. Cooper Sheffield, the pack's security chief, is my father. My dad and Drake are close, real close—which means the League would have your balls in a sling if you even look at me the wrong way."

"Let me give you little piece of advice, Dustin." Jeremy stepped closer, his mouth curled in a wry smile. "Your daddy and Drake don't scare me. The League doesn't scare me. And you and your scrawny little group of pals sure as hell don't scare me."

"Then we'll just have to try harder, won't we?" Dustin murmured, winking at Jillian. Jeremy's fingertips stung with the need to slip his claws, but he held himself in check. Now wasn't the time to go head-to-head with the punk, no matter how badly his beast wanted a piece of the bastard for daring to even look at Jillian.

"I'd be careful, if I were you," he said, slipping his hands into his pockets, his stance as carefree and easy as if they'd been discussing nothing more interesting than the weather. "After all, I'd hate to have to embarrass you in front of all your little friends here." He grinned then, and turned his back on the group as he headed back toward Jillian. She stood right where he'd left her, eyes wide as she kept a wary watch over Dustin and the others.

"Jeremy, how could you just turn your back on them?" she

snapped as soon as he reached her side. "Do you have a death wish?"

"Don't worry, Jillian. They're not going to attack me in the back, for everyone to see." He nodded his head toward the other side of the street. "So let's get out of here before I forget my good intentions not to fight in front of you and go back to kick Sheffield's cocky little ass."

She glared at him, clearly upset, but started across the street. "That was the stupidest thing I've ever seen," she practically growled. "What the hell do you think you were doing?"

"My job," he said in a low slide of words. "So why don't you try to be helpful and explain what's up with the shirts. Since when are rogues considered heroes around here?"

She hunched her shoulders, crossing her arms again, her cheeks pale beneath the rosy burn of the cold. "There's been a lot of talk lately by some of the older members of the pack about the necessity of the Bloodrunners," she began to explain, her tone grim as she rubbed at her arms. "They say that you do more harm than good, blaming the Runners for allowing what they call the 'oppression of the human world' over our own way of life. Stefan Drake and his followers are responsible for a lot of it, but I don't know why the others are so quick to buy in to his rantings." She lifted her shoulders in a baffled shrug. "I wish I did, Jeremy. I've talked it over with Dylan, but we're both at a loss. And Dylan's hands are tied by his position. I think he's afraid. He has to be careful what he says or Stefan will have him voted off the League."

She came to a stop and turned slowly toward him, her face tilted up, eyes shadowed with troubles she'd carried alone for far too long. "Despite how much we argue, the truth is that I really could use your help," she admitted softly.

Such simple words, and yet, the way they affected him were far from simple. "We need to work together, Jillian. We need to find the answers before things get so screwed up they can't ever be put back in order again."

She shot him a searching look, surprise molding her expression.

"What?" he asked, arching one brow.

The corner of her mouth twitched, while a surge of wind caught at her hair. "I just didn't think you, of all people, would want to see things put back to the way they *were*."

Jeremy reached out to hook a wayward lock of gold-spun silk behind her ear as the wind howled around them, scurrying leaves about their feet from the decorative trees that lined the street. "Are you accusing me of being an anarchist?" he asked with a ghost of a smile.

"No." She blinked up at him, velvety brown eyes soft and bright. "But the way things were…and still are, isn't exactly fair, Jeremy. You were right to want to see changes when you lived here. The Silvercrest have to learn to adapt, to change, or we're going to die out because we've buried ourselves in the past."

"Spoken like a true reformist," he teased, following beside her as she set off walking once more.

Her mouth twisted with a small grin, and then she changed the subject by saying, "I never did ask when your indoctrination ceremony is supposed to take place."

He gave a grim bark of laughter. "I decided to skip that bit of hypocrisy. No sense—"

"It's not hypo—"

"Excuse me," said an elderly voice from behind them, "but aren't you Jeremy Burns?"

Together, they turned to find Mrs. Swanson standing before them, a shawl wrapped around her slim shoulders, her cloudy blue eyes troubled beneath her wrinkled brow.

Jillian could feel Jeremy's tension, and knew he was expecting the little old woman to hurl insults at him. Hoping Mrs. Swanson wasn't there to cause trouble, Jillian sent the elderly Lycan an easy smile. "Yes, this is Jeremy."

The woman gave a sharp nod, while the scent of talcum powder lifted to their noses, combined with tea and hair dye. "Good." She shifted her pale blue eyes to Jeremy. "I need to talk to you about my granddaughter Melissa."

"Is Melissa in trouble?" Jillian asked, before Jeremy could respond to the old woman's comment.

Mrs. Swanson's chin trembled as she explained. "She's been missing for over a week now. Along with some of her friends. If she's run off with some human boy," she groaned, "I don't know what I'll do. I couldn't stand to lose my Melissa to one of them. It would be too awful."

A quick glance at Jeremy's expression revealed nothing. He was wearing his "closed" mask, keeping his reactions under lock and key. But Jillian couldn't help but wonder how long it would last in the face of such blatant ignorance and bias. "I'll come to talk with you about Melissa this afternoon," she murmured, "but if you'll excuse us, there's somewhere we need to be."

"You'll let me know if you find anything?" Mrs. Swanson demanded, calling after them as Jillian all but yanked Jeremy down the sidewalk.

"Of course he will," she snapped through her terse smile. "Goodbye."

When they were out of hearing distance, Jeremy slid her a bemused look. "Just where is it that we need to be?"

"Anywhere she *isn't*," Jillian muttered under her breath.

"And what are you going to do when I'm out on my own?" he teased. "Won't be so easy to keep me out of harm's way then, little witch."

Despite the cold, she could feel the heat in her cheeks. She cleared her throat, aware that her heart was pounding, that her blood was throbbing in tender, delicate places that always felt hot when she was around this particular man. "I wasn't…I just… I think you're going to have enough to deal with without getting caught up in all of that." She sighed, jerking her head back behind them, where Mrs. Swanson scuffled herself down the sidewalk.

"We knew Simmons was targeting the teenagers, tempting them to turn rogue. In some cases, even forcing them. But how many do you think are missing from town?"

"Enough for me to worry," she answered honestly, "but not enough yet to be able to make the League take action. Dylan has tried, but Graham and the others take so long to come to any sort of decision. And rebellion in the Lycan community isn't exactly unheard of. Puberty is rough enough to manage without having a wolf to deal with. You know we have a high rate of teenage runaways, but they all come home sooner rather than later. Of course, now that the number of rogues seems to be growing, it's unsettling, to say the least, when one of the teens goes missing, not to mention entire groups of them."

"And here that woman would probably rather her granddaughter be keeping company with those Lycans who have already turned than a human," he murmured, his voice thick with disgust. "Unbelievable. How do you live with these people?"

"Not all of them feel that way," she argued, feeling as if she stood at the top of a towering precipice, with a deep ravine on either side, flanked by craggy cliffs just a leap away. All she had to do was decide in which direction she would jump…and she'd be on solid ground. But instead, she stubbornly refused to move, while the rock beneath her feet tumbled away bit by bit.

Giving herself a mental shake, she finished her argument. "You can't judge us all by a few, Jeremy. That isn't fair."

"Fair? What isn't fair is that their kids are missing, and all they're worried about is that they've run off with a human, when in reality they're probably somewhere doing something that's going to land them in some serious trouble, if not killed. How asinine is that?"

She started to respond, when her cell phone suddenly vibrated in her pocket, signaling a text message. Pulling out her phone, Jillian quickly read the few lines of script and grimaced. "I'm going to have to go. Graham says he needs to see me."

"And just what does ol' Graham want this early?" Jeremy grunted, possession biting at his ass like a mangy dog. Not that he was jealous of the old guy, but he was bitter as hell, knowing that Graham had always been against a relationship between them. The Lead Elder may have been the best friend of Mason's father, Robert Dillinger, but he was still as narrow-minded as the rest of the League. "Is he ready to slap your hand for being seen in public with me?"

She rolled her eyes at him. "I hardly think he even knows yet, Jeremy."

"Graham knows," he drawled. "Trust me, this whole place is on pins and needles, waiting to see what their Spirit Walker will do now that I'm back."

"I'm not going to *do* anything." She blew out a rough breath, not quite meeting his eyes as she said, "To be honest, I've been having problems with the League for a while now, long before they knew you were coming home."

"What kind of problems?"

Her gaze found his then nervously skittered away, focusing on something over his left shoulder. "They've decided that I've gone single long enough. According to the Elders, it's past time I went about the business of producing them a new Spirit Walker."

He made a rude sound in his throat. "Jesus, Jillian. Why don't you tell them to go to hell?"

"It's not that simple," she murmured, and her eyes moved back to his, as if pulled there by the force of his will.

Jeremy arched one brow and moved closer. "Isn't it? Or are you still letting the League call the shots for you? Still letting them control your life?"

"And who should I let control it?" she demanded, her tone as defensive as her body language. She crossed her arms over her middle, shoulders hunched as she nibbled on the corner of that lush, pansy-soft mouth, its pink stain matching the vibrant color in her cheeks. "You?"

"I've never wanted to control you. I've just wanted to f—"

"Don't even say it!" she warned, and he couldn't help but chuckle at the expression on her face.

"What?" He grinned as he held his hands up in innocent surrender. "I was just going to say that I've wanted to *find* a way for us to be friends."

"Yeah, sure you were." She sighed, shaking her head, and he could see the glimmer of laughter lurking in those big brown eyes. Softly, she said, "I don't know how long this is going to take with Graham, but if you're going to snoop around without me today, promise that you'll be careful."

"Worried about me?" he asked, teasing her with a wink.

The corner of her mouth twitched, creating an adorable little dimple that he wanted to press his mouth against. "I worry about *all* my wolves."

"So you *are* worried about me," he rumbled with cocky satisfaction, waggling his brows. He enjoyed teasing her, even when they were going head-to-head with each other.

Jillian rolled her eyes again. "You're impossible, you know that?"

"Yeah, I know. Go on and see what Graham needs. I'll catch up with you later."

She gave him a doubtful look. "What are you going to do?"

"Don't look so worried." He chuckled. "I promise to stay out of trouble. Scout's honor."

"Right," Jillian snickered, too aware of the fact that she did *not* want to leave him. "You were never a Scout."

"Not for lack of trying." His voice lowered, eyes smoky beneath the golden fringe of his lashes. "I've been known to act like a saint on occasion. You should know that more than anyone."

She blushed, remembering the heated embrace he'd tried so hard to keep from going too far when they'd shared that one earthshaking, unforgettable kiss. He'd been so mindful of her age...of her innocence. She'd taken it for granted then, but now, as a woman, she realized just what that restraint had cost him.

Unsure of what to say, she started to walk away, when he touched her arm. "Jillian?"

"Yes?" She turned back to meet his gaze.

"Don't let Sheffield anywhere near you," he warned her. "And be careful around Drake."

"Around Eric?" she asked, frowning.

Jillian watched as his mouth flattened into a grim line. "Around all of them, but especially his father. Until we know more about what's going on, you can't be too cautious."

She sucked in a sharp breath of air, eyes wide. "Oh, my god, you think it's—"

"Shh," he whispered, leaning down to press a chaste kiss to her temple, his breath warm in her ear. "Just promise me that you'll be on guard."

She nodded mutely, the idea that had burst into her brain

spreading like a brilliant ink stain, consuming her mind. Stefan Drake had the hatred; there was no doubt of that. But was it really possible that he was crazy enough to think he could use rogues to…what? What would be his goal? His aim?

Jeremy stared into her eyes and lifted his hand to brush her hair back from her brow, his rough calluses making her shiver with awareness. "We can argue later. Just promise me that you'll be careful."

She wet her bottom lip with the tip of her tongue. "You say that like you really care."

The glowing burn of tenderness in his hazel eyes made her chest feel tight. "I don't want to see you get hurt in all of this, Jillian."

"No, I think you're trying to seduce me," she whispered, her voice thick as she shook her head in silent wonder. It was a statement—one he didn't bother to deny.

He pushed his hands deep in his pockets, all traces of tenderness gone from his gaze as the primitive burn of hunger bled through. "I made it clear what I want last night," he told her, the words gritty and raw with intent.

"Yes, you did." Frustration roared through her, swift and urgent and hot. "And if you'll recall, I told you it wasn't going to happen."

"Then it looks like we're at a standoff." He grinned at her, but the lines around his eyes betrayed the gravity behind his words. He had no intention of backing down. Not until he'd got what he wanted. "We'll just have to see who breaks first, won't we?"

His white teeth flashed in a sharp smile, and he stepped back, her cue to turn and leave.

But as Jillian walked away, it bothered her—how reluctant she was to take it.

* * *

The second Jillian turned the corner, Jeremy leaned back against the brick wall of a street-side shop, gritting his teeth against the dull ache in his lower body. God, he was so on edge, just from being near her, that he knew one touch of her soft little hand on his shaft and he'd have gone over into sweet, mindless oblivion.

Pushing away from the wall, he headed in the opposite direction from which they'd come. At the end of the block, he'd just started around the corner of a building, when he found himself face-to-face with Constance Murphy, Jillian's mother.

Damn.

"Jeremy," she murmured, sounding calm, despite the fact she looked surprised to have run in to him. Maybe she'd thought he'd be skulking around in the shadows...or maybe she hadn't even given a thought to his return. God only knew she'd never had much to say to him before. Some of the most awkward moments of his life had been when he was forced to interact with this woman. "I heard you were back in town."

Yeah, and she sounded less than thrilled with the news. No shock there.

"Mrs. Murphy," he replied, trying to hide his grimace behind a smile, but knowing he failed.

"You don't have to call me Mrs. Murphy, Jeremy. We're both adults. Obviously we should be capable of acting like them, in a civilized manner."

"Yes, ma'am," he murmured, feeling like a boy about to get his ears boxed.

"I heard about last night," she stated, his displeasure evident.

He reached up and tugged at his earlobe. "Yeah, I...uh, figured you would."

Her slender hands clutched at the strap of the brown leather purse hanging over her shoulder, the rouged line of her mouth tight with restraint. "Surely you can understand why it's important for you to stay away from my daughter. You've already caused enough chaos in her life."

"With all due respect, ma'am, Jillian's a grown woman."

Bright flags of color flared in her cheeks, her skin still amazingly smooth for her age, making her look much younger than she was. "Yes, she is a grown woman. One with a soft spot for something that isn't good for her."

"So you think her and Drake are a bad match, too?" he drawled, struggling to keep his face straight. "Glad to hear it."

Her gaze flashed with fire, her expression so brittle, he was surprised she didn't crack. "Don't get smart with me, Jeremy," she snapped. "I want you to stay away from my daughter."

Raw emotion burned through him, making him curse under his breath as he felt the restless shift of his beast. It didn't like being told to stay away from the thing it craved most, any more than his human half did. "I'm afraid I can't do that."

"Can't or won't?"

He shrugged his shoulders. "What does it matter when the answer's the same?"

Her eyes narrowed to slits, mouth pinched, and he felt the chill of her fury rush through him like an angry wind. Locking his jaw, he stood his ground, knowing that if he backed down now she'd take it for weakness and press her advantage. Witches grew more powerful with age, their abilities dependent upon each individual bloodline, and Jeremy knew that Jillian's line was considered one of the strongest. Constance Murphy could become a serious enemy if she chose to, but he hated to be at odds with the mother of the woman he—

Damn it. How about we not go there right now.

He wasn't ready to look too closely at how he felt about Jillian, primarily because he was still trying to figure it out. So much had happened between them since last night…or so little, depending on how you looked at it. But one thing he knew for sure was that something *was* going to happen. And soon.

"This isn't over," she said angrily, and with a cold look, she turned her back on him and hurried away, her movements wooden with fury as her low heels clicked ominously against the sidewalk. Jeremy watched her until she turned and disappeared at the next block, then heaved a sigh of relief before heading in the opposite direction, thinking that if this was the beginning of his day…he wasn't sure he wanted to see how it ended.

Chapter 8

The late afternoon sun was hanging heavily in the sky as Jeremy glanced at his phone for the hundredth time. He kept waiting for word from Jillian, wondering what she was doing. After the unsettling run-in with Constance Murphy, he'd spent the rest of the day snooping around, refamiliarizing himself with the town, aware of the tension hanging over Shadow Peak, as if everyone was just waiting for something bad to happen.

When he'd neared the high school, he caught sight of some more of the controversial T-shirts that he and Jillian had seen that morning. One particular version that caught his eye had read Authority Bites…and So Do I. He'd laughed when he saw it, thinking he'd actually like to own one with that particular saying. Mason would be annoyed as hell by it, but then irritating Mase was too much fun to resist.

For the most part, people made it a point to avoid him, but there were a few who surprisingly made an effort to engage him in conversation. The most interesting bit of news he'd heard had been about the shirts; or rather, the Lycans wearing them. According to one of his father's friends, the teenagers sporting the controversial slogans were part of Stefan Drake's new youth awareness movement. From what Jeremy could gather, the purpose of the movement was the promotion of purity among the Lycans, like a fledgling sect of little neo-Nazis who believed anything less than a pureblooded wolf shouldn't be allowed to live.

Jeremy wasn't surprised by the news, considering the Bloodrunners already knew Drake was twisted in the head. But it still made his blood run cold to think that the bastard's racist beliefs were gaining such momentum among the younger members of the pack. And he wasn't surprised that Jillian hadn't said anything to him about the movement that morning, considering how badly she'd wanted to get him away from Sheffield and his gang.

Apparently Drake claimed he had nothing to do with the shirts the teens were wearing, but that didn't mean anything. If he was the traitor they were hunting, he'd be a fool to openly associate himself with any pro-rogue propaganda. And they knew he wasn't a fool.

Jeremy was nearing the end of Main Street when he finally caught sight of none other than Stefan Drake himself coming out of town hall, the Elder's gray hair shining silver in the weak shafts of sunlight burning through the low cloud covering. For a moment, Jeremy almost didn't recognize him, but then it'd been a while since their paths had crossed—since Drake had been conveniently absent when he'd presented his Bloodrunning numbers to the League. Drake looked leaner than Jeremy remembered him, as if his features had been carved out of stone, his skin stretched over bones with nothing to soften the severity of his expression.

Hatred was probably eating away at the old bastard from the inside out.

Curious to see how the Elder would react to his presence, Jeremy decided to stir the pot. Drake stood at the top of the wide steps set between white painted banisters that matched the stately building's shingled facade. He had his head bent in conversation with Dustin's father, Cooper Sheffield, the League-appointed town security chief, which was really nothing more than a glorified title. In reality, Sheffield was the Elders' muscle when they needed to deal with a pack disturbance and didn't want to dirty their own hands.

As Jeremy approached, he spotted another surly-looking group of teens lounging against the front window of the floral shop, halfway up the block, a cloud of smoke surrounding them as they took dramatic puffs on their cigarettes. One of the thugs caught sight of him, nudging his buddy with his elbow. Keeping the group in his peripheral vision, Jeremy hitched his hip against the base of the nearest banister.

"Hey, Stefan," he called out, smiling when the Elder's shoulders went rigid, his head whipping around to pin Jeremy with a sharp, hawklike gaze. "Throw any good rocks lately?"

For a moment, the Elder vibrated with rage. Then he brought himself under control as he calmly turned toward Jeremy, shot the cuffs on his immaculate white dress shirt and smoothed back the silver at his temples, a thin smile curving his mouth. "Having trouble already, Runner? What a shame."

"So what's next?" Jeremy asked around a grin, mindful of the group of teens beginning to skulk closer. "You gonna get really creative and maybe TP my house? Leave a stink bomb on my front porch? Make crank calls?"

Cooper Sheffield snorted a soft bark of laughter, until Drake's glare choked him silent. Returning his attention to Jeremy, the Elder considered him with a cool look of sinister anticipation. "I don't need to play games, half-breed. When I want you gone, you'll be gone."

"Yeah?" Jeremy murmured, rubbing his hand over his chin as he considered the warning, his afternoon stubble scraping his palm. "I dunno. I gotta say that I think I could take you. And you know why? 'Cause you look old, Drake. I'm guessing that playing the role of an evil mastermind is harder work than you'd thought it would be. Plotting the destruction of this pack wearing you down?"

"Your arrogance is going to be your downfall," the Elder remarked with a knowing smile, the corners of his pale eyes creasing with malevolence. "After all, we each have a weakness, do we not? That one thing we feel we cannot live without."

Jeremy jerked his chin toward the approaching gang of young punks. "Is that why you need your little goon squad over there? Do they keep you safe at night?"

"There's so many ways for accidents to happen," Drake continued, ignoring Jeremy's taunting. "Especially for someone, say, in Jillian's position. The Spirit Walker may have Lycan blood in her veins, but her body is so much weaker than ours. One little misstep, one wrong move," he purred, snapping the fingers of his right hand, "and she could so easily die—just like a pathetic little human."

Hearing Jillian's name on Drake's lips put a fury unlike anything Jeremy had ever known in his blood, violent and raging, seething just beneath the surface of his skin—though it was going to be a cold day in hell before he gave the bastard the satisfaction of seeing it. Relaxing his stance and tilting his head slightly to the side, Jeremy stroked the corner of his brow, careful to keep his anger under tight control. "If you think she's weak," he remarked, his tone mellow and calm, "then you're even thicker than I thought. Jillian Murphy has more power in her little finger than you could ever hope to possess, Drake." He paused, allowing a hard smile to curve the corners of his mouth before adding, "And if you ever threaten her again, I'll make it my number one priority in life to see you dead."

Drake lifted his chin and stared at Jeremy down the thin blade of his nose. "Threatening an Elder is a crime punishable by—"

"Oh, I'm not threatening," he drawled with a smug grin, enjoying the look of outrage slowly reddening Drake's gaunt face. "I'm making a promise. Lay one hand on her, and it'll be the last thing you ever do."

At that moment, Sheffield took an aggressive step forward, his right arm reaching across his bulging abdomen, beneath his jacket, fingers curled around the butt of an automatic handgun. Jeremy arched his brows and gave a low whistle. "That's a fancy-looking piece you've got there, Cooper. Too bad you can't kill me with bullets."

Sheffield's thin lips twisted in a cold smile, his golden eyes burning with malice. "But they hurt like hell, Runner."

The front doors of the town hall opened just then, catching his attention, and the next thing Jeremy knew, a fist with tattooed knuckles went sailing past his face, barely missing his nose, followed by a solid punch to his kidneys from behind. With a laughing snarl, Jeremy grabbed the fist of the first teenager and twisted the punk's wrist until it snapped, then spun with a side kick that knocked the one behind him onto the ground, the guy's body curling into a ball as he clutched at his broken ribs. With their friends incapacitated, four more of the thugs moved in. Fists were flying and bones crunching as the Lycans attacked together, too confident and brash in their youthful arrogance, thinking they could easily take him simply because they outnumbered him.

But they hadn't spent their lives training as a Bloodrunner. Jeremy had had Mase as a sparring partner for years now, and Mason liked to fight dirty—which meant Jeremy had learned long ago how to handle himself in a good ol'-fashioned street fight.

He'd already sent two more to the ground with minor injuries and was just preparing to take out the last two, when someone grabbed him from behind, wrapping their arms around his upper body and dragging him away. He knew from the male's scent that it was Dylan, which was the only reason he hadn't thrown the guy over his head and slammed him into the concrete sidewalk.

"Come on, Jeremy," Dylan muttered in his ear, still dragging him away from the scene. "That's enough!"

"All right, all right," he growled, jerking out of Dylan's hold. Cutting an irritated look at his friend, he wiped the blood from his mouth with the back of his hand. "And it was just getting fun," he complained with a rough laugh.

Sending a furious look at the battered teenagers, Dylan snarled, "Get out of here. Now!"

They sent quick glances at each other, then took off down the street, leaving their broken buddies to crawl after them. When Jeremy glanced up at the steps, he saw that Drake and Sheffield had slithered back inside the town hall.

"Cowards," he muttered under his breath. Turning his gaze back on Dylan, who stood glowering at his side, he leveled a look of accusation on his friend. "What the hell is going on around here?"

"Don't give me that look," the Elder muttered, knowing exactly what he was talking about. "You and the Runners knew what was going down."

"Like hell we did," Jeremy growled. "Yeah, we've known a traitor was targeting the younger Lycans, tempting them to turn rogue. That was Simmons's specialty. But this is out of control. The teenagers in this town, the ones who are still around, are acting as if they've been turned into a bunch of brainwashed Stepford brats."

"Jeremy, we've got it under control," Dylan argued, his face flushed with anger. "Until we have proof they've gone rogue, which we don't at this point, you and the Runners *can't* go after them. Unless you're fighting them in self-defense, you can't even touch them until a kill has been discovered and a Bloodrun assigned. Drake and the rest of the League will have your ass if you do."

"So then this is all for our sake?" he asked with a rough burst of laughter. "You're just trying to protect the Bloodrunners by keeping us in the dark?"

"I'm trying to hold things together around here," Dylan growled through his clenched teeth, taking a step closer, going nose-to-nose with him. Jeremy had never seen the Elder lose his control, but Dylan's face was flushed with anger, his eyes wild as they began to glow an unearthly shade of gold. "You focus on finding the asshole responsible for the rogues and let me deal with the kids."

Jeremy matched Dylan's challenging stare, then rolled his shoulder, wiping at his busted bottom lip again. "Yeah, fine. Whatever," he muttered, turning to leave.

"Where are you going?" the Elder demanded.

Shooting a belligerent look over his shoulder, he snarled, "What's with the inquisition?"

Dylan opened his mouth, bit back whatever he'd been about to say, and blew out a rough breath of air. "Look, I'm on your side, Jeremy. Just promise me that you'll stay out of trouble."

"Sure thing, Mom," he drawled, his tone thick with sarcasm as he walked away, shaking his hands out at his sides.

Beneath his fingertips, his claws still burned with the urge to slip his skin, which was about all of the change he could manage during the day, other than the lengthening of his fangs. It'd been hard as hell to keep from killing the little bastards while fighting them, but he'd made allowances for their youth. God only knew he'd been a pain-in-the-ass at nineteen. True, he'd never been *quite* that bad, but he knew what it was like to want to rebel against authority.

As long as they hadn't gone rogue and hadn't hurt anyone, he'd let them live. Jeremy still thought they were twisted little jerks who didn't know right from wrong, but as Mason was always telling him, you couldn't kill people for being idiots.

Drake, on the other hand, needed to be dealt with. And fast.

As far as Jeremy was concerned, the second the bastard had dared to threaten Jillian, he'd sealed his fate. Pulling his cell out of his back pocket, he punched in Mason's number and filled him in on everything that had gone down that day, starting with the broken window and ending with Drake's threat against Jillian.

Recognizing that he needed to see for himself that Jillian was unharmed and safe, Jeremy headed toward her house, assuring Mason he'd check in with him later. His hair was probably standing on end, he was covered in dust and dirt and blood, not to mention sweat, but he couldn't take the time to go home and clean up. He needed to see her—*now*—because he had the strangest feeling that if he didn't get close to her, he wouldn't be able to breathe.

He couldn't shake the fear that something was going to happen to her.

Drawing a deep breath into his lungs, he concentrated on taking the focus off himself and, instead, worked to pull in the details of his surroundings, like an artist reaching for color with his brush. Hell, he needed something fresh to wipe away the ugliness of Drake's hatred.

He needed something clean—and the second he turned onto Lassiter Avenue, Jeremy found it.

The wind surged past him, and he caught her scent. Fresh. Sweet. Almost innocent, though Jeremy knew that was too much to hope for. A woman as desirable as Jillian Murphy didn't reach the age of twenty-eight as a virgin. He didn't blame her for being a woman…but that didn't mean he didn't want to take every man who'd ever touched her apart with his bare hands.

He could see her in the small driveway at the side of her house, leaning into her car as she took a leather satchel out of the backseat.

Shoving his hands deep in his front pockets to keep from grabbing her, Jeremy managed to scrape a few words out of his dry throat. "I need to talk to you."

She jumped, startled, and spun around to face him. Her eyes went wide as she stared, mouth slack with surprise. "Wh-what happened? What have you been doing?"

His lips twisted with an embarrassed grimace. "Sorry," he grunted, reaching forward to take the heavy satchel from her arms. "I'm grimy and smell like hell."

"No." Her voice was soft, her cheeks flushed. "You just look as if you've been fighting."

"Huh," he snorted, heading for her front door. "Go figure."

Groaning, she followed behind him. "Please tell me you haven't been in a fight."

At his telling silence, Jillian moved past him and unlocked her door, mumbling under her breath. "Come on inside," she said wearily. "You look as if you're about to drop."

"Thanks," he said tightly, his male pride irritated that she thought a little scuffle with some street thugs could leave him sapped. "At least I was able to walk away," he muttered, setting the satchel on her coffee table. "Can't say the same for Drake's goons."

She paused in the act of taking off her jacket, her face pale. "You were fighting with Stefan?"

"Not really." Jeremy lifted his shoulders in a shrug. "Just some of the thugs from his little 'youth movement' I heard about today. And they started it."

Jillian closed her eyes. "Of course they did," she agreed, though her tone was wry. "God knows you'd never try to provoke someone into a fight."

Jeremy watched her hang the jacket on a peg behind the door, the tension in his gut easing with every second he spent near her. "So where have you been?" He could see the shadows under her eyes, sense the underlying fatigue in her movements.

"After my meeting with Graham, who expected a full accounting of the fight with Danna last night," she told him, rolling her head over her shoulders as she braced her hands against the back of a chair, "I had to go out to the Harvey farm. Mrs. Harvey delivered her fourth child this afternoon."

Damn, no wonder she looked exhausted. Jeremy knew that as the pack's Spirit Walker, it was Jillian's duty to assist in all births, lending her powers to the mothers, easing their way through the labor. Then once the infant was born, she had to give the ceremonial birth rites of protection and health to the newborn child.

"Did it go well?" he asked, perching himself on the edge of the sofa.

A small smile played at her lips as she took a seat in the chair. "It was tough there for a bit, but they're both fine."

"That's good, then." He ran his hands back through his

hair, then exhaled a shaky breath. "Look, I came by because I need to talk to you about something."

"Okay," she said softly. She must have sensed his tension because she stood up and moved to stand in front of the window, the pale shafts of light spilling through the muslin curtains painting her with iridescent stripes of color.

Jeremy braced his elbows on his spread knees, staring at his hands clasped loosely together. His jaw locked, the vein in his temple throbbing with worry. Drake's threats were echoing in his head, and she needed to be warned.

Feeling as if he had a frog stuck in his throat, he finally said, "I'd stay away from you, but it wouldn't matter at this point. They all know that we're…"

"That we're what?" Jillian asked when his voice trailed off, while a swift jolt of panic stabbed through her middle.

His head shot up, eyes swirling with a glowing blend of colors as he stared at her, daring her to stop being a coward. "They all know that we're *mates*. Not saying it out loud doesn't make it any less true. And the fact we've never had sex doesn't change it. We *are* mates, Jillian. Which means the second I set foot back in this town, your life and the way they look at you changed."

Oh, yeah, something bad had happened. "What are you talking about, Jeremy?"

"Drake threatened you," he admitted in a low, almost silent rasp, "as a way to get to me."

"That's impossible," she whispered. "He couldn't possibly get away with—"

"He did and he could. Dylan was there with me, as well as others, and that didn't stop him. He's arrogant enough not to care who heard him. If he thinks it will hurt me, he'll hurt you." He made a gruff sound of frustration that wasn't quite a growl or a laugh, but caught somehow in between. "I guess using you to get to me is more important to him than seeing you matched up with his son."

Jillian wrapped her arms around her middle, hating the cold, slithering sensation of fear slipping between her shoulder blades, inching its way down her spine. "Great," she muttered through stiffened lips. "What am I supposed to do about it? What do you want from me, Jeremy?"

His mouth tightened. "I want you to be careful."

"I always am," she said unsteadily.

"And I want *you*." His expression became fierce, the angles sharpened by a vicious, visceral intensity and purpose as the guttural words seemed to just pour out of him. "I've barely been back in town a day and I'm already burning, Jillian. I can't be near you like this and not ache inside with the need to touch you. To have you under my hands, my mouth, my body. I want to lay you down and lose myself in you until we're so exhausted we can't even walk."

"Jeremy," she rasped, the sound of his name thick in her throat, crowded by the same impossible lust he'd spoken of. "We—we can't."

"Why?" he demanded, his brows pulling together over the masculine line of his nose. "We're both adults. We both know the score. Why the hell shouldn't we take what we *both* want?"

Jillian pressed her hands against the heat in her face, wondering what she could say to make him understand...without having to spill the truth. Because once out, it would reveal far more than she was willing to give him. "Dammit, Jeremy, it isn't that simple!"

He started to stand, when her cell phone began buzzing. Glaring at her pocket, he growled, "I'm really starting to hate that thing."

Turning her back on him, Jillian pulled out the phone and read the text message from Graham. Groaning, she shook her head in disbelief.

"What is it?" he asked, rolling to his feet as she looked at him over her shoulder.

"Drake's got some kind of rally going on in town." She turned, slanting him a hard look of frustration. "You really got him stirred up today, didn't you?"

Jeremy shoved his hands in his pockets, his gaze sharp beneath lowered brows. "I'm not here to sit and twiddle my thumbs, Jillian. Stirring up Drake is going to be the least of my plans. I have no doubt he's the traitor, and once I can prove it, I'm taking his ass down."

"Yeah, well, I've been ordered to make an appearance at the rally," she told him, heading toward her jacket. "Graham doesn't want me giving the pack any reason to be suspicious of my loyalty right now."

"And why would they question that?" he asked in a quiet drawl.

Pulling on the dark blue jacket, she said, "You know damn well why."

"If they'd asked me," he muttered bitterly, "I could have told them that nothing was more important to you than your duty to this pack."

She paused for a moment, just staring at him, then ripped opened the front door. "I don't have time to argue with you about this right now, Jeremy. I have to go."

"Not without me you don't," he growled, following her outside.

"I'm perfectly capable of taking care of myself," Jillian warned through her clenched teeth, clearly irritated with him as she locked her front door.

"Whatever you did before is in the past," he explained in a soft voice as he waited behind her. "That's what I'm trying to get through to you, Jillian. I'm home now, which means everything is different, for both of us."

"No, it isn't," she argued, whipping around. "It's not as if you'll be staying. The second you have your madman or traitor or whatever the hell he is, you'll be back at the Alley. Everyone knows it, Jeremy."

"They don't know jack," he grunted, sliding her an irritated look as they set off down the sidewalk together. "You want an answer about my intentions, then ask *me* the questions. But don't waste your time listening to small-town gossip. I would've thought you'd learned that lesson by now."

She pressed her lips together, but remained silent, and he locked his jaw, unwilling to back down. The tension between them remained strong, combustible, until they approached the end of the block and a little girl in pigtails ran from the front yard on their right, her tiny legs hurtling her toward them. "Jilly!" she squealed, throwing her arms around Jillian's leg and offering up her chubby cheek for a kiss.

"Hey, sweet pea," Jillian said with a smile as she knelt down, giving the little girl a quick hug and kiss on the cheek. "Are you being a good girl for your mommy today?"

The child gave a gap-toothed grin, her baby blue eyes shining with mischief. "Uh-huh. Mommy even let me ride my bike again!"

Jillian laughed, and the happy sound made something in Jeremy's chest clench *hard,* the burning sense of tension in his body replaced by something softer…sweeter, and yet, infinitely more powerful.

"That's wonderful," Jillian told her, straightening one of the child's lopsided hair bows. "I'll have to come and watch you as soon as I can."

"Promise?" the little girl squealed, deep dimples showing in both cheeks as she smiled and clapped her hands together.

"I promise." A dark-haired woman waved from the front yard, smiling at them, and Jillian waved back. "See ya later, sweet pea."

"'Bye," the cherub-faced child called out, sending a shy smile at Jeremy before she turned and ran back to her mother.

Jeremy chuckled softly under his breath as they set off back down the sidewalk. "Looks like you've got a fan there."

Waving goodbye one last time, Jillian glanced at Jeremy as she explained. "Kelsey broke her arm last week and I helped it heal. She'll be eternally grateful," she added wryly, "since riding her bike is her favorite thing to do."

They'd just turned onto Mitchell Lane when she realized he was staring at her strangely. "What?"

His gaze slid away, focusing on the cracked sidewalk. "They rely on you," he offered in a low, husky voice, "more than I had imagined. You belong here."

"You belong here, too," she stated softly.

The corner of his mouth lifted in a lopsided grin, but she could see the shadow of bitterness in his eyes as he met her gaze. "No, I don't. And that's always going to stand between us, isn't it?"

"I…I don't know, Jeremy," she said after a moment, wishing she knew what was going on behind those mesmerizing eyes.

He blew out a hard breath, pulling his gaze from hers once again, hands still shoved deep in the pockets of his jeans. "Maybe the fact that we never got together was for the best. I mean, let's face it. You were never going to give up all of this for me."

She was painfully aware of the butterflies taking flight in her belly. "Would you have asked me to?"

His shoulders shifted, jaw working as he stared at the butter-yellow sun sitting low on the horizon. Finally, he said, "I don't know how you could have been married to us both—me and the pack."

Despite the fact he was only voicing her own thoughts, Jillian felt a flare of frustration at his words. "Is there never any middle ground with you, Jeremy?"

The sensuous line of his mouth curved in a wry smile as he glanced her way. "Not where you were concerned. But then you didn't have any middle ground, either. Did you, Jillian?"

She wanted to disagree, but he was right. She'd been so immature, expecting him to make all the sacrifices, and tensions had been so strong between him and the pack. He'd already begun training to become a Bloodrunner and his days in Shadow Peak had been numbered.

Had she jumped at the chance to rid herself of an uncomfortable situation? Because she'd been a coward?

And if so, had anything changed?

No, she admitted, because she was still afraid. Terrified, actually, of having sex with him and making herself so vulnerable. Of allowing him to see in to her heart and know just how much he meant to her.

Like it or not, she couldn't get over the fear that he would take that love and use it to destroy her. Not in an evil way, no. Just by being himself. Jillian knew he didn't love her, and without that bond, her own emotions wouldn't be enough to hold him. All it would take was one woman—one slip—and her heart would be crushed.

And what of the pack? Even though he was home now, Jillian understood that it was only temporary. He'd be back in the Alley as soon as he could, once again avoiding the town and the pack, and what then? Jeremy wouldn't want her involved with the Lycans any more than the Silvercrest would tolerate their Spirit Walker living in the Alley with a Bloodrunner.

No, she couldn't take the risk. No matter how badly she wanted to.

Frustrated with the entire situation, she shook her head, saying, "I may have had unrealistic expectations, but I was young."

"That you were." He sighed, sounding tired. He squinted toward the setting sun again, the brilliant spectrum of colors painting his hair and face in an ethereal glow that made him look like some primeval creature escaped from the forest. "But even now, your life is still tied to them."

She wanted to argue, but he was right.

They turned at the next corner, and the town hall loomed in the distance like a symbol of everything that stood between them. "We probably shouldn't head in together," he rumbled, motioning for her to go on ahead. "I'll come in after a minute or two."

Jillian wanted to tell him that she didn't care what people thought, but she knew everyone would be waiting for the opportunity to set the gossip wheel rolling. "I'll wait for you afterward," she said huskily, and not looking at him, Jillian headed toward the steps.

The instant Jeremy walked into the rally, Jillian could feel the energy in the room crank higher.

As if he didn't notice the rabid attention of the townspeople focused on his tall form, he took up position by the wide double doors, propping his shoulder against the wall, his heavily muscled arms crossed casually over his chest. It was a relaxed pose, but the way he immediately found her, watching her from beneath his lashes, made her breathless. The intensity of his stare made her feel exposed, as if he could see all her secrets.

Did he know how close she was to giving in? How badly she wanted to?

God, she hoped not.

Graham had motioned her toward the stage when she'd come in, but Jillian had refused to take a seat beside the Elders, choosing instead to remain on the small stairs that led up the side of the raised platform. She'd wanted to be able to see Jeremy when he came in, but now she tore her gaze away from his unsettling stare and looked out over the crowd, stopping suddenly when she spotted Elise standing in the back corner.

Even with the length of the room between them, Jillian could read her friend's troubled expression. She made a move to head toward her, but Elise shook her head, a shuddered look of warning firing out of her deep blue eyes. Frowning, Jillian wondered what was going on, when she realized Elise's reaction had been noted by a group of middle-aged women standing close by. They were gossiping about Jeremy and Elise supposedly having a late-morning tryst in her office that day, their painful words reaching Jillian's ears as they raised their voices to be heard over the others, while everyone waited for Drake himself to take the podium.

Leaning heavily against the wall, Jillian felt her stomach go hollow, while her pulse began to roar in her ears like a great, monstrous freight train speeding down the tracks. There had to be some explanation, but she couldn't stop the decade-old scene from playing through her mind. As if it'd happened only yesterday, she could hear that deep, trusting voice as it said, *"I saw it with my own eyes, Jillian. He was with Danna, and the embrace was hardly a platonic one. We tried to warn you, but you just wouldn't listen."*

She wanted to argue with herself that Elise was her friend, but she knew more than anyone how hard it was to resist

Jeremy. And suddenly she knew that she had to get out of there. Shaking, she rushed down the stairs, struggling to make her way through the crowd as the noise level reached deafening proportions. Looking over her shoulder, she saw that Drake had finally taken the stage, his eyes burning with maniacal hatred as he began speaking into the microphone. He wasted no time, but went straight to the heart of his argument, raging over the dangers that human society posed to the Lycan way of life.

"We are forced to their limits and restrictions, like dogs being collared by their owners! How long are we going to live in fear, hiding what we really are? How long will our way of life here in our sleepy little town survive while we allow them to control our existence?"

A round of applause went up from the room, only making the sick feeling in her stomach intensify as Jillian wondered just how many of the pack members actually believed his nonsense, and how many were simply caught up in the mob mentality of the moment. While she struggled to make her way toward the exit, Drake continued to incite the crowd, referring to what he called "Bloodrunner Propaganda," claiming that Anthony Simmons had been framed by the Runners to further their own conspiracy theory that rogue Lycans were growing in numbers.

Just as she reached the door, Jillian felt a hand close around her elbow. Lifting her gaze, she found Jeremy watching her with a questioning expression. "I've heard enough," she mouthed, unable to scream loud enough to be heard over the crowd.

Drawing his brows together with an unspoken question, he gave her a sharp nod, then pushed open the door and followed her into the comforting silence of the night.

Chapter 9

The metallic sound of pans banging together in her kitchen pulled Jillian from a restless, exhausting sleep. Rubbing her eyes, she stretched to a drowsy wakefulness, a deep breath of air allowing her heightened senses to identify the source of the god-awful racket.

Jeremy.

Snuggling deeper into her pillow, she thought about the conversation they'd had the night before. They'd walked home beneath an oppressive veil of silence, but when she'd opened her front door and he'd followed her inside, she'd heard herself say, "There was talk tonight at the meeting. About you and Elise."

He'd slanted her a hard look, knowing from her tone what the talk had been. "It wasn't like that, Jillian."

She'd shrugged, as if it didn't matter, and a coarse sound of frustration had rumbled deep in his throat. "I'd ask you to trust me, but we both know that isn't going to happen, don't we?"

Her voice had come as little more than a whisper. "That's not true."

"Like hell it isn't." His tone had been grim, belligerent. Then he'd sighed, running one hand back through his hair. "Jesus, Jillian. Give me more credit than that. If I wanted to screw Elise, I'd hardly go waltzing into her real estate office in the middle of the morning, for everyone to see."

"Then why were you there?"

"For the same reason I've come back to the pack. I'm here to find answers, and Drake is at the top of my list, just like I told you. I figured Elise was as good a place to start as any."

"And will you question Eric, too?"

His mouth had thinned. "Eventually."

"Did you learn anything from Elise?"

"Only that she's terrified of her father," he'd admitted with a scowl.

"He's not…very kind to her," she'd told him, "which isn't hard to believe, considering he's not only racist, but misogynistic, as well. He calls her weak, because she's refused to shift ever since her attack."

The dark spill of anger and surprise spreading over his features had been genuine. "What attack?"

"Elise was raped by a group of wolves. It happened three years ago, and she almost died."

Jeremy had stared at her, his look so intense, she'd felt as if he were peering in to her soul. "You healed her, didn't you?" he'd finally rasped. "That's how the two of you became friends."

She'd nodded, and he'd asked, "Why weren't the Runners told about the attack?"

"It was considered best handled in-house, but Sheffield botched the investigation from beginning to end."

"Why the hell didn't Eric do anything about it?"

"He tried, but Eli, their older brother, made Eric promise to let him handle it on his own. Eli was able to track down and kill one of them, but it was without the League's permission and that's why he was banished from the pack."

For a moment, he'd just stared at her, his eyes dark and bright all at once, his gaze moving slowly over her features, one by one, until he'd quietly said, "When you healed her, did you…"

She'd nodded, shivering with the memory. "Yes, I saw it in her mind. But I couldn't tell who they were."

He'd cursed hotly under his breath at her admission, pacing from one side of her living room to the other. Then they'd argued over her safety. He'd wanted to stay, even if it meant sleeping on her sofa, but she'd been adamant about him going home. He'd been furious, but he'd finally left, and she'd tried to get some sleep.

Not that it had worked worth a damn.

Blearily, she pulled on her robe and scuffled out of her bedroom, following the thick, enticing aroma of coffee. "Am I still sleeping?" she asked in a throaty rasp when she stood in the kitchen archway. "Because I don't remember inviting you in."

He sent her a cautious grin over his broad shoulder, the long, ropey muscles in his arms flexing as he moved a frying pan to one of the back burners, the cotton of his T-shirt clinging to the mouthwatering line of muscles down his back. "That's probably because I don't remember asking. Yesterday, I helped myself to the spare house key you keep on that little hook by your phone over there," he told her, nodding toward the white phone mounted on her kitchen wall.

Sure enough, her spare key was missing.

Too tired to get angry, Jillian settled herself into one of the white kitchen chairs at her small table, propping the side of her face up on her hand. Enjoying the fine view of his tight backside wrapped up in soft denim, she gave a loud, jaw-cracking yawn that had those broad shoulders shaking with silent laughter.

"Trouble sleeping?" he asked, while the early morning sunlight slanting through the blinds set his golden head alight, turning his blond hair the warm, gleaming color of honey.

"Don't you know?" she mumbled around the edges of another yawn.

"Wouldn't have a clue," he remarked easily, bending to pull something out of the oven. "I left you, remember? Just like you wanted."

Softly, she said, "I won't be spied on, Jeremy."

He paused in the act of taking down a coffee cup, having obviously already familiarized himself with her cupboards, and muttered a low curse under his breath. "How did you know?"

"That you were watching my house last night? I just...*felt* you. The sensation was so strong that it pulled me out of sleep. When I peeked around my curtains in the living room, I saw your truck parked out on the street."

"I went home and tried to sleep, but it wasn't happening. So I went out for a drive, just to take a look around," he said after a moment, moving to pour her coffee.

"Right," she snorted, before saying, "I lay in bed listening for you to drive away. It was hours before I fell asleep— and you were *still* out there."

He blew out a rough breath. "Okay, truth?"

"That would be nice," she replied drolly, starting when he glanced over his shoulder and caught her staring at his perfectly muscled backside. She blushed, and with a ghost of a smile, Jeremy turned back to stir cream and sugar into her coffee, then brought it to the table. She took it with a murmured thanks and lifted her gaze to his face.

"Maybe I just wanted to make sure Eric didn't stop by for a late night tryst," he told her in a gravelly voice. "When I was sure that he wasn't heading over to crawl into bed with you, I took my tired butt home to my lonely bed and grabbed some z's. Satisfied?"

She couldn't look away from the greedy, smoldering look of hunger in his eyes, his irises glowing with a warm, swirling blend of green and gold, the way they did when his wolf was lurking beneath the surface, taking an interest in his surroundings. "You may have been jealous, but that wasn't the only reason."

He nodded slowly, watching her with that same predatory awareness that never failed to ramp up her heart rate. "You're right," he said quietly, his voice little more than a low, warm murmur. "That wasn't the only reason. I was worried about you, Jillian. I wanted to make sure Dustin and his pals didn't try to get anywhere near you, acting on Drake's orders."

"Thanks for telling me the truth," she whispered, as if afraid of breaking the spell, even though she didn't know *what* the spell was. She just knew that when he stared at her like that, she wanted it to last forever.

His head listed to the side as he studied her, thumbs hooked in the front pockets of his jeans. "There's been enough lying in our lives, Jillian. I don't think we need to add to it now."

Before she could think of what to say in response, he turned back toward the stove and started filling two plates. Minutes later, he'd nearly finished his breakfast while she was still staring down at the heaping mound of food he'd placed before her, a bemused expression on her face.

"What's wrong?" he asked when he realized she hadn't touched her breakfast. "Don't you like it?"

Jillian shook her head, her tone one of baffled amazement. "I'm sure it's wonderful. I mean, it smells delicious. I just…" She paused, shrugging her shoulders. "I guess I'm just surprised that you can cook like this. It seems too domestic for a guy like you."

"A guy's gotta eat, you know." He wiped his mouth with a napkin and leaned back in his chair, giving her a warm, knowing look. "And contrary to what you seem to think about me, there's no harem of love slaves stashed away at my cabin waiting on my beck and call." His white teeth flashed in a slow, sexy smile. "If I want to eat, I have to make it."

"How surprising." Grinning, she reached for her fork and scooped up a mouthful of fluffy scrambled eggs. "And here I thought they probably ran around in little French maid outfits, with names like Fifi and Lola."

His deep chest rumbled with laughter. "Damn, woman. You must think I'm pretty impressive, to warrant a whole harem of Fifis and Lolas."

"Oh, I've never doubted your virility," she murmured dryly, before taking a bite of toast. Had she doubted his feelings for her? Yes. His willingness to accept the importance of her job? Yes. His ability to be faithful? Oh, yeah. But never, ever had she doubted his sexuality. Jeremy Burns was one of those men who wore his potent masculinity and rugged good looks with such an easy grace, women couldn't help but be drawn to him, herself included.

And fighting him was only getting harder with every second she spent in his company.

"So you've never doubted my…uh, virility," he drawled with a boyish grin, his hazel eyes glittering with humor. "Good to hear. And just to let you know, in case you wanted to check out my virility firsthand, I'm free for a sleepover whenever you feel up to asking me."

She almost choked on her second bite of toast, but took a quick sip of coffee to wash it down, then sent him a narrow look. "Call me crazy, but something tells me that inviting you to a sleepover wouldn't guarantee much sleep."

"On the contrary," he countered, hooking his hands behind his head, his pose one of indolent leisure, as if he had all the time in the world to sit there with nothing better to do than keep her off balance. She tried to keep her admiring gaze off the round perfection of his bulging biceps, so prominently displayed by the raised position of his arms, but knew she failed.

Arching one golden brow, his voice lowered to a deep, smoky rasp as he continued his seductive torment. "When you invite me to your bed, I'll promise to restrain myself to a few hours at the most, and by the time I'm ready to wrap you up in my arms and snuggle under the covers, you'll be syrupy and soft, your muscles like noodles. All those knots of tension you've been carrying around reduced to a state of hot, liquid bliss. You'll sleep like a baby, Jillian, and then I'll wake you up in the morning with my head buried between your legs. Nothing but slow, sweet torture, until you're ready to beg for…"

His voice trailed off in a deliberate tease, and she swallowed dryly, knowing her face was cherry red. She was so turned on she was panting, her throat tight, muscles locked against the need to jump over the table and tackle him to the kitchen floor. "B-beg for what?" she heard a voice that sounded suspiciously like hers ask, while her body temperature spiked, her robe too warm and heavy against her skin.

Jeremy leaned forward, bracing his elbows on his knees, eyes smoky with desire. "Uh-uh," he whispered, grinning like the wicked bastard that he was, confident in his power over her, in his ability to wear her down until she gave in. He didn't have to worry about *making* her want him—he was already sure of it. "That's part of the magic. Part of the mystery. I've got to keep you guessing."

"Jerk," she muttered under her breath, and he gave another deep, rough laugh that made her shiver with awareness. Wetting her bottom lip with her tongue, Jillian turned her attention back to her plate and picked up a crisp piece of bacon. "So what's on the agenda today, or did you just come over to make me breakfast because you missed me?"

"I always miss you," he said softly, leaning back in his chair again. When she glanced at his expression, all traces of humor and teasing had fled, the look in his eyes one of pure, unadulterated purpose and intent. But instead of pushing, he picked up his coffee cup and said, "I want to take a look at the records room before they open, which means we still have a few hours."

Jillian took a bite of the bacon, enjoying the salty burst of flavor. "And how were you planning on doing that? Pack records aren't available to the public."

Jeremy met her stare over the rim of his mug. "I know."

"So we're going to break in, then?"

"Looks like it." He grinned before taking another drink. "Nothing like a little B and E to get the day started, eh?"

"If you want to visit," she said, after thinking about it for a moment, "you could just ask my mother. She's friends with Carolyn, the record's clerk. It wouldn't be easy, but she could probably get permission for us to look around."

He snorted, a half-smile playing at his mouth as he gave a dramatic shiver. "Thanks, but no thanks, sweetheart. Your mother still scares the bejesus out of me."

Jillian couldn't help but laugh at his expression. "You're a grown man now, Jeremy. Twice her size."

"Doesn't matter," he murmured, his tone wry, cheekbones flushed with a dull shade of embarrassment. "When she looks at me, I feel like she can see straight into me."

"Hmm…she probably can," she teased, enjoying watching him squirm.

He closed his eyes, holding up one hand. "Oh, god. *Don't* tell me that. I'd rather not know."

"Don't worry." She laughed, taking mercy on him. "I don't *think* she can. Not just by passing you on the street. If she touched you—" her shoulders lifted in a shrug "—maybe."

He gave another dramatic shiver. "Then remind me never to let her touch me. That woman would kill me for the things I've fantasized about doing to her beloved daughter."

Snuffling a soft laugh under her breath, Jillian perched her chin on her fist as she studied him. "You really are afraid of her, aren't you?"

"Not nearly as afraid as I am of you." He gave her a slow, sexy wink as he stood up and reached for her plate. "Now, go get ready, and I'll clean up in here. I want to get an early start, before the town is crawling with people."

"I'm still not sure why you need me there," she said around another yawn.

"To save my ass in case we *do* end up getting caught," he offered with a cocky grin, somehow managing to look ruggedly masculine with a sponge in one hand and bottle of dish soap in the other.

"I'm not buying it," she murmured. "I think it has to do with everything that happened yesterday. I think you want to keep an eye on me."

"No argument there," he said lightly, flashing her a killer smile over his broad shoulder. "God knows I like having my eyes on you."

With a delicious shiver warming her body from head to toe, Jillian grabbed her coffee and hurried out of the room.

"I can't believe I let you talk me in to this," Jillian huffed, twisting her body through the oblong window that sat five inches above street level, opening into the basement storage room of the hall of records. Luckily, the window was located on the backside of the building that faced an alley, so they were relatively hidden from view.

Her legs cleared the window first, and Jeremy grabbed her waist, helping her to the floor, trailing his hands up her sides until they settled at the outer curves of her breasts. "Give me an inch and I'll take a mile," he murmured, pulling her closer to his hard length.

"I'll remember the warning," she muttered, jerking out of his hold.

"You do that," he drawled, giving her a slow smile. "'Course, it won't do you any good," he added with a lift of one shoulder. "I'm not above taking advantage of the situation whenever I get the chance."

Jillian tried to ignore the way he was looking at her, but it wasn't easy. Since the moment she'd found him in her kitchen, he seemed to be in full seduction mode. His gaze traveled over her with such delicious intensity, it made her feel stripped down to nothing, even though she wore a pair of low-slung jeans, a thick worn leather belt and a thin boat neck sweater in a rich, golden green that reminded her of Jeremy's eyes when he was turned on. She'd been the recipient of that look too often when she was younger—and finding herself caught in that deliciously smoldering stare again had her feeling restless and on edge.

Of course, that restless feeling of unease *could* have been attributed to the fact they'd just broken in to a private building. What the hell was she thinking?

Shifting her gaze away from him, Jillian took a deep breath and tried to settle her thoughts. "Do you want me to find the lights?" she asked, thinking that the sooner they got what they'd come for, the sooner they could get out.

"Naw," he drawled, moving behind her to lift the blinds

on the second basement window. "We should have enough sunlight to be able to read."

Looking out over the rows and rows of filing cabinets, Jillian shook her head at the daunting task ahead of them. "So where do you want to start?"

"Let's see if we can find files for the League members."

"Even Dylan?" she asked, sending him a surprised look over her shoulder.

"Everyone," he said in a low voice, his attention already on his task as he pulled open the nearest cabinet to see how the files were organized. "Looks as if everything is in alphabetical order according to last names, so we should be able to move pretty quickly. You start with Graham and Clausen on the far side of the room, and I'll pull Dylan's, Pippa's and old Summers's."

"What about Drake and the others?" she asked, moving two rows over, before opening a drawer to see where she was in the alphabet.

"We'll work our way through all of them, but I'm saving ol' Drake for last," he grunted.

Forty minutes later, they'd been through the files of every member on the League, save Drake, and had nothing. "One more to go," she said, watching as Jeremy pulled the last file from its drawer. Since it also contained documents dealing with his wife and children, Drake's file was the thickest of all, a musty smell rising up from its yellowed pages as Jeremy dropped it on top of the filing cabinet. "What are you hoping to find here?" she asked, when he started thumbing through the thick stack of pages.

His eyes narrowed, and he pressed the file flat, his focus on a pale blue page that sat about halfway through the hefty volume. "I'm looking for motive," he answered in a low voice.

"Motive?" she echoed. "But we already know how he feels about humans. Rogues hunt humans, and the traitor you're trying to find has been enabling the rogues to grow in number, even encouraging wolves to turn. What better motive do we need than that?"

"But we don't know why," he responded, turning another page. "And that could be the key to all of it. We know he hates humans. And if he *is* the Elder behind this surge in rogue wolves, if he's the one who's teaching them how to dayshift, then we can assume that he hates humans enough to want them dead. But why? That's the part of the puzzle that still needs to be solved."

"So you want the motive for his motives?"

"Exactly." He lifted his head and sent her a flash of a smile, before turning his attention back to the file. "If we can get to the bottom of his hatred, maybe we can understand where he's coming from. Maybe we can…" His voice trailed off, and he quickly turned the page he'd been reading, then flipped back a few pages before it. "Son of a bitch," he rasped under his breath. "Could it really be that simple?"

"What?" she asked, trying to see what had caught his interest. "What'd you find?"

"It's not what I found," he drawled, shaking his head while a slow grin spread across the sensual line of his mouth, "but what I *didn't* find."

"Which would be?" she growled, glaring when he arched one brow at her disgruntled tone.

"There's no death certificate for his wife," he told her, his grin melting into a smile at the look of surprise on her face.

"That's impossible," she whispered, grabbing the file and turning it toward her. "There has to be one in here. Helen Drake died in some kind of accident when the kids were still little."

"Not according to the file, she didn't. You know what this means, don't you?" he asked, reaching out to tuck a lock of her hair behind her ear as she flipped through the pages of the file, backward and forward. But sure enough, it wasn't there.

"No death certificate could mean she isn't dead," Jillian whispered, lifting her gaze to his, "but if that's the case, then where is she? What happened to her?"

"That's what we need to find out."

She watched him return the file to its proper place in the drawer, while a cold knot of dread settled into her stomach. She didn't know what would come of everything, but whatever it was, Jillian had no doubt that it was going to be bad. They needed answers, and she knew the best place to find them. "I think we should talk to Pippa."

His eyes went wide. "Pippa Stanton? The Elder?"

"I know it sounds crazy, but hear me out. Pippa and Drake have been going head-to-head lately. And she's one of the oldest members of the pack. If anyone around here knows what really happened to Helen, Pippa will."

Jeremy held her stare for a long, hard moment, then finally said, "Not that I think there's a chance in hell she'll talk to us, but do you trust her?"

"As much as I trust any of them. But Pippa's the only one who didn't support Graham when he first threatened me with a Mate Hunt." Jillian shivered at the memory, remembering her horror when she'd been called before the League and told they were growing impatient with her, reminding her that it was her duty to provide the pack with their future Spirit Walker. If a Mate Hunt were voted into action, the unwed male wolves would be given the chance to hunt her down, and she would be wed and bonded to whomever caught her first.

"What do you mean, she was the only one?" Jeremy

demanded, his brows pulled together in a deep V over the golden-green of his eyes. "There's no way in hell Dylan would've agreed to something like that."

She shrugged. "I didn't think so, either, but Pippa was the only one who made an argument that the Mate Hunt was an arcane tradition that should be abolished."

He started to respond, when a sudden noise had them both freezing, breaths held tight in their lungs.

"Let's get the hell out of here," Jeremy rasped, lifting the window.

"Good idea," she whispered, and he hoisted her up to the street.

The quiet house was as quaint as the woman who lived within its antique white walls. Pippa Stanton took the chair across from the love seat where Jillian and Jeremy sat, her long, signature silver plait of hair coiled around the top of her head like a crown, her posture equally regal as she made herself comfortable. After making it out of the records room undetected, they'd headed straight to her house on the outskirts of town, careful to make sure they weren't seen walking to her door.

To Jillian's infinite relief, the Elder had been more than happy to invite them in. "Tell me," Pippa said in a soft, husky voice that had ripened like a fine wine, "what did you think of Drake's rally, Mr. Burns?"

With his hands clasped between his knees, Jeremy sent her a charming, lopsided grin. "I thought it was the biggest load of bullshit I've ever heard."

Jillian poked him in the ribs, glaring, but the Elder threw back her head and chuckled. "And if you don't agree with Drake," she said a moment later, when her laughter had died down, "then what's your answer to the tensions rising within the Silvercrest?"

Jeremy shook his head. "I don't claim to have the answers. I only know what I see. The pack's insistence on defining itself by what it is and what it isn't gives power to those who seek their own personal ambition. Is there an easy answer? An easy solution? Of course not," he rumbled. "But focusing on the differences between your race and the humans will never lead to either. It will only bring bloodshed and destruction to this town and to the pack itself."

"I agree, Mr. Burns. We are not human, and yet, we are not monsters. We are, in fact, charged with a greater purpose. If we chose, we could do wonderful things. Instead, we focus on bitterness and differences…when in fact, we are more alike than different. We want to be safe. We want love, protection and happiness for our families. Things that hate will never produce."

Jillian was aware of Jeremy's expression mirroring her own surprise at the Elder's words. She had expected Pippa to be civil, but she'd never dreamed that the woman would actually share such opinions with them. "But that's a discussion for another day," the elderly Lycan murmured, inclining her head in a graceful gesture. "I assume you've come for information."

"You're right," Jeremy told her. "It's about Helen Drake. We've seen the family's file in the hall of records and there's no death certificate for Stefan's wife."

Slim gray brows lifted over piercingly sharp eyes the color of a mountain lake. "Uncovered that particular little tidbit, did you?" she remarked. "It's one thing to see something that's there—and quite another to see something that isn't. I'm impressed."

"Can you tell us what happened?"

Pippa leaned back in her chair. "Oh, there's not much to tell. Helen fell in love with another man and left Drake and the children, which was bad enough in Drake's opinion. But the fact she abandoned them all for a man who was human was intolerable. That was the beginning of the end for Drake. The Lycan he was has been lost to hatred as virulent as a disease."

Jeremy's golden brows drew together in a deep ridge. "What happened to Helen?"

"I don't know, but I imagine she got as far from here as possible. Drake asked us for permission to have her assassinated, but the League refused." She paused, the corners of her mouth turning in a thoughtful frown. "You know, he's never forgiven us for what he called our 'desertion in his quest for justice.' He was furious, accusing us of turning our backs on him in his time of need."

"How is it that nobody knows the truth?" Jillian asked, hyperaware of Jeremy pressed against her side on the small love seat—of his heat and hardness and the heady scent of his skin filling her head.

"Oh, there are those who know, but they're forbidden to tell. Drake refused to let the children even speak her name, but they know what really happened. As for the League, we supported his story that she'd been killed in an accident because it served our purpose to do so. We wanted the whole sordid affair forgotten, though Drake has never been able to get past it." She rose out of the floral-printed chair, an unspoken signal that the visit had come to an end. "Now, if you'll excuse me. I'm expected at Graham's in fifteen minutes, and he's a crotchety ol' bastard when forced to wait."

Rolling to his feet, Jeremy gave a quiet laugh. "We understand, and we appreciate your talking to us."

"You've been more than helpful," Jillian added. "Thank you."

The Elder gave them a wondering smile, looking from one to the other. "You know, I always thought it was a shame you two couldn't see past the nonsense that tore you apart."

Jillian blinked in surprise, aware of her face going hot. She'd always assumed that Pippa supported the League's ultimatum that she break things off with Jeremy, that the decision had been unanimous. Had she been wrong? If she'd spoken up and fought for the right to make her own choices, for what she'd wanted, would she have had an ally in this woman?

And not for the first time since Jeremy had returned, she questioned her decision ten years ago. Had she grabbed at the ready answer, at the easy way out, allowing fear to rule her actions? Is that why she'd let rumors and the League's disapproval tear them apart?

Rumors? Her own thoughts surprised her. Was that what she now believed? That his cheating with Danna *had* been a lie? And if so, why? To keep them apart?

Regret twisted her insides and Jillian tore her gaze away from Pippa's knowing stare. "Again," she said quietly, "thank you for talking to us."

"If Drake learns what I've told you," Pippa drawled airily, moving toward the door, "he'll have my head."

"Don't worry," Jeremy assured her. "We have no intention of involving you."

"Oh, that's a thin promise, Mr. Burns," the Elder commented with a wry smile. "We're all involved, are we not? At any rate, my soul is at peace with my choice. I've done the right thing today, and at this point in my years, that's all that matters."

She opened the door, giving an uncharacteristic wave goodbye, and Jillian shook her head in wonder as she and Jeremy headed down the sidewalk. "I can hardly believe she was so willing to talk to us," she whispered, when the Elder had closed her front door.

Pushing his hands into his pockets, Jeremy rolled one shoulder, his tone thoughtful, as if the wheels in his brain were going at full speed. "You know, I used to think she was a scary old crone, but she's really not so bad. And I think she talked because her conscience was weighing on her. She knows Drake's rotten, and she knows the League has let him get away with murder lately. Hell, he's been wreaking havoc in Shadow Peak for years."

"I can't believe what she told us about Helen," Jillian murmured. "It explains so much. Why he's such a misogynistic bastard. Why he blames humans for all the troubles in our world. He's never gotten over the humiliation of being abandoned for another man."

Jeremy nodded toward the thick line of trees at their right, saying, "Let's take a shortcut through the woods."

A few minutes later, they were following one of the worn footpaths that wove through the forest, the autumn wind whistling through the trees while the damp scent of the earth filled their heads. "So what now?" Jillian asked as she followed behind him on the narrow pathway, the thin shafts of pale sunshine muted by the towering trees overhead.

"I need to go to the Alley and talk to Mason," Jeremy said in his deep, husky baritone. "I don't want to risk putting this out over the phone."

Jillian narrowed her eyes on his back. "You mean, *we* need to talk to Mason, right?"

He stopped so suddenly that she nearly plowed right into him. "Are you sure you want to do that?" he rasped, turning and pinning her with a heavy-lidded look, his eyes suddenly burning the golden-green of his wolf. "The pack isn't going to like you hanging out at the Alley, Jillian. You can bet they'll have something to say about it."

"I don't care," she whispered shakily, wetting her bottom lip as she stared up at him, acutely aware of just how alone they were in the secluded woods, surrounded by nothing but the primal pulse of the forest and its rich, earthy heat. "I—I know that's probably hard for you to believe, Jeremy, but you're just going to have to trust me."

Chapter 10

Jeremy exhaled a shaky breath of air, then another, and the next thing Jillian knew, he was pushing her across the forest floor, his hands gripping her upper arms, her feet barely touching the ground. Wearing a visceral, urgent look of craving, he pressed her against the smooth bark of a tree, trapping her with his muscled strength at her front. She opened her mouth, only to lose her words on a throaty gasp as he grabbed her wrists, stretching her arms up high over her head, pinning her there. "You want my trust, Jillian?" he whispered, the velvet-rough timbre of his voice melting into her like the smooth, sweet burn of whiskey. "Fine. But it works both ways, sweetheart."

Jillian drew in a deep breath of his dark, rich scent, and the stab of desire that shot through her was instantaneous and hot, so intense she nearly screamed. It was as if she'd been left in a constant state of anticipation, just waiting for him to make a move and flip her switch. "Wh-what are you talking about?" she stammered, while her body struggled with a mind of its own, her hips rolling against the brutal shape of his cock as he pressed his lower body against her. She needed to be higher, dammit. Needed to be able to feel that breathtaking ridge where she needed it most.

"Why don't you read my mind and tell me? Let's see you put those powers of yours to good use."

"I would never—"

"What's the problem?" he whispered, his breath hot against the sensitive shell of her ear, making her shiver as each husky word curled against her skin. "Scared of what you might find?"

"You know I can't just crawl into your head," she snapped with frustration. "My powers don't work that way!"

Jeremy shifted back just enough to be able stare into her eyes. He didn't need to hold her with his hands and the hard press of his body—that look alone could have trapped her. It was *that* powerful...*that* compelling. "But you want to get inside my head," he whispered in a dark, smoky rasp. "You'd love to be able look inside and snoop around, discovering for yourself whether or not I'm worthy of your trust."

Unable to deny it, she asked instead, "Wh-what is it with you and pushing me against trees?"

"I don't know. Must be the animal in me," he drawled, his eyes bright with laughter, triumph and the savage burn of lust. He leaned down, nuzzling the softness of her throat, sending tingles over her skin, while a smooth warmth coursed just beneath her surface, setting her on fire. "I've spent so many years wanting you," he confessed in a low, wicked slide of words. "Wanting to touch you, taste you. You're all grown up now, Jillian. I don't have to be careful anymore."

His open mouth pressed against the base of her throat, his tongue flicking in a slow, carnal caress against the fluttering of

her pulse, and she gasped, her breath catching at the pure eroti-
cism of the act. "I don't have to watch what I say. Don't have
to worry about going too far. You're no longer that innocent
little eighteen-year-old who the boys were afraid to kiss."

"You weren't afraid to kiss me," she moaned, arching her
neck to give him better access.

"That's because I wanted you so badly, I was willing to risk
your mother's fury," he admitted with a gritty laugh, nipping
the tender tendon that ran down the side of her neck to her
shoulder.

"Jeremy," she breathed out unsteadily, searching for the ar-
guments she knew she had to make, but her own hunger was
making her crazed. Then he shifted her wrists to one big
hand, and the other settled at her waist. Her heart beat so fu-
riously, Jillian thought it would explode. And before she
could draw her next breath, Jeremy shoved her sweater up to
her chin, baring her belly and chest to the blistering heat of
his gaze.

"God, you're beautiful," Jeremy breathed, staring in a hazy
state of lust at her lace-covered breasts, the sound of his pulse
roaring in his ears, vicious and violent. Before Jillian could
protest, he leaned down and captured the tip of her left nipple
in his mouth, wetting her through the delicate French lace, desperate to get to the even softer flesh beneath. Her back arched
at the touch of his tongue, and she cried out, the shaky sound
of his name on her lips the sweetest thing he'd ever heard.

"Want you," he groaned, panting, aware of his beast growing restless as her lush, sweet scent filled his head. "All of
you, Jillian. Everywhere."

"Yes," she gasped, her petal-soft skin hot, slick beneath his
tongue as she vibrated with arousal, the fine tremors telling
him just how badly she needed him.

Satisfaction pooled hot and thick in his blood, making him want to howl…because finally, after all this time, he had her.

The thought spun deliciously through Jeremy's mind with stunning, headspinning force, nearly bringing him to his knees. Sensations flooded in on him, provocative and rich and warm, overwhelming him with the need to get close to this woman…and stay there.

Wanting to imprint the moment on his memory forever, he took a handful of seconds just to stare at her, to soak in every detail, every soft, delicate curve and shade. Studying her face, he could see the dark, rosy flush on her cheeks that betrayed her desire, mesmerized by the way her teeth sank into the damp cushion of her lower lip. Curious to see what she'd do, he released her wrists, and watched as she blinked her eyes open and slowly…*shyly* drew her arms over her breasts, while her blond hair fell around the shadows of her face like a veil.

"Don't cover them," he rasped, leaning down to nuzzle her arms away, pressing tender kisses along her skin. "I want to look at you, Jillian. You're so beautiful like this, in nothing but watery sunlight. Just let me look at you, sweetheart."

Taking a deep, trembling breath for courage, Jillian forced her arms to fall gently to her sides, her fingers fluttering, restless with nerves. Jeremy pressed his face closer to her chest, until his teeth caught the edge of her lacy cup and tugged, releasing her breast. His lips closed around the hard ache of her nipple like a wet, liquid heat, suckling at her, pulling that warm, pulsing glow of pleasure in her belly up closer and closer to the surface, and then he pulled back to stare again, as if fascinated by the sight of her.

"Oh, god," she panted, and she didn't even recognize the ragged sound of her voice.

His lips were damp, slightly parted for the rush of his breath, eyes burning so bright, they were almost more golden than green—and the way he stared at her breasts made everything inside of her pull tight. He made her feel like a siren, like a goddess, her body the instrument with which she could tame the beast. She liked the feeling, liked the power…but then, it worked both ways. The more she took from him, the greater his power over her.

With hurried movements that betrayed his urgency, he unhooked the front clasp of her bra and pushed the open cups out of his way. Then he ran his tongue over her nipple with a slow, tasting rasp, before shifting to the other, pressing the swollen tip to the roof of his mouth, rubbing at her with his tongue while a rough, animal sound vibrated in his chest. His right hand found her hip…and moved lower, pressing possessively between her thighs, cupping her sex.

"God, Jillian. You're so hot I can feel you through your jeans," he growled, and then he was ripping at the buttons, his big, warm hand slipping beneath the top of her panties, pressing low, until he was touching tender flesh, so sensitive she couldn't hold back the sharp cry that surged up from her lungs. "You're swollen…*wet*," he said in a guttural, nearly soundless voice, while his fingertips stroked, learning her by touch, before working one thick finger into the clenching tightness of her body.

Jillian stiffened, sensations rushing over one another in a brilliant, chaotic jumble, too fast to catch or control, and she could have sworn that there were stars at the backs of her eyes, blinding her to everything but the breathless, provocative feel of his finger thrusting in shallow movements. "Damn, you're so tight," he rasped, pressing the damp heat of his forehead to hers, before leaning away, and she could feel the press of his eyes on her face. "Look at me, Jillian. I want your eyes open."

Lifting her lashes, she saw that his own eyes gleamed, the smoky green burning like a dark fire, jewel-toned and mesmerizing.

She wanted to scream from frustration when he pulled his hand away—wanted to demand he put it back and finish what he'd started—until she realized he was lifting his glistening finger to his mouth. Wearing a hard, savage look of hunger, he closed his lips around the slippery digit and his eyes drifted shut, a low moan of pleasure rumbling deep in his chest.

Jillian panted harder, unable to draw in enough air, everything in her body feeling heavy and hot, until she burned with sensation from the top of her head down to her toes. Staring at her through the thick, golden fringe of his lashes as he opened his eyes, he pulled his finger free and cupped her jaw with the damp heat of his palm, stroking the pad of his thumb against the corner of her mouth. "You taste incredible, Jillian. Hot, sweet, like goddamn honey."

She made a murmur of embarrassment, but he was already thrusting his finger back into her, going deeper as he added another, her muscles clenching around him as if to hold him inside. Fitting his mouth over hers, he kissed her deeper, as well...*harder,* his tongue mastering hers with destructive skill.

"I want to make you come," he groaned against her lips, the words gritty and breathless. "I want you to spill into my hand...want those sharp little cries in my head as you go over."

She gasped, feeling disoriented, like someone who'd been spinning in a circle, going faster...and faster...and faster. He was ragingly beautiful in his lust, the angles of his face sharpened by hunger. Suddenly, she heard herself saying, "J-just do it."

"What?" he rasped, his gaze questioning as he stared into her eyes. "What do you want, Jillian?"

"You. Us. Now," she panted…pleading. "I can't think straight anymore, Jeremy. Please…just do it."

His eyes narrowed, the crest of his cheekbones marked with violent color. Slowly, he shook his head. "No."

Jillian blinked, stunned by his refusal.

"No," he repeated, the word shaky and raw. "Not here, like this, because once I have you, you're *mine*. I'm not going to bang you against a tree and then watch you walk away from me. From the moment I get you under me, Jillian, you're going to stay there until I've had my goddamn fill of you."

She wanted to scream at him, to yell and shout and demand that he give in, but he took her mouth in a ravaging kiss, stealing her breath, her mind. She pressed her fists against the solid wall of his chest, and his fingers flexed deeper inside of her, thrusting, making her cry out. He swallowed the sound as he pressed his thumb through her slick, tender folds, until he was touching that most sensitive part of her, stroking her with the callused pad, while using his fingers to rub a place deep inside of her that made her stiffen in shock. She saw nothing but a stunning, infinite darkness that seemed to overtake her mind, everything inside of her pulling tighter…and tighter…until that perfect, shattering moment when she crashed over the edge.

Jillian went wild…and the forest erupted into chaos around them.

Breaking her mouth from his, she threw back her head and screamed in the violent wash of ecstasy as a churning, roaring whirlwind surged up from the leaf-covered ground. She opened her eyes to see Jeremy staring at her in stunned awareness, while the ground beneath their feet began shaking, the wind whirring faster…and faster. The pleasure in her built higher, stronger, until they were caught in a maelstrom of wind and leaves and the dark, rich scents of the forest. The dry leaves prickled against their skin, lashing at them, the pine needles stinging and sharp. It went on…and on, until finally the last ripple faded and she went boneless in his arms, while the leaves and needles fluttered quietly back to the ground.

"What the hell was that?" he demanded, breathless, his hand still buried between her legs, cupping the liquid soft heat of her sex. His eyes were glowing within the darkness of his face, the hazel green edged by a dark ring of molten gold, and Jillian knew his wolf had awakened.

"I—I don't know," she panted, running her tongue along her lower lip. He stared intently, as if he were trying to decide whether or not to believe her. "Honestly. I—I don't know what that was, Jeremy. I swear."

"In that case, we should see if we can make it happen again," he whispered huskily, smiling, lifting his hands to cradle her face. Jeremy knew he shouldn't tempt fate by touching her, not unless he wanted their first time to be against that goddamn tree, but he couldn't stop. His cock was so hard he could barely see straight, much less think. Her orgasm had been explosive…breathtaking…awesome, and he wanted to experience it again…and again. Right now. That very second. Pressing a tender, searching kiss to her mouth, he reached for her jeans, ready to push them down her thighs, when the quiet of the forest suddenly exploded with a sharp crack of sound. The air around them sizzled with a blinding strip of heat and something smashed into the trunk behind her, sending shards of bark skittering into the air.

His brain had two seconds to register the fact they'd just been shot at, and then he was wrapping himself around her, protecting her with his body. The second bullet ripped into his shoulder at an angle, coming out the front in a clean strike that felt like liquid fire. They stumbled from the impact, and

Jeremy used every ounce of his strength to shove her behind the massive trunk of a nearby oak, before landing on top of her, her small body squished between his full weight and the prickly floor of the forest.

Through a fog of pain, Jeremy was dimly aware of Jillian shoving his heavy weight to the side, her small, cool hands moving frantically over his body. "Oh, my god, Jeremy, some-one shot you! Can you hear me? Jeremy, say something!"

He let out a groan, gritting his teeth against the black burn of pain searing across the landscape of his consciousness. The sound of his heartbeat pounded in his ears like the roar of a fighter jet, endless and excruciating, and he ground his jaw, refusing to pass out. If he could just breathe his way through the worst of it, he knew he'd be okay.

And then, through the thick cover of darkness spreading over him, he felt her hands on his temples, the coolness of her skin giving way to the blistering wave of heat that seemed to be radiating out from the bullet wound, engulfing him— and he suddenly realized what she was doing. Gripping her wrists, he jerked her hands away. *"No!"*

"What? Why?" she demanded.

"That nifty little slipping-into-someone's-brain thing that you do when you're healing them," he rasped, his words rough-ened by pain as he released his hold on her. "You told me you can read their minds when you do it. See into their heads."

"Only to get what I need to help them," she said in a choked voice, "or to get information about their injury. But I don't go snooping, Jeremy. That would be wrong and an abuse of my power."

He managed to crack his eyes open and give her a lopsided smile. "But too much to resist if you were given the chance to poke around in my head. Just think of the things you could go looking for."

Her eyes glistened with tears as she reached under him, grasped a handful of fabric, and applied pressure to the bleeding wound, before duplicating the process to the front of his shoulder. "Jeremy, you're not thinking straight. Let me help you."

"No way, Jillian." He lifted his left hand, rubbing his thumb over the damp, dewy softness of her lower lip, wishing she hadn't pulled down her sweater, missing the breathtaking view. "You wanna ease my pain, go to bed with me. But until then, stay the hell outta my head, sweetheart."

"Of all the stupid, stubb—"

He grasped her wrist, his grip controlled, careful not to hurt her. "No cheating," he murmured, snagging her shimmering stare and holding it, unwilling to let her look away. "When you decide to trust me, I'll be more than happy to give you what you want and let you look around in my head. I've got nothing to hide. But I'll be damned if I'll let you do it so that you can test the waters."

Her mouth thinned, and she gave a frustrated shake of her head, sending her hair cascading over her shoulders. "I can't stand to see you in pain," she said thickly.

"I'll be fine," he grunted. "It stings like a son of a bitch, but I'll live."

"Fine, have it your way." She sighed, her eyes bright within the paleness of her face, damp with tears. "Do you think you can move?"

His lips pulled back over his teeth in a grimace, and his brow was covered with beads of sweat that trailed down the sides of his face. "Not yet. Just give me a second for my stomach to settle."

"Okay," she whispered, pulling her wrist from his hold to wipe his forehead for him, careful to keep the stinging trails of sweat out of his eyes. Staring at the dark stain of blood seeping through the fabric of his shirt, she gave a weary shake of her head. "God, Jeremy, how many enemies do you have? You've been back in Shadow Peak for little more than a day and already they're trying to kill you."

"They?"

"Who do *you* think it was?"

"Hell if I know," he rumbled, unable to pick up anything other than Jillian's mouthwatering scent and the coppery smell of his blood. "But I've already had my share of threats since yesterday, including one from your mother."

She gasped, suddenly looking as if she wanted to hit him, her concern giving way beneath a wave of indignation. "My mother did not shoot you, you idiot!"

"Don't go getting all prickly," he wheezed, trying not to laugh. "It's the honest to god's truth that she hates me enough to shoot me."

"She doesn't hate you," she argued, pushing the words through her clenched teeth.

He didn't even bother responding to that one.

"And even if she did," she huffed, "she's powerful enough just to fry your circuits. She wouldn't need to resort to a bullet."

"Jillian, a bullet isn't going to kill me." His breath hissed through his teeth, the pain in his shoulder burning like fire. "Not unless I bleed out, but that isn't going to happen from one shot. This was a warning."

"So then we can add Drake to the list?"

"Stefan *and* Eric."

"What is it with you and Eric?" she practically growled. "He does *not* want you dead!"

"But he does want me *gone*," Jeremy grunted, putting the emphasis on the last word. "And come to think of it, maybe he *does* want me dead. I know I wouldn't mind seeing *him* dead and buried."

She gave him a priceless look of confusion. "For god's sake, why?"

His own look said the answer to that question should be obvious. "For touching what belongs to me."

"You can be so thickheaded sometimes," she muttered. "I already told you that there's nothing serious going on between Eric and me. *We. Are. Friends.* Nothing more."

"Well, if that's true, Mommy's gonna be crushed to hear it."

Jillian sighed at his stubbornness. "You still don't believe me, do you?"

"Irritating, isn't it?" he asked, arching one brow. "Not having the trust of those you care about."

"Who says I care about you?" she grumbled out the side of her mouth.

He managed a low rumble of laughter, though the sound was strained. "I do," he said lightly. "Which is why you're going to help me home and take care of me, because this thing is starting to hurt like hell."

Sending a furtive glance in the direction the shots had come from, she said, "Do you think it's safe now?"

"Yeah, it's getting late enough in the morning that the pack's going to be moving around. Whoever it was got what they wanted. They're long gone by now."

"Can you walk if I help you?" she asked, putting her arm around his shoulders as he struggled to sit up, his shirt saturated with a fresh surge of blood.

"Just get me to your place. It's closer," Jeremy told her… and for once, she didn't argue.

Chapter 11

The walk to her house was painfully slow, but thankfully uneventful. Jillian sat him down in one of her kitchen chairs, cleaned and dressed his wound while he sipped on some "medicinal" Scotch to dull the pain, then helped him to her bed. If his shoulder hadn't been burning so badly, he'd have taken the time to tease her about helping him out of his clothes, but by the time he was stripped down to his black cotton boxers, Jeremy was done for. The second his head hit the pillow, exhaustion swept over him, but he struggled to stay awake long enough to call his partner.

Mason picked up on the second ring, and Jeremy quickly filled him in on the shooting, as well as the fact that he had information that he didn't want to share over the phone. His partner was furious that he'd been shot, but he assured Mason that it wasn't serious. He was going to be back in working order within hours, a day at the most, since the bullet had gone clean through. Their Lycan genes allowed the Runners to heal at a far greater rate than humans, which was a convenient genetic bonus, considering the physical demands of their jobs.

While he finished up with Mason, Jillian closed the blinds behind her sheer bedroom curtains, casting the room in deep, dusky violet shadows. Jeremy set his phone on the bedside table, and his gaze moved back to where she stood by the window, her arms crossed over her middle. With the pale streaks of light sneaking around the edges of the blinds at her back, it was hard to read her expression, but he knew she was upset, maybe even a little bit afraid.

"You okay?" he rasped.

"It's all related, isn't it?" she asked unsteadily, her voice a whispery thread of sound as she moved slowly toward the bed. "The rogues, the dayshifting, the teenagers, Drake's wife, you being shot. All of it, everything, it's all tied together. Someone's trying to destroy us, aren't they?"

He reached out with his good arm and grabbed hold of her hand, her fingers cool within the feverish heat of his grip. "If it is Drake, and I don't see how it can't be, we're going to find the proof we need to nail his ass and put a stop to all of this once and for all. The Runners won't quit until that happens."

"I know. I'm just worried about you," she whispered, staring at their joined hands while she made that telling confession, before daring a shy glance up at his face.

"I like the sound of that," Jeremy teased in a deep, suggestive rumble, waggling his brows at her, glad when he saw her lips twitch with a small smile. "And I promise nothing's going to happen to me. I'm not going to give the bastard the satisfaction of taking me down."

She nodded, and took a step back, pulling her hand from

his. "You should rest now," she told him. "I'll check back in on you in a little while."

"Don't be too long," he murmured, closing his eyes, re-opening them a moment later when she walked back into the room, carrying a tall glass of iced water. Jillian set it on the bedside table, and turned to leave as silently as she'd entered. But when she reached the door, she stopped, one hand on the frame, and looked back at him, her velvety brown eyes full of questions.

Jeremy watched as she wet her bottom lip with a quick swipe of her small, pink tongue, and softly said, "Why is it still…"

Her voice trailed off, but he picked up the question for her, knowing instinctively what she'd wanted to say. "You mean, why do our bodies still scream that we belong together, even though we've both been with other people?"

A strange look darkened her eyes, but she only said, "Yeah."

"I don't know for sure, but I assume it's because we never completed the bond. We never had sex…and I never took your blood. You know as well as I do that when a true lifemate takes a lover who isn't his or hers, it can sever the connection. But our connection was never made, Jillian—we've just put it on hold for all these years."

She nodded, but didn't say anything as her gaze slipped away from his, and he wondered if she was thinking about the forest. About the way she'd begged him to take her when she'd been wild with need, too hungry to fight what her body so desperately craved.

"But I wish I'd made love to you that afternoon when you kissed me," he confessed in a sudden rush, driven by a sharp sense of urgency to get the guttural words out before she turned and left. "I could have made you give in to me, Jillian, but I went easy on you. But if I had, if I'd pushed for what I wanted, we'd have made it. I'd have had that bond to fight with, to make you believe in me when everyone else was working to keep us apart."

She blinked, the movement rapid, as if trying to hold back tears. "Maybe believing in *you* was never the problem," she whispered brokenly, and before he could respond, she pulled the door shut behind her.

Before Jeremy had so much as opened his eyes, he knew that Jillian was close. He drew in a deep breath, and savored the sweetness of her; that lush, provocative scent that called to every part of him and made him burn.

Cracking his eyes open, he found her lying beside him in the bed, her head cushioned on her folded hands, her eyes open, but hazy with the remnants of slumber, as if she, too, had only just awakened. "What time is it?" he asked, his voice scratchy from sleep.

"Late afternoon. I hope I didn't bother you. I came in to check on how you were doing, and you looked so peaceful, I couldn't resist lying down for a nap."

"It hardly bothers me to wake up next to a beautiful woman," he told her with a lopsided smile, reaching out to thread his fingers through the soft, silken tresses of her hair, enjoying the way it caught the shimmering sunlight that edged its way around the blinds. "You know, I've always wondered what you would look like if I were able to wake up next to you, when my eyes were still sleepy."

"Pretty scary, huh?" she joked, obviously trying to lighten the moment.

"No," he confessed with a grin. "To be honest, you're more beautiful than ever like this, with your hair falling around your face, eyes soft, mouth softer. I've always thought you were the most beautiful thing in the world." He drew in a deep,

Jillian-scented breath, and lifted his thumb to the corner of her mouth, watching as he stroked the seductive swell of her lower lip. The curve of her mouth was too petal-soft to resist, moist and pink and delicious. "I never forgot you, Jillian." His words were hushed…solemn. "God knows I wanted to, but I couldn't."

Her eyes blinked slowly closed, cheeks turning a soft shade of rose. *"Jeremy…"*

"No, let me get it said," he rasped, cutting her off. "I know you're scared, but—"

The ringing of his cell phone on the bedside table interrupted his words, and she sat up, quickly handing him the phone.

"Burns," he growled, ready to howl with frustration as Jillian slipped off the bed and padded softly from the room.

Mason's low laugh rumbled over the line. "I see your sunny disposition hasn't suffered any."

"Piss off," he grunted, dropping his head back on the pillow, half wishing he could strangle his best friend for interrupting what had been leading up to be…*a moment*. He didn't know what "kind" of moment, dammit, but he'd sensed that something powerful was about to happen.

"I know you're not feeling too hot," Mason rumbled, "but I wanted to let you know that we've got a new development. I don't want to get in to details on the phone, either, but it's one that's related to the case Cian and Brody are on."

"Shit," he groaned, scrubbing his hand down his face, knowing that another human victim had been found. There'd been two other murders in the past few weeks, both blond, blue-eyed human females whose hearts had been eaten out of their chests, and at both crime scenes, no traceable Lycan scent had been found, only a sharp acidic odor that was produced when a wolf dayshifted. Anthony Simmons had known about the killings and had even staged a similar murder of a woman whose hair had resembled Torrance's, trying to mess with Mason's mind. Before Simmons's death, he'd told Mason that the deaths would continue, and that the Runners wouldn't be able to stop the Lycan responsible.

And now they had a third victim. "I have a really bad feeling about this."

"Me, too." Mason sighed. "I'll give you a call back when I have all the info, okay?"

"I'll be waiting," he said, then disconnected the call. Jeremy thought about his options for a moment, and then, making sure to move as carefully as possible, he rolled to his side, relieved when his shoulder didn't flare up with a fresh surge of pain. Instead, there was a low, annoying ache, but it was definitely manageable. Reaching for his jeans at the foot of the bed, he pulled them on, and had just stood up to finish buttoning his fly when Jillian came back into the room.

Her eyes went wide when she saw him. "What are doing? You need to be in bed."

"Something's come up and I can't discuss it on the phone," he told her, realizing he didn't have a shirt to wear. "I need to head down to the Alley for a bit to see Mase, and since I'm not leaving you alone after what happened this morning, I guess you're coming with me."

She crossed her arms over her breasts and glared at him. "Jeremy, you're not going anywhere. You need to give your body time to heal."

"I can heal later," he countered, "when we don't have this shit breathing down our necks." He pushed his fingers back through his hair, hopefully dealing with any bed-head he might have. "You don't happen to have an extra large T-shirt I could borrow, do you?"

She moved stiffly to her dresser, rummaging through the

bottom drawer while growling, "You've been shot, dammit. You may be an almighty Runner, but you're not invincible!"

He waited until she'd turned around to face him, tossing a wash-softened Pearl Jam concert shirt at his chest, before saying, "The only way I'm staying in that bed is if you're in it with me. *Under me,* Jillian. Your sweet little body laid out, wide-open, with me buried deep inside of you. Got it?"

"God, you're impossible," she huffed, but he could see that the image he'd created fascinated her. Bright flags of color burned in her cheeks, and her eyes had that hazy glow of hunger again.

"Not really," he shot back, the sound muffled as he carefully pulled on the shirt. "I just know my own limitations. Trust me, dragging my ass to the Alley is going to be a hell of a lot easier on me than lying here the rest of the day, driving myself crazy thinking about you."

"Impossible…*and* oversexed," she muttered, grabbing her brush off the top of her dresser and ripping it through her hair so viciously, he actually winced for her poor scalp.

"Can't be oversexed when I'm not getting any," he drawled, the corner of his mouth kicking up in a crooked grin when she stopped and cut him a sharp look from beneath her lashes.

"Oh, and by the way," he remarked casually, sitting down on the bed so that he could slip on his boots, "we'll need to take your car. The truck is out of commission. Can't get anyone out to fix it until tomorrow."

"What's wrong with it?" she asked, her eyes narrowing in suspicion.

He sent her an innocent look as he tied up his right boot, determined to ignore the pain in his shoulder. "Nothing's wrong with the truck itself, but the tires aren't doing so hot."

"What happened to them?" she demanded.

"Someone slashed them up a bit last night." He reached for his other boot, careful to hide his smile, since for some reason he was taking perverse enjoyment at seeing her so bent out of shape on his behalf. Maybe it meant she *did* care. God, he hoped so.

"A bit?"

He lifted his good shoulder. "That's one way of putting it."

Jillian closed her eyes, shaking her head. "You've had rocks thrown at your parents' house—"

"That was probably just Drake's little thugs," he interrupted.

"Had your tires slashed," she went on, clearly on a roll.

"Thugs again."

"And been shot at," she growled through her clenched teeth, opening her eyes to glare at him.

"*That* I'm still trying to figure out," he murmured, enjoying the fire blazing in her eyes. "But I'm placing my money on Drake again, or Cooper Sheffield. So that's three for three for the psychotic headjob. Guess he's in the lead, then."

She stood completely still for a beat of ten seconds, breathing slowly in…then out. "Fine, I'll drive you to the bloody Alley," she finally said, her menacing tone making him want to smile as she prowled forward, poking him in the chest with her finger, "And in exchange, how about you just try not to get yourself killed?"

"Will do," Jeremy agreed, unable to hold in his grin any longer…but she was already walking out of the room.

Despite its unusual name, Bloodrunner Alley was a picturesque, gently sloping glade located on Silvercrest pack land, several miles down the mountain from Shadow Peak, with the ceremonial clearing sitting equidistance between the two. The only structures it boasted were the fully modernized cabins where the Runners lived, the rugged homes surrounded by the wild, natural beauty of the forest, perfectly suited to their environment.

As they made their way down the private roads that connected Shadow Peak to the Alley, Jeremy finally told Jillian about the latest human victim, and the ones who'd come before. At first he'd tried to convince himself that he hadn't told her about the gruesome, ritualistic murders because he didn't trust her enough to tell her *everything* about the Runners' investigation—but he knew that'd only been a lie to cover the real reason.

The truth was that he'd kept this last bit of information to himself for the simple fact that he'd known it would upset her. Stupid, but there it was.

And it *did* upset her. At first, she got pissed that he'd kept the killings to himself, considering they were supposed to be working together, but then she'd admitted that she'd known there was a last piece of the puzzle he hadn't shared with her yet. She could have pressed him about it, but she'd been waiting for him to tell her himself, which he'd just done. Then, the reality of what they were dealing with sank in, and she went quiet, a strange, unsettling stillness settling over her body that made him want to take her into his arms and crush her in his embrace.

Unfortunately, when they pulled in to the Alley, Mason and his wife, Torrance, came outside to see who was there and he never got the chance. Mason gave him a hard time for getting out of bed after he'd been shot, and Torrance fussed over him, which only irritated his partner even more. But once inside, the four of them settled into the kitchen, and Jeremy went over what he and Jillian had learned at the hall of records, as well as from Pippa. While he talked, the other three worked together to make some cold-cut sandwiches, which they paired with chips and beer for an impromptu dinner.

Taking a long swig of an ice-cold Corona, Jeremy nodded his bottle toward Mason before setting it down. "So now that Jillian and I have shared our news, what did Brody have to say?"

Mason placed his sandwich on his plate, then leaned back in his chair with a tired sigh. "It isn't good. We found out about the body from a member of the pack. Dawson's youngest daughter, Sophia. She's been hanging around down in Covington for kicks, mixing in with the rave scene. Enjoying the sex, drugs and rock'n'roll."

"Christ," he muttered under his breath. "The more Lycans we have prowling around down there, the greater the risk of discovery. At this rate, it's only a matter of time before everything blows up in our faces."

"Yeah, well, you'll get no argument from me on that score," Mason grunted. "Anyway, Sophia dropped by the vic's house to score some weed and found the body. She's pretty much a mess right now, but was able to keep it together enough to know that she should call us. Brody and Cian were already down in Covington, following some possible leads on where the rogues might be hiding, so they were able to act quickly. Once they arrived on the scene, they got Sophia calmed down and took her to the Doucets. Michaela's going to let her hang out with them for a while, until she's ready to head back up to Shadow Peak."

Michaela Doucet was Torrance's best friend, and Jeremy knew that Jillian had met the friendly Cajun at the Dillingers' wedding, since Mic had been the maid of honor. She and her brother Max had been put under Bloodrunner protection after Simmons had made his first attempt on Torrance's life, and later trashed Michaela's business. Jeremy's friends Wyatt Pallaton and Carla Reyes were the Bloodrunning team who had been assigned to the Doucets' protection, and they would remain with them in the city until the threat had been eliminated.

"So the vic was found in her home?" he asked Mason.

"An old Victorian house that's been renovated into studio apartments, all artists and musicians. Brody said the music's so loud, it's not surprising the cops weren't called. You wouldn't have been able to hear her scream, and he probably took her throat out first."

From the corner of his eye, Jeremy watched as Jillian and Torrance both turned green, pushing their plates away. With a sigh, he shoved his partner in the arm. "Watch it, you idiot. They're trying to eat."

Mason glanced at the women, and immediately apologized. "Damn, sorry about that."

"That's okay," Torrance murmured. "We know this is important."

"Uh, so that's all we have so far." Mason picked up his beer, but he didn't take a drink. Instead, he turned the bottle around in his hand, and Jeremy knew he was thinking about the killing and what it meant. "Last I heard, Brody was on his way to the Alley with the body. He left Cian down at the scene until we get a unit in to clean up. Last thing we need is one of her neighbors stumbling into her apartment and finding all that blood."

"So then the killer left her body to be found by…anyone," Jeremy said quietly, not liking where his own thoughts were taking him. "He had no way of knowing that the vic would be found by a Lycan. That had to have been pure coincidence, which means that the killer doesn't give a crap if the humans discover our existence. He's playing with us, screwing with our heads."

"Either that," Mason muttered, "or he's so messed up he doesn't realize what he's doing."

Blowing out a hard breath, Jeremy said, "Whichever one it is, we're screwed."

"No shit."

Jeremy lifted his beer, then paused with the bottle halfway to his mouth, cocking his head to the side. "I think I hear Brody's truck."

Without a word, everyone pushed away from the table and headed out of the kitchen. Mason opened the front door and they all filed outside, waiting for Brody's truck to make the last bend and come in to view. No one said anything, but then, there didn't seem to be anything to say.

Moments later, the dark blue Ford appeared, pulling to a slow stop in front of the Dillingers' cabin. "Drive seemed as if it took forever," Brody grunted, climbing out of the cab, "but I didn't wanna push my luck and go over the speed limit." Wearing a grim look that only made the childhood scars slashing across his face seem more prominent, he jerked his chin toward the tarp-covered bed of his truck, where the victim's body had been placed. "Can you imagine coming up with a good excuse for something like that if a state trooper pulled me over?"

Jeremy moved forward to give the giant auburn-haired Runner a welcoming slap on the shoulder. "That took some balls, man."

"Didn't have much of a choice," Brody explained, beginning to undo the hooks that secured the tarp. "We had to get her out of there so that the clean-up crew could get in before anyone gets suspicious and goes to check up on her."

Taking a step toward the bed of the truck, Jillian asked, "What are you going to do with the body?"

"We burn them," Jeremy said as gently as possible, noticing how pale she was, but it didn't help. She still flinched, looking as if she'd been slapped. And suddenly, he realized just what it was costing her to be there, coming face-to-face with the ugliness of his world. He wanted to pull her into his arms and take her away, shelter her...protect her... But as Brody peeled back the tarp, revealing the bloodied remains of the victim, he knew it was too late.

The smell of death hung over the body with the darkness of a shadow, close and damp, like a slick palm clasping the back of your neck. It made Jillian shiver from somewhere deep inside of her, the trembling slowly spreading outward, until her skin was covered with chill bumps, her teeth chattering from the frigid sensation of cold.

"Are you okay?" Jeremy asked by her side, his voice soft while Brody stepped away from the group, one finger stuck in his ear while he answered a call on his cell.

The sharp scent of marijuana still lingered on what was left of the girl's clothes, mixing with the thick smell of blood, and her stomach roiled.

"I'm fine. I'm just not..."

She'd been about to say that she wasn't used to seeing death, but that wasn't true. As the pack's Spirit Walker, she knew death well, from illness, injury and old age. It was part of her job to know death—to use her powers to prevent it— and when unable to heal her patients, to give them the proper rites that would lead them into the afterlife. She even knew violence and bloodshed. No one living within a Lycan pack could be shielded from the more physical side of their natures.

But she didn't know murder. She didn't know cold-blooded butchery; the kind that made your skin crawl. And now she stood beside blatant proof that such evil existed, that it had reveled in this poor girl's violent death.

"I didn't mean for you to have to see this," Jeremy said, shoving his hands into the pockets of his jeans, while his dark gaze studied the blond victim, taking in every detail. "I'm sorry."

"It's not your fault," she whispered, the words shaky, since she couldn't seem to keep her chin from trembling. "And as much as I hate it, maybe it's something that I needed to see. I don't think I would have truly understood how this was affecting you, if I hadn't seen for myself what this monster is capable of."

Brody rejoined the group then, flipping his phone closed. "Sorry about that," he rumbled, shaking his head, the sun-lit strands of his auburn hair shifting across his shoulders. "We found a flyer from one of the local raves, and Cian went to check it out once the cleaning crew showed up."

Jeremy sent him a sharp look. "Find anything?"

"It's in the warehouse district," Brody told them, rolling his shoulder. "That's all we've got so far."

"The warehouse district? Isn't that where you suspected Simmons was hiding out while he was in Covington?" Torrance asked.

"Yeah." Glancing at the body, Brody's expression turned to one of barely restrained fury. "Her living room was covered with bongs and beer bottles. Drunk and stoned makes for one hell of an easy victim."

"She never even stood a chance, did she?" Torrance whispered, while her husband pulled her into his side, pressing a tender kiss to the top of her head.

"We're going to get him, sweetheart," he told her. "I promise you."

"I'm worried about Michaela," the petite redhead murmured, and Jillian didn't blame her. If she'd had a human best friend living in the city that was slowly becoming a killing ground, she'd have been concerned, too.

"Don't worry about Mic and Max," Mason murmured, his deep voice lowered to a warm, gentle rasp. "Pallaton and Reyes aren't going to let anything happen to them. I promise, baby."

Torrance nodded, and put her arms around her husband's middle, and it was like watching a miracle, seeing the look of love on the imposing Runner's face as he cuddled his wife, offering her his comfort.

It made Jillian feel…alone. Bereft.

"Jeremy," she said unsteadily, taking a step back from the truck. She couldn't do this, not now. Her emotional reserves had been sapped from the constant push and pull with Jeremy since he'd walked back into her life—and now she was caving in on herself.

"Jillian?" he rasped, his voice cut with concern. One big, capable hand curved around the back of her neck, as she struggled to draw in a deep breath of air.

But she was choking on the scent of death…of madness.

"I'd like to go home now," she croaked, and without a word, he pulled her into his chest, one strong arm wrapped around her shoulders, and led her away.

Chapter 12

He was an idiot.

That was his only excuse. Jeremy knew he should have considered what it might do to her to see something like that. Jillian dealt with hope and healing. Yes, she knew how to deal with loss, but for the most part, the darkness of his world didn't touch her.

And that was as it should be; protecting those within the pack was the true reason for the existence of the Bloodrunners.

Opening the passenger side door of Jillian's car, he tucked her into the seat and pushed her hair back from her face, giving her a small smile. "Hold tight for a few seconds and let me go grab some things from my cabin, okay?"

"No prob," she said with a wobbly attempt at a grin, but he knew she was freaked out. Her brown eyes were huge within the hollows of her face, lips trembling, skin as pale as the silvery moon now slowly rising in the evening sky, the blood-orange sun finally vanishing on the distant horizon.

"I'll be fast, I promise," he told her. Shutting the door, he lifted his hand to Brody as the Runner drove by. Brody would take the truck onto one of their private dirt roads, until he found a good spot to burn the body, then return to the city to help his partner look for clues. Jeremy made a mental note to call them tomorrow, just to make sure they were doing okay. They were both tough bastards, but they'd had to deal with some really messed up shit in the past few weeks. He knew too well how easy it was for stuff like that to screw with your head.

Jogging up to his front door, he was fishing his keys out of his pocket, when something made him pause. He lifted his head, eyes closed, and drew in a deep breath of air, searching for the faint trace that had snagged his attention. The wind had shifted for just a brief second, and then resumed its strong westerly flow, but he knew he hadn't imagined it.

Lycan musk. Thick and rich. Which meant only one thing. A wolf was near.

He was already yelling at Mason as he ran back toward the car. "Someone's in the woods. Get the women inside. Now!"

Ripping open the door, he yanked Jillian out of the car, practically shoving her toward Mason as his partner shouted for Torrance to get the hell inside of the cabin.

"What's happening?" Jillian demanded breathlessly, at the same time Mason muttered, "You've been shot, Jeremy. You should let me go."

"The shift will do me good," he grunted in a hard scrape of words, the anticipation of the hunt already burning through his veins, roughening his speech. "This bastard is mine."

Mason must have agreed, because instead of arguing, he gave him a sharp nod, then grabbed on to Jillian and began pulling her back toward his cabin, where Torrance stood in the doorway. "Just watch your back and don't do anything stupid," his partner growled.

"Stupid? This whole idea is stupid! Jesus, Jeremy, you can't face a rogue on your own!" Jillian shouted, struggling against Mason's hold, but unable to break away. She stared at Jeremy with a wild look of outrage, as if she wanted to get her delicate little hands around his throat and throttle him. "You're still healing, you idiot!"

"It isn't a rogue," he told her, and then he forced himself to rip his gaze away from her ravaged expression, knowing that he had to trust the man he loved like a brother to keep her safe.

"You're crazy!" Jillian shouted after him as he set off at a loping run toward the woods, relying on his instincts to lead him to his prey. The late afternoon had already given way to early evening, darkening the forest with long, purple shadows as the moon climbed its way into the stormy, cloud-mottled chaos of the sky, and the wind shifted again, just for a second, but it was enough. Jeremy raced into the trees, and let the primal, visceral surge of energy riding beneath his skin break free. Denim and cotton ripped with a hissing wail of sound as muscle and bone expanded, the surface of his skin prickling as thick, golden fur rippled over his body. The smells of the forest exploded into sharper focus as he took the powerful shape of his beast, his senses heightened in full Lycan form. He could hear the heartbeat of the forest; feel its movement, its breath.

His prey was running about two hundred yards to the east, already slowing from fatigue. With a burst of speed, Jeremy sprinted ahead to the north, the heavy muscles in his thighs and calves flexing and pumping as he sped over the forest floor, then cut back, bursting through a copse of birch trees and taking the lumbering Lycan in a head-on attack, pinning its body to the moss-covered ground.

"Son of a bitch!" he snarled, shaking his hulking head with disbelief, his words guttural within the muzzled shape of his mouth. "I thought that beer-soaked scent was yours. What the hell are you doing at the Alley?"

Magnus Gibson stared back at him through a pair of glowing, bloodshot eyes. His breath rattled in his chest, and like the air being slowly released from a balloon, the mangy body of his beast melted away. Knowing the heavy weight of his wolf would crush the idiot in his human form, Jeremy lurched to his feet.

"Don't freak out," Magnus croaked, shifting himself into a sitting position, his dark hair tangled around his ashen face, eyes so bleary and red, they looked painful. "I c-can explain," he mumbled, wiping the back of his wrist under his nose, reminding Jeremy of a petulant two-year-old.

"Explain when we get back to the Alley," Jeremy growled, reaching down to curl his claws around Magnus's thick arm and hauling him to his feet. Whatever explanations the guy had to make could wait until they got back, since he knew Jillian would be going out of her mind with worry.

He allowed his own wolf to slip away as they walked, retaking his human shape, and snuffled a soft laugh when he thought of what Jillian's reaction would be to two naked men walking out of the woods. He figured it'd be funny as hell, but couldn't embarrass her that way, especially not in front of others. So when they came across the clothes he'd shredded when he'd shifted, Jeremy reluctantly snatched them up. He was able to wrap the tattered remnants of Jillian's Pearl Jam shirt around his waist, ordering Magnus to hold what was left of his jeans over his groin.

It wasn't much, he thought with a crooked smile, knowing they looked like idiots, but at least they were more or less covered. He only hoped Jillian appreciated the gesture.

As they broke through the edge of the forest, Mason

opened his front door, a sardonic smile twisting his hard mouth while Jeremy dragged Magnus toward the Dillingers' cabin. "Well, well, well," his partner drawled, "what do we have here?"

Jillian shoved her way past Mason, then immediately came to a screeching halt on the porch the second she set eyes on him. "What happened to your clothes?" she demanded, pointing a finger at the ruined remains of her shirt.

A gruff laugh broke from his chest, and he shared a smile with Mase. "After everything that's happened, Jillian, you're worried about my clothes?"

"What clothes?" she hissed, waving her hand at his bare torso and legs. "You're practically naked! And you destroyed my favorite shirt!"

"You act as if you've never seen a naked man before." He chuckled, clucking his tongue.

She glared a blistering look at him that would have shriveled most men, but Jeremy prided himself on being made of sterner stuff than most. "I've never seen *you* naked, you oaf!"

The corner of his mouth tipped in another smile. "In that case, I guess I understand," he rumbled with a dose of wry, velvety arrogance. "But in my defense, I *did* try to conceal the more shocking parts."

"Stop teasing her and just cover yourself," Torrance called out as she came through the front door and tossed a towel in his direction.

"Yes, ma'am." Jeremy laughed, releasing Magnus so that he could tie the length of soft, white cotton around his hips. His chest and calves were still bare, but at least he no longer looked like some demented version of Tarzan in a loin cloth.

"So," Mason rasped with a hard smile, "what's his story?"

Crossing his arms over his bare chest, Jeremy looked at the man standing beside him, who was quickly covering himself with the towel Torrance had just tossed his way. "I wasn't gonna hurt anyone," the Lycan grumbled, sending him a belligerent glance from beneath his heavy brows. "I was just supposed to keep tabs on you and the witch."

Jeremy's eyes narrowed. "And just who were you supposed to keep tabs on us for? Drake?"

Magnus rolled his shoulder, then gave a reluctant nod, sending his hair back into his eyes. "I owe Cooper Sheffield some money, and he said I could clear the debt by keeping an eye on you for Drake."

"So you're Sheffield's little gopher boy," Jeremy murmured with disgust. "And do your duties go beyond spying?"

Magnus's bleary gaze skittered away. "I don't know what you mean," he muttered, chewing on the corner of his mouth.

Jeremy took a step closer. "I mean, the bullet," he drawled with pure menace.

Magnus' shaggy head shot up with a hard snap, as if he'd been clipped on the chin with a solid undercut. *"What bullet?"*

Holding the Lycan's wide-eyed stare, Jeremy pointed at his healing bullet wound. "The one that went clean through my shoulder this morning."

"It wasn't me," Magnus gasped, while fresh beads of sweat broke out across his forehead. "I swear to God. What do you think I have, a death wish? I messed with your parents' house and slashed your tires, but I swear, I haven't hurt anyone!"

"And what about Danna?" Mason asked. "Maybe Sheffield pressed your wife for a little favor. Does she have a gun?"

Magnus lifted his watery gaze up to Mason, blinking with stunned outrage. "You think I'd let that woman have a gun?" he shouted, his horrified expression making Mason chuckle under his breath.

"She could have gotten one without you knowing about it," his partner drawled.

"Dammit, it wasn't Danna!" Magnus argued. "I know she's crazy, but she's got her hands full with family stuff right now."

"Even if one of you didn't shoot me," Jeremy grunted, "the fact remains that you've been a real pain in the ass, so here's how it's gonna be. First, you're going to pay for my mother's front window."

The Lycan's shoulders fell, but he nodded his agreement. "I'll pay for it."

"*And* my tires."

At that, Magnus's complexion started to look a little green, but he mumbled, "Yeah, the tires, too. And I guess you'll want your parents' house cleaned, as well."

Jillian groaned, while Mason just shook his head. "What the hell is wrong with my parents' house?" Jeremy demanded.

Magnus flicked him another quick look from the corner of his eye. "I kind of egged it this morning, after you left."

"You egged my parents' house?" he shouted, aware of a vein throbbing angrily in his temple.

"Not by choice. I'm telling you, it was all on Sheffield's orders. I think he got the idea from that kid of his."

He started to take a step forward, his muscles flexing, hands fisted, when Mason casually said, "Jeremy."

"Yeah?"

"I know it's tempting, but you can't kill him."

He took a deep breath, and slowly forced himself to relax. Mason was right, of course, but that didn't mean the urge to knock some sense into Magnus wasn't any less of a temptation. "I wanna give you some advice," he said in a low, deadly rasp.

Magnus shuffled a step away. "What is it?"

"Grow some goddamn balls."

"That's what Danna's always telling me," the Lycan grumbled.

"Yeah? Then maybe you should listen to her."

"That's easy for you to say," Magnus huffed. "You don't have to live with her."

"Yeah, well, neither do you tonight," Mason rumbled. "Because you'll be spending it in lockup."

"That's what I figured." The Lycan sighed, then rubbed his chin. "Won't be so bad, I guess, though. At least that way Danna can't get to me."

"I know it's a pain in the ass, but can you take him up for me?" Jeremy asked, glancing at Mason.

His partner nodded, a slow grin curving his mouth. "No problem. Torrance and I will run him up to Shadow Peak and deliver him to Dylan."

"Thanks, man. I owe you."

"That's what you always say." Mason laughed.

Shifting his gaze to Jillian, he said, "Do you mind coming up to my cabin with me while I get cleaned up?"

She murmured her agreement, stepping into place beside him as they waved goodbye to Torrance and Mason, but didn't say anything more until he was opening his front door. "Do you think Magnus followed us to Pippa's house this morning?"

"Damn," he muttered, rubbing at the back of his neck. "I'll give her a call when we get back to town and warn her to be careful. If he didn't know about the shooting, I doubt he knows about Pippa. But it's better to be safe than sorry. She needs to be on guard."

"I think you're probably right." She sighed, tucking her hair behind her ears.

Jeremy moved to turn on a light, and the living room filled with a low, mellow glow. Nodding toward the black leather sofa that sat against the back wall, he said, "Just chill out for a bit, make yourself comfortable, and I'll go grab a quick shower."

Jillian sat with her bottom perched on the edge of the soft leather sofa in Jeremy's living room, her hands clasped between her knees, while her pulse drummed a heavy, thundering beat through her head. She breathed deeply, slowly releasing the air from her lungs, but it wasn't helping her to relax. Too much had happened since that morning, and her emotions were in a constant shift from one extreme to the other. Suddenly, it was all catching up with her, and she felt ready to crawl out of her skin.

Glancing toward the bathroom door that she could see just down the shadowed hallway, she knew what she wanted…what she needed. So far today, she'd known fear, anger and passion, and this evening she'd seen death. Now she wanted to feel alive.

She wanted Jeremy.

As if answering her unspoken call, he came out of the bathroom in nothing but a well-worn pair of faded jeans, droplets of water still glistening on his skin, muscles rippling in his arms as he ran a dark gray towel over his head.

Lust hit her so hard that her knees nearly gave out, and with a soft gasp of surprise, she realized that she'd rushed to her feet and was no longer sitting.

Wetting her bottom lip with a nervous flick of her tongue, she stared at the dark, golden beauty of his chest, the satiny skin stretched tight over hard, firm muscles, the wound in his shoulder little more than a raw, pinkish mark that would fade within a week. On his ribs, paler scars from his last run-in with the rogue wolves shone faintly against the deeper tan of his skin, the bite on the side of his throat all but healed. He was so perfectly, ruggedly beautiful that it took her breath away, and she blinked against the hot wash of tears she felt at the backs of her eyes, even though she knew she wasn't crying. It was just excess emotion, everything welling up inside of her, growing harder and harder to contain.

"Jesus. Do you know how long I've waited to see you look at me like that?" he asked with a slow, sexy smile, watching her as he propped his bare shoulder against the wall, the flexing of muscles across the broad expanse of his chest and rippling abdomen making her light-headed.

She drew in an unsteady breath, her voice a husky whisper of sound as she said, "Do you know how long I've waited to see you like *this?*"

The corner of his mouth twitched, eyes bright with sensual awareness. "Like what?" he asked softly, staring at her with a possessive intensity that made her feel completely… wanted. Needed.

She wanted that. Wanted him to need her, crave her… *hunger for her.*

She wanted to push him to the edge, push him until he forgot to be careful, until he lost his control. She wanted his guttural growl in her ear, his body wild for her.

Jillian found herself standing in front of him, with no recollection of stepping around the low coffee table and moving across the room. Reaching out, she pressed her hand to the smooth skin of his chest, right over the pounding of his heart. "You're so beautiful, Jeremy."

"You're the beautiful one, sweetheart."

"I can't compare to you," she said dreamily, her voice thick. Oh, yes, she knew what she wanted; and she was going to take it. She might be too cowardly to let him make love to her, but that didn't mean that she couldn't sate her own hungers. That she couldn't touch and taste and feast, drawing him into her, taking as much of him as she could. Savoring him.

Even *loving* him.

Her fingertips grazed his chest with the teasing lightness of a feather, the firm muscles beneath his dark skin so hard and warm, vibrating with a fine tremor. His breath came slightly faster, almost panting, the press of his stare hot against her face…warming her like a physical source of heat, though she kept her gaze focused on the path of her fingers. If she looked up, she'd lose her nerve, and she wanted this so badly. Had to have it, or she was going to go out of her mind, all this raging, tumultuous need breaking her down, leaving her wrecked and damaged.

She lost herself to the exploration of his body, smiling inside when his breath hitched as she grazed his right nipple. Pulling her lower lip through her teeth, she pressed both hands over his chest, the small tips of his nipples hard against her palms, then trailed them lower, across his ribs. Her thumbs skimmed over the silky, honey-colored hair that arrowed down the center of his abdomen, whorling around his navel, before it disappeared beneath the faded denim of his jeans, the top button left undone, while a thick ridge distended the fly.

"Jesus," he moaned under his breath, his lips pulling back over his teeth. "What are you doing, Jillian?"

"Touching you," she told him, proud that her voice didn't shake apart like the trembling feeling inside of her. "You're so warm, Jeremy. So hot. Hard."

A rough laugh jerked from his throat. "Yeah, you've got no idea."

Her mouth twitched into a smile, and she lowered her gaze to the stunning bulge at the front of his jeans. "You have a problem inside your Levi's, Mr. Burns."

"If you're wondering what to do about it, I have some *really* good ideas," he volunteered with a low, rumbling chuckle, casting a wry look down at his groin.

She shook her head as silent laughter bubbled up from the warm, churning glow of excitement in her belly. "I'll just bet you do," she murmured, her shoulders shaking. "It's just that…well, it's a little on the *extreme* side," she pointed out, wondering just who the playful tease was that had commandeered her body.

"Don't know about that, but I've never had any complaints before. I think it may even be a bit bigger than usual," he added with a dark laugh, "but then I've never wanted anyone this badly before, either."

"I bet you say that to all the girls," she said softly, shaking her head.

He tipped her chin up with the edge of his fist in time for her to see the deep look of tenderness that melted into his eyes, and her knees shook. God, she was so easy when it came to this man.

"I've never said anything even close to that to a woman," he admitted gently, curving his palm along her jaw, so that he could rub his thumb against the corner of her mouth. "And I wouldn't lie about it, either. You…affect me, Jillian. In ways that I can't even explain. You always have."

He touched his thumb to her lower lip, then leaned forward and the heat of his breath, of his mouth, touched hers, shaking her apart inside. Everything roiled and tumbled together, a chaos of emotion and craving and raw, overwhelming need.

Her trembling, shivering hands struggled with the stubborn buttons on his jeans, while his hands cupped her face, his mouth claiming instant, carnal possession of her own with a blistering kiss that made her toes curl. With a throaty groan, Jillian broke away from the kiss to shove his jeans over his lean hips, her groan growing deeper as she watched him take himself in hand, gripping himself so tightly that the veins on the back of his hand thickened beneath his skin, like the swollen, distended veins pulsing beneath the velvety skin of his cock.

She licked her lips as she dropped to her knees, a purring sound of pleasure vibrating in her throat as she caught the richer, heavier source of his scent, salty and sweet and warm. Leaning forward, she pressed her lips against the violent heat of his skin, moaning at the decadent taste of him.

"Oh, god," he growled, breathless, trembling. "This is gonna kill me."

He placed both hands on either side of her head and pushed past her lips, sinking into the damp silk of her mouth, and she stroked him with her tongue. He pushed deeper, and she made a quick sound of panic. "Don't be afraid," he gasped, baring his teeth. "I won't push too far. Just…harder, Jillian. Like that, baby. You won't hurt me."

His legs tremored, muscles rigid and hard, as her mouth worked over him, her tongue stroking his skin as if she couldn't get enough of him. And she couldn't. It was too good, too hot…the perfection of him in her mouth and the possessive way he watched her pleasuring him made her feel too much. Everything about him intoxicated her. The sinewy tension in his neck and shoulders. The way his head lowered as he watched her, his fingers clenched in her hair. She loved it. Loved the power of him throbbing against her tongue. Loved the trust implicit in such a blistering, provocative act of intimacy. Loved his salty-sweet taste, the musky, masculine smells of his skin and sweat and the dominant strength in his long, hard body that he tried so hard to control. His eyes drifted shut for a moment, and then he lifted the dark smudges of his lashes, revealing a gaze that was bright with fever, glittering with lust and hunger and tender, breathtaking emotion.

"Can't hold it," he growled, and his head fell back, spine arching as the dark wave of energy roared through him. His muscles jerked as he came, a rough shout breaking from his throat, back arched, his rich flavor too sexy to resist.

And then his body was moving, his hands pulling at her until he lay on the hallway floor and she was spread out over him like a blanket. Jillian struggled to get her bearings, but his hands were everywhere, stroking her backside, dipping under her sweater to stroke the shivering skin of her stomach, the backs of her thighs, his urgency tugging at her heart.

"I'm going to make love to you all night long," he growled, and then his hands reached between them, attacking the button at the top of her jeans, and the reality of how close she was to giving in suddenly crashed through the sensual haze clouding her mind, shocking her into instant awareness. In that moment, she couldn't get past the knowledge that he could make her whole world come apart, destroying her, without even meaning to.

Her muscles tensed, and Jillian grabbed at his wrists. "Stop," she whispered.

His hands instantly lifted away, eyes shadowed beneath the heavy veil of his lashes. "What's wrong?"

She swallowed the thick feeling in her throat, and struggled to get the words out. "I…can't."

He went completely still beneath her, not even breathing, just watching her, waiting for her to explain. "What the hell's going on, Jillian?"

"I—I didn't mean for things to go so far," she said shakily, slipping off of him. "I just wanted to make you feel good."

The golden line of his eyebrows pulled together in a deadly scowl, his mouth hard, savage. "You went down on me because you felt it was owed, like some kind of goddamn payment?"

"No!"

A gritty, sarcastic sound rumbled in his throat. "Then explain it, honey, because I'm having a helluva time figuring you out."

Jillian closed her eyes, wanting to block out his presence, but she couldn't. The loss of sight only made her other senses that much more attuned to him. He vibrated with a sexual frequency that pulled on her, made her want to throw caution to the wind and dive on him, ravenous for each hard, mind-shattering, delicious detail.

She scooted away until her back hit the wall, opening her eyes as she wrapped her arms around her knees. With greedy fascination, she watched the muscles in his abdomen ripple and flex as he sat up, his skin burnished a deep, golden brown in the low light spilling from the living room. Clearing her throat, she said, "I—I just need more time, Jeremy."

He thrust both hands back through his hair, so hard that she winced. "God, Jillian, every time I think we're moving forward, it's like slamming into a brick wall. Just one more obstacle shoved in my path. What do I have to do?" he demanded in a gritty rasp, his expression ravaged, his eyes wild. "Just tell me and I'll do it, but don't keep shutting me out."

She blinked rapidly, rolling her lips together. "I'm sorry. I—I just can't do this."

"Because of Eric? Christ, Jillian, he's wrong for you and you know it!"

"It has nothing to with Eric," she insisted in a low voice, wishing she could feel hollow inside. She wanted to welcome that comforting nothingness that had been her companion for so many years, but it seemed impossible to go back and find that steady, lifeless state of existence. Jeremy had destroyed the calm, like a violent storm sweeping across a dead sea, stirring chaos in his wake. Now all she could do was try to survive and stay intact, without being crushed beneath the force of the waves. If she stopped struggling, she would be pulled under the surface, taken down deeper…and deeper.

"Is it me, then?" She flinched, the hurt underlining his rough words cutting her to the quick. "Is that it? Can't have damaged goods touching the pack's little angel?"

"No!" she gasped, hating that he could even think that of her. "I admire you more than any other man I know, Jeremy, no matter what his bloodline. But I *can't* take what you're offering. It's too dangerous for me."

"What the hell does that mean?" he demanded, his voice raw, his eyes glittering and bright. "Dammit, Jillian, I'm trying so hard to understand but you won't give me anything." He was silent for a moment, the only sound that of their breathing and the howling wind rushing against the roof of the cabin, and then he quietly said, "I *need* you, Jillian."

She understood what he was trying to say—but it wasn't enough. "Lust is not love, Jeremy."

She watched the muscles in his face tighten, his golden brows pulling close as he worked over her words. "And if I told you that it was more than lust?" he rasped, the hoarse words thick with emotion.

"It wouldn't matter," she whispered, shaking her head, "because it's not."

"So now you're the expert on how I feel?" he shot back, the brackets around his mouth deep with frustration.

"No…it's just that… God, I'm sorry." Pulling a tissue out of her pocket, Jillian shoved it under her nose. "I wish…I wish things could be different, but they can't."

"Things can always be different," he grunted, staring at her with such intensity, she felt as if he were trying to see right in to her. "If we think they're important enough to fight for, we find a way to *make* them different."

A choked sob escaped her throat, tears streaming from her eyes, leaving salty trails over her skin. "I wish that was true, but it isn't. Not this time."

He didn't respond…didn't argue…didn't even look at her.

With his expression cast in stone, he just pulled himself to his feet, buttoned his jeans and headed into his bedroom.

When he came back, he was dressed and Jillian was waiting for him in the living room. "Come on, I'll drive you home," he rumbled. She nodded, unable to meet his eyes, and followed him outside.

Chapter 13

Jillian spent the rest of the night and following day with her emotions careening between frustration and the churning, aching feeling in her gut that she'd screwed something up. Just let it slip right through her fingers.

She knew she'd made the wrong choice. And why? The answer to that was easy—the only easy answer she had.

She was a coward. Too chicken to take a chance, to make the leap.

It reminded her pitifully of a nature show she'd watched on TV the week before, when she'd been trying to fall asleep. It had been all about these arctic birds that were born on the side of a craggy, towering cliff. When old enough, they had to jump off the ledge and soar to the water below, without ever having learned how to fly. If they wanted to survive, they had to take that blind leap of faith and trust their instincts to get them safely to the sea.

It was beyond depressing to know that if she'd been one of those birds, she'd have died of starvation up on that rocky cliff, never taking that breathtaking leap toward her destiny.

And that's what life felt like without Jeremy. She was starving. Starving for the emotional connection, the physical contact, that exhilarating rush and piercing sensation of being *alive* that she felt whenever she was with him. Colors were more intense, smells sweeter, food richer.

He simply made her life better. Made it whole. Complete. Made *her* complete. And like a cowardly fool, she'd pushed him away. Again. She hated how pathetic that made her, but she didn't know how to fix it.

She couldn't change what she was.

So while the storm that had been building for days finally unleashed its wrath upon the mountains, she moved around her house in a daze, putting in a load of laundry, vacuuming, dusting, anything to keep her body busy, desperately trying to keep her mind blank. But it wasn't working. She kept replaying the scene from the night before over and over, wishing she'd handled it differently. Wishing she were brave enough to reach out for what she wanted and hold on to it. Fight for it. Gnash her teeth and challenge anyone who tried to take it away from her.

But the thing she wanted was Jeremy's heart, and how could she *make* someone love her? She didn't have to be a genius to know the answer to that timeless question: she couldn't. Love was either there or it wasn't. She couldn't "make" it do anything.

When her house was so clean it would have made Martha Stewart proud, she popped a bowl of popcorn and curled up in front of an old Cary Grant movie, needing something to keep her mind off the mess she'd made of her life. She'd just started to doze off, when she heard a knock on her front door, and her heart leapt into her throat. Was it Jeremy? She could feel her pulse hammering, her cheeks going hot as she wondered what to do.

Oh, god. You coward! How long are you going to keep running?

Taking a deep breath, Jillian wrenched open the door and came face-to-face with Eric. "Oh," she breathed out on a sharp stab of relief that felt suspiciously like disappointment.

His dark gray eyes glittered with humor, and the corner of his mouth twisted into a knowing smile. "Let me guess. You were expecting someone else?"

"No." She sighed, moving aside to let him in. "I'm not expecting anyone."

He took a moment to glance at the movie, then the half-eaten bowl of popcorn sitting beside a box of tissues, and turned back to give her a slow once-over. "Not that the bunny slippers aren't adorable, honey, but you look wrung out."

"Thanks. It's been an eventful few days," she muttered, flopping down on the sofa. "At this rate, I can only imagine what kind of shape I'll be in by next week."

"That bad, huh?" he asked, taking a seat in the matching leather chair.

Jillian arched a brow in his direction. "If you're going to try and tell me you haven't heard all about it, I should warn you now that I won't believe you."

A low, husky chuckle rumbled deep in his chest. "Yeah, I heard. The whole town is gossiping about you helping a blood-covered Burns to your house yesterday morning, then traipsing off to the Alley with him in the afternoon. Just what the hell were you two up to?" Her gaze slid away from his, and his laughter deepened. "I'd say from the look on your face that you were definitely up to something."

Jillian lifted her chin, trying to figure out how much to tell him. She trusted Eric…but she knew what Jeremy would want her to do. Giving him a tense, half-hearted grin, she finally said, "It seems that Jeremy is always up to something. Life is certainly never boring around him."

Eric watched her with a wondering stare, gray eyes dark beneath the heavy fringe of his lashes, and it was as if he knew she was keeping something from him. For a moment, it looked as if he'd press her, but then he leaned forward and braced his elbows on his knees. "Look, there's a reason I came by."

Dread settled like a weight in her belly. "What's wrong?"

"I'm worried about you," he told her, his expression suddenly a concerned mixture of anger and frustration. "I want you to stay sharp and keep your eyes open, Jillian. Something bad is coming, and I have a feeling my father is going to be right at the center of it. I want you stay on guard around him, always."

"I will," she whispered, her thoughts racing, "but what about you? And Elise?"

His mouth twisted. "Don't worry about us. We'll be okay."

"I want your promise that you'll be careful, too," she told him. "And I'm here if you need anything, Eric. Whatever happens, I know this isn't going to be easy on your family. I want to be able to help."

He shook his head, while another soft, wry laugh rumbled deep in his chest. "You're something else, you know that, Murphy? I come to warn you that your life could be in danger from my own father, and all you're worried about is how you can help my family."

"We're friends, Eric. I care about what happens to you and Elise."

"I'm worried about her," he admitted, his tone becoming grim. "You know I can't stand him, but I put up with his bullshit to protect her. The more I argue with him, the harder it is for her. She puts on this act of being so tough, but on the inside she's still hurting from what happened to her."

"I know she is," Jillian whispered. "I can feel the rage inside of her. And the fear."

Eric's jaw worked, his lip curling with anger. "And my father does everything he can to grind her into the ground. He's done his best to systematically strip her pride. The fact that Elise refuses to stand up to him only incites his cruelty. When she was raped, he told her it was her fault for being weaker than they were. I nearly killed him, but that only upset her more because she was worried about what would happen to me. Now I just keep my distance. She may be our little sister, but Elise is militant about protecting me and Eli, and he uses that to manipulate her."

"He's good at manipulating others," she pointed out, thinking of his followers. "You've seen what's happening, Eric. The fear and animosity is spreading through the pack. It's like a sickness. And if it keeps growing, not even the Runners will be enough to stop him," she added softly, staring at her lap as she thought of Jeremy. "That's what scares me the most."

Reaching out, Eric lifted her chin with the edge of his fist. "You love him, don't you?"

She blinked, her mouth twisting with a wry smile. "It doesn't matter if I do or I don't. Jeremy and I don't have a future."

He ran his thumb over her chin in a gentle caress, then pulled his hand away. "You sure about that?"

"Pretty sure," she murmured. "I think I've blown any chance by being a coward."

"Look, god knows I'm no expert on relationships," he drawled, lifting his dark brows at the vastness of that understatement. "But I know enough to believe that when you find love, it's worth taking a risk or two. Don't run away from it because you're afraid, Jillian."

Her smile fell, and she pulled her knees up to her chest, wrapping her arms around them. "I wish it were that simple, Eric."

"Well, if you need a friend to talk it over with, you know where to find me." He rolled to his feet with an easy grace for a guy his height, and reached for his jacket.

Pressing a kiss to her cheek, he stepped out the door and headed toward his truck. Jillian waved to him as he drove away, then shut the door and made her way to the kitchen to put on the kettle for some tea. She'd just turned on the stove, when her phone rang.

"We need to talk, Jillian," her mother said in a low, suffering tone, before she'd even had the chance to say hello.

"About what?" she asked, knowing very well what her mother was calling to gripe about.

There was a stifled pause, and then her mother said, "I heard that you were at the Alley last night. What were you thinking?"

"I know this may come as a surprise to you—" she sighed "—but I know what I'm doing."

"Is it worth it, Jillian?"

She sniffed and reached for a crumpled tissue in the pocket of her robe. "A broken heart won't kill me, Mother."

"I was lucky, Jillian. I found your father just before I dried up inside, but who will you find? My mate was still out there, waiting for me to find him. But Jeremy *is* your mate, no matter how unfair—"

"It's not unfair," she argued.

Her mother made a brittle sound of frustration, then took a deep breath. "What I'm trying to say is that I was able to recover in a way that you may not be able to."

"And if I never take the risk?" she asked in a soft voice, staring down at her pink bunny slippers that Sayre had given her as a joke the year before on her birthday. "What do I do then?"

"You and Eric are good together," her mother murmured.

A sharp crack of laughter burst from her chest, taking her by surprise. "Oh, god. And is that fair to Eric? Is it fair to me? I don't love him, Mother. And he doesn't love me. His mate is out there somewhere, waiting to be found. Would that be fair to either one of us?"

"I don't care if it's fair!" her mother snapped, obviously losing her tenuous hold on her temper. She was angry, but Jillian knew her anger was self-directed for the mistakes she had made…and couldn't let go of. Despite the happiness in her life, Constance Murphy had never figured out how to forgive herself for falling in love with the wrong man. Her mother's voice cracked, and she said, "I don't want to see you hurt, Jillian."

"I've been hurting for the last ten years," she said tiredly, surprised to hear herself admit it. "So enough already. Maybe it's time I just get on with my life and stop hiding from what I want."

"He'll never be there for you," her mother rasped. "He'll break you and then he'll leave. If he doesn't get you killed first."

Jillian gripped the phone so tightly, she was amazed the plastic didn't crack apart. "You should have more faith, Mother."

Whoa…and isn't that like the pot calling the kettle black?

"Jillian, what happened with your biological father nearly killed me, and he wasn't even my lifemate. Think how much more painful it will be for you with Jeremy. Do you really want to put yourself through that?"

Pushing her hair up from her forehead, she muttered, "I'm not a masochist."

"Be sarcastic if you want, but before you decide what to do, ask yourself this, Jillian. Do you trust him enough to give him the keys to your soul, to hand him that kind of power? Because he'll see it all. Do you trust him enough for that—do you trust yourself to be able to handle it when he breaks your heart?"

"I don't know," she whispered, shoving the tissue under her nose again, wondering how long it was going to take before the blasted tears dried up. "But I know that he doesn't want to hurt me," she heard herself say, the words welling up from some unknown source buried deep inside of her, taking her by surprise again.

"You're going to destroy your life, Jillian."

"But it's my decision to make, Mother. Not yours," she whispered, hanging up the phone. It rang again almost immediately, and she snatched up the receiver, snapping, "What?" into the plastic mouthpiece.

"Jillian," a deep, craggy voice rumbled from the other end of the connection, "this is Graham. I realize it's late, but I wanted to warn you that the League is aware of your whereabouts last night."

Clutching the phone to her ear, she was conscious of her heartbeat steadily gaining speed, like a train barreling its way down a track. And yet, she didn't sound afraid as she said, "Is that so?"

Silence greeted her firm tone, and then Graham cleared his throat, sounding a bit uncertain, and she almost smiled at the thought that she'd rattled the powerful Lead Elder. "Yes, well…er, what do you have to say for yourself, young lady?"

Jillian rolled her eyes, while an airy sensation seemed to expand in her chest, bringing the strangest feeling of freedom. "With all due respect, Graham, I'm a grown woman. One who doesn't answer to you or to the League. Which begs the question of why exactly we're having this discussion."

"I'd be careful of the stand you take on this issue, Jillian," the Elder grunted. "It's been called to our attention that your actions of the past few days have been…questionable, at best."

"I've done nothing I'm ashamed of," she stated with firm conviction.

"Jillian, you have a great deal to lose if you follow this course."

She narrowed her eyes on her kitchen window, where her reflection stared back at her in shocked astonishment. "Are you threatening my position, Graham?"

"You know we're impatient to see you mated and married," he replied carefully.

"You've made your position clear, yes."

Graham's sigh traveled heavily over the line. "You've left us no choice, Jillian, but to invoke the Spring Rites. Come the Spring Equinox, a Mate Hunt will be called, and you *will* be awarded to the one who hunts you down."

Fury poured through her veins at his words, moving with the swiftness of a ravaging storm, raging and violent. Suddenly, things became so clear, as if Jillian had finally put on a pair of glasses that set the world into a clearer, sharper focus—one that propelled her into a blinding awareness.

All her life, she'd been the outsider. The one who was Lycan in blood, and yet had no wolf. She was Silvercrest, and yet, she was different, set apart by her power as much as Jeremy was by his bloodline. But where he had the strength to stand up to the pack, she'd been a coward. She'd let fear and feelings of inadequacy color her perception, until she only now realized she'd been trying to earn the approval of the League for all these years to prove that she was worthy.

But she didn't need their approval, dammit.

She was so tired of it. Tired of everything. Tired of fighting her feelings for the powerful Runner. Tired of her parents and the pack trying to control her life. Tired of feeling as if she was lacking, of always putting everyone else's needs before her own. Dammit, wanting fulfillment in her life didn't make her a bad person…or a bad Spirit Walker. It meant she was alive! That she had a heart and a mind, that she had a soul hungry for connection.

She *was* worthy, whether they approved of her or not, and if she had half a brain, she was going to do everything she could to set things right. And she needed to start by standing up for herself and telling the arrogant browbeaters what they could do with their archaic threats.

"Well," Graham snapped impatiently. "What do you have to say?"

Taking a deep breath, Jillian smiled at her reflection in the window. "I say you can all take your ridiculous threat and shove it, Graham. And you can quote that to the rest of the League when you tell them that it will be a cold day in hell before I ever again allow them to tell me what to do with my life!"

She hung up then, surprised to feel her legs were steady beneath her. She'd expected her knees to be knocking, she was so full of nerves and excitement, but somehow, she felt amazingly at peace, as if a cool, calm cloud had wrapped around her, sheltering her from the storm.

She'd never, in all her life, been brave enough to take a chance and go after what she wanted. She'd always played it safe. She'd always done what was expected of her.

But now, finally…after all this time, all of that was about to change.

Early morning mist curled lazily around her ankles as Jillian knocked upon the side door of the Burns's house,

while soft, featherlight raindrops gathered on her lashes like
shimmering jewels.

She listened to the metallic sound of a lock being turned,
then the door pulled open, and her breath froze in her lungs.

Ohmygod. He was so impossibly gorgeous, and she
wanted him so very badly—wanted him with every fiber of
her being. If she'd had a white flag, she'd have waved it in
surrender.

Jeremy's hazel eyes darkened when he saw her, the
grooves around his mouth tight with strain. "What's wrong,
Jillian? Is everything okay?"

She opened her mouth, but her throat wouldn't move. She
barely managed a nod, the grin playing at the corners of her
mouth feeling shaky and off balance. God, she was so pathetic. Why couldn't she just grab him and demand he put an
end to it?

Reaching out, Jeremy grabbed her upper arm and pulled
her into the small entryway as he kicked the door shut with
his foot. "Jillian, say something," he commanded, the corners
of his eyes crinkling in that way that she found so sexy, so
intense. "What are you doing here?"

"I have to talk to you." She licked her bottom lip, flinch-
ing from the chill of her skin, so at odds with the hot burn of
anticipation in her cheeks. "I'm sorry for what happened
before, at the cabin. I'm just… I mean I… The only thing I
know is that I need to be close to you, Jeremy. I'm so tired
of being alone. I don't want to keep fighting it—I don't want
to be afraid anymore."

His eyes narrowed, the hazel all but lost in the glittering
darkness of desire…in the savage burn of a decade spent in
hunger. "Are you sure?" he demanded, the set of his mouth
grim, determined. "I can't do this if you're going to turn
away from me again. You have to be sure, Jillian."

"I am," she promised, her voice breathless. "I'm so nervous, Jeremy, but I won't run. Not again."

"It's about damn time," he groaned in a ragged tumble of words, sounding like a man who'd been tortured for far too long, and then his strong, powerful arms wrapped around her back, pulling her into the shocking heat and hardness of his body with an urgency that made her cry out. "Shhh," he crooned, pressing soft, tender, reverent kisses to her lips, her cheekbones, her tear-damp lashes. "I swear, I won't hurt you, Jillian."

The scratchy stubble of his morning beard teased her skin with every word that he spoke, and she lifted her arms, winding them around his strong neck as she tried to climb her way up his body.

"Shh…" he told her again, when a low, husky moan broke from her throat.

She blinked up at him. "Wh—"

"I don't know if they've bugged the house," he whispered, nipping her chin, the fragile line of her jaw. "And I don't want anyone but me hearing those sexy little sounds you make."

She blushed, and he buried his nose in the curve of her throat, breathing deeply. "God, you smell good."

Jillian shook with silent laughter, her eyes hot with tears that surged up from that warm, liquid glow pouring through her, until their surroundings were nothing but a hazy, buzzing nothing. The only point of reference in the world was Jeremy. Her anchor. The thing she kept swimming toward, like a beacon, a light. The source of everything that could make her feel alive. "I t-took a shower before I came over," she breathed out, the words almost soundless. "It's my soap. My shampoo."

"Uh-uh," he growled huskily, taking a playful, provocative lick of the sensitive skin beneath her ear. "It's you. Your skin, your hair, that creamy piece of heaven melting between your thighs. It gets me so hard, I feel dizzy from lack of blood to my brain."

She smiled, trembling as a breathtaking burst of happiness welled up inside of her, like the rising of a phoenix from his ashes, making her feel reborn. Jeremy pressed his mouth to hers, kissing his way into her, his tongue wicked and hungry and bold, and then he pulled away with a low, fractured groan. "I don't want to leave," he panted, his breathing ragged, "but if I don't go now, Dylan is going to show up looking for me and I don't want you to be embarrassed."

Shaking her head with confusion, she struggled to make sense out of what he was saying. "You're leaving? Now? But I thought we could... I mean, I thought we were..."

"I'm meeting Dylan in town and we're heading to the Alley for a meeting with Mason," he whispered in her ear. "I think Mase intends to pressure Dylan about getting more involved with the investigation."

"I just... I can't believe you have to go."

"I know, but...maybe it's for the best." His voice was rough with lust, and yet soft with tenderness, his lips even softer against her ear. "I'm not taking you like this our first time, up against a goddamn door. I need hours with you, Jillian. Days. Go back home and wait for me. I promise I'll be there as soon as I can."

"Okay," she said shakily, wondering if she looked as disappointed as she felt. She lowered her gaze and finally noticed that he was wearing a jacket, his long legs already wrapped up in jeans, scarred hiking boots on his feet. If her head hadn't been in the clouds when he'd opened the door, she would have realized he'd been getting ready to head out.

His fingers speared into her hair, cradling her skull, and she lifted her gaze to his, trapped by the searing intensity of his stare. "I won't let you change your mind," he warned her in a deep, sexy rasp. "Not this time, Jillian. I'm not letting you run away from me anymore."

"In case it escaped your notice," she whispered back, "I ran to *you* this morning."

His dark eyes practically glittered with victory as he stared down at her, the primitive look as possessive as it was male. "And don't think I'll ever forget it." He pressed another tender kiss to her mouth, then lifted his head, a pained expression settling over the rugged beauty of his face. "God, they owe me for this big-time."

"Yeah, and *you* owe *me*," she teased.

Jeremy went completely still, his breath suspended, and the look he gave her all but buckled her knees. His eyes... *burned.* There was no other word for it. "You better be ready to back those words up when I get back."

She didn't even bother playing coy. "Don't worry. I will be."

He moved in to kiss her again, when a low knock rattled against the door, making her jump. "Do you think that's Dylan?" she asked, blushing as she slipped to the side so that he could open it.

"Probably," he said with a grin, winking at her as he reached for the door.

Standing so that she would be behind the door when it opened, Jillian quickly combed her fingers through her hair, trying to restore it to some kind of order. A wry smile began to curl across her mouth as she thought of what Dylan's expression would be when he found her at Jeremy's house so early in the morning, until she heard someone say, "Are you happy to see me?" The words were spoken in a soft, sultry voice, and Jillian froze, blinking in surprise.

"Happy to see you?" Jeremy repeated, sounding confused.

"I know you said to call first," the woman murmured, "but

I couldn't wait to be alone with you again. What we had the other day was too good not to repeat." Her voice lowered, and she said, "Don't worry. I made sure no one saw me, since I know you don't want Jillian to know about us."

A shiver slipped down her spine. She *knew* that voice.

"Elise," Jeremy growled, "what the *hell* are you talking about?"

"Wh-what do you mean?" she stammered. "Did I come at a bad time?"

"Looks like it," Jillian said tightly, stepping out from around the door.

Elise's eyes went wide the second she saw her. "Oh god, Jillian, I'm so sorry," she mumbled, her face so pale, she looked like a ghost. "I didn't know you were there."

Elise pressed her hand to her mouth, turned around and ran away from the house, the morning fog swallowing her form by the time she'd reached the end of the drive.

Jillian stared after her, feeling dead inside. Elise was gone, and now she was left to deal with the man who'd destroyed her for the last time. Her hand pressed over her heart, as if she could will it to keep beating, despite breaking apart.

"Jillian, it's not what you think," Jeremy said in a low, urgent voice, touching her shoulder.

"Oh, that's a good one." She laughed, hating the thickness of tears she could hear in her throat. She didn't want to cry in front of him. Didn't want to let him see how damaged she was. But she was caving in on herself.

His eyes narrowed, skin tight over his cheekbones. "Just what the hell do you think is going on here?"

"I don't have to think anything, Jeremy." She lifted her arm and pointed at the spot where Elise had disappeared into the fog, and the heavens opened, the rain coming down in a hard, vicious downpour. "I saw it with my own eyes. Heard it with my own ears!"

"Did you now? And what exactly did you see? A woman I barely know standing at my door, putting on one of the worst acts I've ever seen? Jesus," he growled, ripping his hands through his hair. "Tell me you weren't buying that load of bullshit."

"It didn't sound like bullshit," she shot back. "It sounded as if she came here expecting some action."

"Yeah, that's me," he rasped bitterly, something dark and ugly and painful flashing through his eyes that made her cringe. "Just the neighborhood stud, at your service. If you have an itch, I'm the faithless half-breed who'll be more than ready to scratch it."

"I think I should go now," she said, the words so soft, they could barely be heard over the slashing rain hammering away at the side of the house.

"Don't do this, Jillian." His voice was low, rough, stripped down to raw emotion.

"I'm not doing anything, Jeremy. I'm just leaving."

His jaw locked, hands fisting at his sides. "Ten years ago, I asked you to believe in me, to have faith, not to turn your back on me, and you did it anyway. I won't ask you again, Jillian. If you walk out that door, I'm leaving. And this time, I'm *never* coming back. Are you sure that's what you want?"

She could feel the salty sting of tears spilling down her face, but couldn't stop them. His urgency tugged at her heart, but she didn't trust herself. And obviously, she didn't trust *him*. "There isn't any other way."

"When you realize how wrong you are, it'll be too late." His words rang with solid, uncompromising finality, making her flinch. "When you learn the truth and want to come after me, don't."

She nodded and stepped out the door, the first drop of rain

settling on her cheek like a tear. "Do me a favor and be careful," he said to her back, his tone brittle and cold. "Until this night-mare is over, Shadow Peak isn't safe, not even for you."

"I can take care of myself."

A bitter sound jerked past his lips, angry and hard. "Yeah, you do that."

Jillian walked down his drive, down the street, making her way home cocooned within a thick, impenetrable bubble, not even feeling the rain that soaked through her clothes, drenching her. She walked up her front steps, opened her front door and locked it behind her.

Then she slipped to the floor in a wet, sodden puddle, and buried her face in her hands.

Chapter 14

Dragging her wilted body through her front door the following afternoon, Jillian dropped her jacket on the living-room floor, not even bothering with the peg on the wall. Not wanting any interruptions, she managed to make it to the kitchen so that she could take her phone off the hook, then powered off her cell and tossed it onto the table along with her keys. After that, she kicked off her rain-soaked shoes, stumbled into the living room and collapsed on her sofa. Staring at the blank screen of her television set, she shook her head in amazement at the day she'd already had.

She'd awakened that morning feeling like death warmed over. After standing beneath the burning spray of the shower until the hot water ran cold, she'd wrapped herself up in her robe and cuddled up on her sofa, staring at nothing…while her mind tortured her by running through yesterday's wrenching scene, over and over and over.

She didn't know how long she might have stayed like that, if Sayre hadn't come knocking at her door. She hadn't seen her little sister since the night of the challenge fight, and it seemed like a lifetime ago. So much had happened since then, so much had changed, and yet, so much had remained exactly the same.

Jillian had no doubt that rumors were flying around town about what had happened the morning before, so she guessed she should have been expecting her sister to stop by and check up on her. Like a merciful angel, Sayre had come bearing fresh baked cinnamon rolls, steaming cups of coffee and a friendly face to take her mind off Jeremy.

Of course, once they'd finished their breakfast, she'd learned that Jeremy was *exactly* what Sayre had wanted to talk about. Amazingly, her sister refused to believe that Jeremy Burns wasn't madly in love with her, and argued her case with the same boundless energy that she did everything in life.

By the time Sayre had left, Jillian had felt more confused than ever. She'd just gotten dressed and cuddled up on her sofa again when another round of knocking, this one pounding and hard, had rattled her door. Praying it wasn't her mother, she'd shuffled to the door, blinking in stunned surprise at the sight of Danna Gibson standing on her front porch.

"If you're here to try and kill me again—" she'd sighed "—can it wait 'til tomorrow?"

"I know you have every right to hate me, and I don't blame you," Danna had said in a low, ragged voice, and Jillian had suddenly realized how devastated the other woman looked. "But...I need your help."

Jillian had blinked, unable to believe what she was hearing. "You need *my* help?"

Danna had given a jerky nod, her expression strained while dark circles gave her eyes a hollow appearance. "It's about Carly, my little sister. She's been missing for over a week. We didn't tell anyone, because we...we didn't know what she was doing and we figured she was with a friend of hers named Melissa who went missing at the same time." She'd rolled her shoulder in an angry gesture, and pushed both hands back through the tangled mess of her hair. "Melissa brought Carly home last night, and she's hurt. I can't get the bleeding to stop and I don't know what to do. I know I've been a bitch to you and that you must hate me, but I need you to come and help her. *Please.*"

"Where's she bleeding?" she'd asked, already grabbing her sneakers from beside the front door and pulling them on her bare feet.

"I think she's been raped," Danna had said, her voice breaking as a dry, choking sob broke from her throat. "She says she was with some human guys down in Covington, but I think it was... I think she was with some of the rogues everyone's whispering about. The guy she was dating, he got in tight with Simmons before Simmons turned. I warned her to stay away from him, but you know how well teenagers listen," she'd groaned, while Jillian grabbed her jacket and pulled it on.

"Did you drive here?" she'd asked, grabbing her house keys. Danna had nodded, and Jillian had locked her front door behind her, the brutal chill of the morning freezing her to the bone as they'd run to Danna's car parked on the side of the road. They'd made it to Danna's parents' house within minutes, and the rest of the morning had gone by in a gruesome, nightmarish blur. Carly had been in bad shape, but Jillian had finally been able to stop the bleeding and get the teenager's condition stabilized. She'd tried, while healing her, to get an idea of who was behind the crime, but the details had been fragmented in Carly's mind, nothing but a chaotic jumble of brutal, horrifying images.

The young Lycan was going to be weak for a while, but her body would heal, and with the support of her family, hopefully her spirit would, as well.

Since the rain was coming down hard again, Danna had driven her back home. After they'd pulled to the curb in front her house, she'd reached for the door handle, ready to climb out, when Danna had leaned over and grabbed hold of her elbow.

Casting a questioning look back at the Lycan, Jillian had listened with a wary sense of caution as Danna had said, "There's something I want to tell you."

Hoping like hell the woman wasn't about to challenge her to a fight on her front lawn, she'd asked, "What is it, Danna?"

The other woman had swallowed, her complexion turning a sickly shade of green, before croaking, "I didn't…I've never… Hell, this isn't easy. I've never been much good at apologizing, but I want you to know that I'm sorry for the way I've acted."

Jillian knew she couldn't have been more shocked in that moment if she'd been whacked upside the head with a shovel. "Uhh…thanks."

"There's more," Danna had muttered, taking her hand from Jillian's elbow and crossing her arms over her bountiful chest.

"Okay."

Her mouth grim, Danna had growled, "Burns never touched me once you came back to town."

Jillian had blinked, shaking her head in confusion.

"Not once, and believe me, I used to try everything to get him to break. We all did, even most of your so-called friends. But after you came home from school, he wouldn't even look twice at any of us. I just thought it might help for you to know that. You deserve the truth, after everything you did for Carly."

Somehow, Jillian had managed to struggle past her shock long enough to stammer, "I—I don't know what to say."

Danna had given a weary laugh. "Hey, like I said, I owe you the truth after what you did today. And who knows. Maybe your boy is one of the few exceptions to the golden rule that *men are pigs.*" A wistful look had entered her weary eyes, and the corner of her wide mouth had actually tipped in a smile. "God knows it'd give me hope to think that there's at least one man out there who knows how to keep his pants zipped when away from home."

"Thank you, Danna, for telling me the truth," Jillian had murmured numbly, and finally climbed out of the truck.

Now, as she sat on her sofa, exhausted from the long hours spent healing Carly, Jillian accepted that she didn't know with any certainty if Danna's story was true—and if it was, then she had to accept that the person who'd told her about Danna and Jeremy all those years ago had lied. For all she knew, Danna felt guilty and was simply trying to ease her conscience. She had no proof, no evidence. No, the only way she would ever truly know the truth was if she looked into Jeremy's mind, but that was never going to happen.

God, the thought of Jeremy made her chest hurt, and she pressed her hand between her breasts, as if she could stop the ache. But this was a wound that she couldn't heal—one she wasn't even sure she could survive.

Pulling her tired body from her sofa, Jillian had just turned toward the hall, thinking she'd lie down for a while, when her door rattled with yet *another* knock. For a split second, she was sorely tempted just to ignore it.

But the knocking came again, louder this time, and she quietly muttered, "I'm coming, dammit. Hold your horses."

Yanking open the door, Jillian almost slammed it shut again when she found Elise Drake's big blue eyes blinking back at her. Chewing on the corner of her lower lip, Elise said, "Can I come in?"

Jillian crossed her arms over her chest. "Are you here because of what happened yesterday?"

"I need to talk to you. Please, Jillian," she begged, the Lycan's eyes glistening with a sheen of tears as she held her cold gaze. "It's important, but I can't talk about it out here. I need to explain what happened."

"You're welcome to try—" she sighed, stepping aside to let her in "—but it won't change anything, Elise. I thought you were my friend."

Elise came inside and stopped with her back to the front window, arms wrapped around her middle, her sleek silver leggings and long charcoal-gray tunic giving her a wraithlike appearance. "I *am* your friend, Jilly. Which is why I'm going to tell you what happened. All of it."

With a frown tugging at the corners of her mouth, Jillian closed the door.

Eighty-nine. Ninety. Ninety-one.

Jeremy's knuckles were bruised from the endless beating they'd taken as he pounded the hell out of his punching bag, but he kept going, kept pushing. He didn't have a choice. He needed the physical burn of pain to keep his mind blank. The second he slowed down and gave himself time to think, he knew he was going to fall apart, and this time he didn't know if he'd be able to pull himself back together again—or if the rage would simply overtake him, destroying who he was.

Too much of a risk. And so he kept pounding away at the bag.

Mason had dropped by earlier, wanting an explanation for

his return to the Alley, but he hadn't been able to deal. Thankfully his partner knew him well enough to understand when to leave him alone, and had gone back home to his wife. Probably losing himself in married bliss, Jeremy thought with a sneer, switching to his right leg for high kicks. It was unfair of him to be snide, but he couldn't help it.

Finally, his muscles demanded a break from the relentless torture. Exchanging his drenched sweats for a pair of jeans and T-shirt, Jeremy slipped on his boots, wrapped a towel around his neck and headed into the kitchen. Standing at his sink, he watched the weak threads of sunlight struggle against the heavy storm clouds scarring the horizon. The promise of more foul weather matched his mood, irritable and on edge, with an uneasy heaviness in his gut…as if he were waiting for a hammer to fall.

And it was headed straight for his head.

He wanted to pace from one side of his cabin to the other, but the key to control was remaining still, reining in the driving, visceral urges of his beast. Like heat building from the bottom of a pan set over flame, it roiled beneath the surface of his hot skin, eager for the chance to prowl…to rage…to seethe. It wanted to rip itself from the confines of his flesh and sink its claws into something. Wanted to experience that rich, drugging rush of pleasure that came with the savage act of pure, mindless destruction. But he was a man, as well as a wolf; he'd learned long ago to control that darker side of his nature and temper it with reason.

Unfortunately, his reserves of reason and restraint were already running low.

When he heard a knock on his front door, he wondered if Mason was back for another shot at getting the sordid story out of him, but found Sayre Murphy standing on his doorstep instead.

"Sayre?" he rumbled, shaking his head with surprise. "What are you doing here?"

"Hi, Jeremy," she said shyly, her pale cheeks tinged with a soft flush of color. "I hate to bother you at home, but I really need to talk to you."

His muscles cramped, and Jeremy knew it wasn't from his work out. No, it was the thought of having to sit here and talk about Jillian, but he couldn't be a bastard to Sayre and send her walking. The kid was just looking out for her sister; she didn't deserve his anger. "Do your folks know you're here?" he asked her, stepping out of the way so that she could come inside.

"No…" she sighed, while he grabbed the end of the towel, rubbing the remaining drops of sweat from his face "…and I'd like to keep it that way."

"Just promise me you're going to be careful," he lectured, making his voice stern. "You shouldn't be out by yourself. There's too much weird stuff going on in the mountains right now. It isn't safe."

"I know," she said with a small shiver. "I was careful, I promise. I just really needed to see you," she told him, the look in her big eyes too solemn for his peace of mind.

"It's good to see you, Sayre," he breathed out on a soft burst of air, "but if this is about Jillian, I don't wanna hear it."

"Please, Jeremy," she implored. "She doesn't know that I'm here. In fact, she's probably going to kill me for interfering, but I really need to talk to you."

He cursed a silent string of words in his head, then jerked his chin toward the kitchen. "Come and take a seat at the table. I'll put on some coffee."

Sayre followed him into the kitchen and folded herself into a chair while he went about putting on a fresh pot. When the machine began to gurgle and hiss, steam rushing from its top,

Jeremy propped his hip against the counter and crossed his arms over his chest. "Okay, I'm listening."

She shifted nervously, her hands folded together on the tabletop—to keep them from shaking, he suspected. "Um, has Jillian ever told you about our mother?"

He arched one brow, wondering where this was going. "What about her?"

"If you have to ask," Sayre murmured, a crooked smile on her lips while that sad look still lingered in her eyes, "then she hasn't told you. I'm also guessing that she hasn't told you about the way of a witch and her heart."

The way of a witch and her heart? What the hell did that mean?

"I'm trying to keep it together, Sayre, but if you don't just spit it out, I'm gonna lose what little of my sanity is actually left. Have mercy and just say whatever it is that has you grinning like a little urchin."

For the next few minutes, Jeremy found himself listening, stunned, as Sayre told him the story of the man Constance Murphy had fallen in love with while away at school; the Lycan who was Jillian's biological father.

"You see, Jeremy, when a witch opens herself sexually to a man," she explained in a low, soft voice, her face burning with embarrassment, "he's given insight into her soul…into her very heart, right down to every emotion, every private thought and feeling that she holds for him. All of it, every intimate detail, is shared through their connection. When Jillian's father realized how thoroughly our mother cared for him, he used that love against her, because he didn't love her in return. He didn't cherish the gift he'd been given, and though she's happy with my father, there's a part of her that's never healed."

Silence settled between them, followed only by the cracks

of thunder rolling in hard and fast, heralding the sudden arrival of another violent storm. Jeremy stared at the gleaming finish on his kitchen floor, his mind taking him back over a decade ago, to the time when he'd fallen in love with a golden-haired imp who made his heart soft and his body hard; who turned his entire world on its ear. "So all this time, Jillian has pushed me away because she was afraid of me seeing…"

"How much she loves you," Sayre finished for him, her voice watery with the silent tears rolling down her cheeks. "All her life, our mother has been warning Jillian of what would happen if she gave her love and her body to a man who didn't return that love."

Oh, god, he thought, while a searing pain crushed through his head…through his heart.

Christ, it all made such perfect sense now that he could see the pieces that had been missing. He'd been so intent on protecting himself, that he'd never opened himself up to her, never revealed his feelings. Not then. And not in the past few days.

He'd told her that he wanted her, that he needed her. Hell, dozens of times. But he'd never—not once—admitted that he felt something more for her than lust.

"I've got to talk to her," he rasped, taking the towel from around his neck. He'd just tossed it on the table when Sayre suddenly reached out, grasping his right wrist with both hands as he moved past her.

"Jilly is in trouble," she whispered, her eyes shocked wide in fear, voice so soft he could barely hear her.

"What?" he grunted, staring down at her, but she was… gone, her eyes glazed…her mind in another place. "Sayre," he barked, taking her shoulders and giving her a gentle shake. "Sayre, come back, honey. What are you talking about? What's wrong with Jillian?"

Blinking rapidly, she lifted her gaze, staring up at him while a cold look of horror spread over her fey face. "I—I don't know how to explain it, Jeremy. I just…feel things… sometimes. I can't control it. But something in my head is screaming that she needs you. That she's in danger!"

"Goddamn it," he growled, grabbing his keys and cell phone off the nearby counter, cursing a foul streak of words when he saw that his battery was completely dead. Tossing the useless piece of technology back on the counter, he rushed out of the kitchen as Sayre followed beside him, her eyes huge in the paleness of her face. "I want you to get Mason and tell him to meet me at Jillian's as fast as he can," he told her, pulling open the front door as he gave her a hard look. "Then you stay at the cabin with Torrance, Sayre. No matter what, you're not to head off into the woods alone. You understand?"

She nodded, trembling, clearly terrified for her sister, and Jeremy's heart turned over in his chest. "It's going to be okay, honey." He tried to give her a reassuring smile, but knew it looked strained by his own fear. "You just do what I said, and then start trying to get through to Jillian on the phone. If you can get her, tell her I'm on my way."

"I don't expect you to forgive me," Elise rasped, glancing nervously out the front window, while Jillian settled back on the sofa. "But I want to explain the reason I went to Jeremy's house yesterday."

Turning away from the window, she said, "My father is having both this house, and Jeremy's house, watched. When he saw you leave yesterday morning, he waited to see if you would go to Jeremy. When you did, he called me and told me that I was going to help him get the Runner out of town once and for all. Said he had important plans and that Jeremy couldn't be around to get in his way."

"And you agreed?" Jillian asked, shaking her head in confusion.

A wry sound that was too brittle to be laughter fell from Elise's lips. "At first? No, I told him to go to hell. But he's lost his grip on reality, Jillian. He told me that if I didn't do as he said, he'd make sure the Runners turned their sights on Eric, said he'd fix it so that evidence turned up that would incriminate my brother and make it look as if he was in league with the rogues. I panicked, and so I…I did it. I only live around the corner from the Burns's house. Like a puppet," she sneered, curling her lip with disgust, "I jumped to do his bidding and put on that stupid, horrible act."

Jillian wet her bottom lip with the tip of her tongue, a strange tingling sensation surging through her limbs, her skin feeling shivery and hot at the same time, while ideas tumbled over themselves, one after the other in her tired mind. "So then…it was all an act? It was a setup, because Drake wanted Jeremy out of Shadow Peak?"

Elise nodded, looking miserable, and lifted one shaking hand to tuck the burgundy fall of her hair behind her ear. "Think about it, Jilly. I may not shape-shift, but I'm still a Lycan. I could scent you the second he opened the door. I knew you were there, even though I couldn't see you. I'm so sorry," she sniffed, and Jillian held up the box of tissues. Elise took one with an unsteady smile, then collapsed into the chair beside the sofa. "Anyway, I panicked and didn't know what else to do," she confessed in a low, broken voice. "I couldn't let my father do that to Eric, and he would have. I know he would. He'll use any of us, any way he chooses, so long as it gets him what he wants, and he's angry at Eric for refusing to support him.

"Then, this afternoon," Elise rasped, a fresh surge of tears spilling from her eyes, "I heard him talking to Cooper Sheffield, and I knew it was about you. You're in danger, Jillian. I don't know what they have planned, but they said something about using you as an example of what happens to those who befriend the Runners. I think—"

A jarring burst of laughter came from the street, and Elise flinched, the slim line of her brows pulling together in a frown as she glanced toward the front window. Standing, she went and looked around the edge of the sheer curtains. "I guess there's a challenge tonight," she murmured. "There's a crowd out on the street, heading toward the woods."

It was nearly impossible to pull her mind off Jeremy and Drake and what she'd just learned, but Jillian closed her eyes, trying to remember. "This whole week has been a blur, but now that I think about it, I think there *is* a challenge planned for tonight." She opened her eyes, frowning. "I should be there, but I'm not up for it."

Elise slanted her a weary look. "Me, either." She sighed, rubbing at her forehead. "And we need—" In the next instant, she screamed, stumbling forward, and then she went down hard on her hands and knees, her body jerking as if she were having a violent seizure.

"Elise!" Jillian shouted, rushing forward, but Elise's head shot up, her top lip pulled back over teeth that were slowly lengthening into fangs. "Don't!" she moaned, while tears poured from her eyes, drenching her face. "Oh, god, Jillian. Don't come near me. I don't... I don't know what's happening."

A raw, wrenching sound of pain ripped out of Elise's throat, another hard wave of spasms racking her body, and Jillian could see the ridges of her spine shifting beneath the thin cotton of her shirt. Elise whimpered, her words garbled as the delicate bones in her jaw began cracking... lengthening. Blood poured out of her nose, and trickled from her left ear in a thin, meandering trail. "Jillian, get out! I c-can't…can't control it. It's coming. Get out of here!" she growled, her voice growing deeper, more guttural, and Jillian finally registered the danger she was in.

If Elise couldn't control the change, there was every chance she wouldn't be able to control her wolf, either. Which meant that the second her shift was complete, Jillian would become her prey. Squeezing her eyes shut, Jillian hesitated. She wanted to help her friend, but she knew she would be no match for a feral werewolf. Elise could rip to her shreds within seconds, and Jillian would die without ever getting the chance to set things right with Jeremy.

Oh, God…Jeremy. She didn't want to die without seeing him again—without ever telling him how much she had always loved him. How sorry she was that she'd allowed so many things to stand between them.

A crackling surge of lightning struck the top of her house, jarring the walls, at the same time Elise let out a sharp, sinister howl…and Jillian suddenly realized she was already too late.

Her time had just run out.

Chapter 15

Knowing her only chance for survival lay in a sprint for the door, Jillian opened her eyes and found a fully formed werewolf blocking the exit, its long claws flexing sinisterly at its sides, reddish gold fur rippling as it drew in each deep, bellowing breath. Above the muzzled length of its snout, blue eyes glowed like the inside of a flame, its upper lip curling to reveal the long, deadly length of its fangs.

Now she was going to have to fight her way out, when she knew she was still too weak from healing Carly to win, and hope she could make it to her car before Elise caught her. Jillian knew she didn't stand a chance, but for Jeremy, she was willing to try.

"Elise?" she whispered, but there was no flash of recognition in the beast's eyes, only the steady, relentless burn of savage aggression, its nostrils flaring as it scented her fear. Jillian shook her hands out at her sides, searching for every last ounce of power she could scrounge up from the depths of her soul, when suddenly there was a terrible banging against her front door. The wolf lurched at the sound, and Jillian nearly collapsed with relief as a deep voice roared her name.

"Jillian! Are you in there?" Jeremy shouted, and the door rattled so hard that the frame began to crack. "Open the goddamn door!"

She cried out at the sound of his voice, the pour of relief flooding through her veins so intense, she felt light-headed. The wolf snarled in reaction, then threw back its head and let out an unearthly howl that shook the glass in her front window…and had Jeremy shouting even louder, his deep voice stark with terror.

"What the hell is going on in there?" he roared, and something solid and heavy hit her door, like his shoulder, and she knew he was breaking it down.

The werewolf's head lowered at the noise, a coarse chuffing sound surging from its chest, and Jillian took a step back, sensing that it was only a matter of time before it attacked. "Hurry!" she called out, and the seething beast instantly lunged for her, taking her to the ground with its overpowering weight, slamming her into the floor. Screaming, Jillian watched as its long, deadly fangs flashed toward her throat, glinting silvery white in the pale light of the room. She called up every ounce of power she could find lingering in her body and mentally pushed at the wolf, at the same time she lifted her arms, sinking her fingers into its warm fur as she fought to hold it at bay…but she wasn't strong enough to throw it off.

Searching deeper, Jillian shoved with everything she had, feeling as if she were turning her body inside out. Blood began trickling from her nose while a dull roar filled her head, the pressure intense, as if her skull would crack in two. She had no idea how many seconds her power bought her, but suddenly Jeremy was crashing through her door, the splintering wood cracking with a sickening wail. With a single, piercing glance, he took in the situation, and without any hesitation, he threw himself at the crouching wolf. His hands transformed into deadly claws as he slammed into the beast, and together they crashed to the side, rolling over her living-room floor, while the sky broke open again with another thundering strike of lightning. Rain began coming down like a great, roaring waterfall beyond the open doorway, drumming against the roof, its fresh, crisp scent washing over the nightmarish scene with the surging breeze, while Jeremy and the wolf battled in a vicious, violent striking of claws and gnashing fangs.

Tears filled her eyes when she saw the werewolf's sharp claws slash across Jeremy's chest and his arm. She pressed her hand to her trembling mouth, torn between the need to help him and the fear that she'd only get in his way, when a blur of movement brushed past her from the doorway, and Mason joined his partner. Together, the two Bloodrunners quickly subdued the rage-filled wolf, shoving it face-first against the floor and pinning its powerful arms behind its back.

With a low snarl, Mason's claws reached for the beast's neck, and Jillian shook herself out of her stupor. "No, don't kill it!" she screamed, and the Bloodrunner sent her a sharp look of surprise. "It's Elise," she gasped, struggling to draw in enough air for her explanation. "Something's wrong. She d-didn't want to change. I d-don't know what happened, but this isn't her. I mean, it's her…but she can't control it! It just…overtook her. One minute we were talking, and in the next she was…changing."

The Runners shared a dark look, but neither said a word. Pulling back his right arm, Mason's claws shifted into a clenched human fist. Jillian knew he meant to knock the snarling, bucking wolf unconscious with a blow to the temple, but just before he struck, the beast's shape bled away and Elise regained her human form. Releasing her arms, the men shifted away from her shivering body, and Jillian grabbed the baby-soft afghan from the end of her sofa, wrapping it around Elise's trembling shoulders as her friend curled onto her side, keening like a creature in pain. "It's okay," Jillian murmured in a low, soothing voice. "It's okay now, honey. Everything's okay."

Lifting her gaze, she found Jeremy staring down at her with an arrested expression on his face. His terror and concern for her were evident in his shattered appearance—his mouth grim, a torrent of emotions flashing through the glowing depths of his eyes. "Are you all right?" he asked, pulling her into his arms and holding her so tightly, she could barely breathe in his crushing embrace.

"I'm fine," she assured him, gazing up into his ruggedly handsome face, while everything that had happened, everything that she'd learned and experienced that day, crashed through her mind in a dizzying, chaotic jumble of details. "God, Jeremy, I have so much to tell you. Elise…she came here to confess that it was all a set-up, that scene at your house. Her father put her up to it, because Drake wanted you out of town."

His eyes narrowed with anger, but before he could comment, she said, "And before Elise got here, I had a visit from Danna Gibson."

"Danna?" he croaked, his hazel gaze going wide in surprise.

"I'll have to tell you about Carly, her little sister, later. What I want to tell you now is that Danna apologized for… everything. She told me that you never touched her after I came home from school."

"Did you believe her?" he asked, his expression guarded, and yet somehow tender, without any trace of the anger or bitterness she had expected.

"I wanted to believe her," she told him, "but I knew that the only way I was ever really going to learn the truth about what had happened was if I looked inside of you. And then, when I thought I was going to die, I finally realized that—"

Suddenly, her confession was interrupted by a series of unearthly cries coming from the street, spilling in through the open doorway, making her heart clench with terror all over again. Jeremy moved to slam the broken door shut, while Mason peered through the front window. "I don't believe it. We have more Lycans shifting in the street," the Runner growled.

"Wh-what do we do?" Jillian stammered, her jaw shaking so badly she could barely control it.

"We get the hell out of here," Jeremy muttered, cutting a sharp look at his partner.

"I've got Elise," Mason grunted, bending down to lift the trembling woman into his arms.

"Stay behind me," Jeremy ordered, opening the door, one hand clenched around Jillian's wrist, holding her close to his back. The Lycans were still contorting in the street, their changes not yet complete, tortured bodies straining in agony as they writhed upon the rain-drenched asphalt. "Your truck's closer, Mase. We need to make a run for it. Now!" Jeremy shouted, and Jillian struggled to keep her footing on the slippery sidewalk as they ran out into the rain, sprinting for the truck. Jeremy pulled open the driver's side door and shoved her up into the front, while Mason laid Elise out over the backseat. Jumping in behind the wheel, Jeremy caught the keys that his partner tossed his way and cranked the engine. Mason jumped in on the passenger's side, slamming his door as the first werewolf charged the truck.

Through the windows, Jillian could see her neighbors opening their doors to those who were searching for a safe place to hide, while the feral wolves began closing in. Jeremy floored the gas pedal, sending the tires squealing while the end fishtailed, and then they finally found purchase and the truck surged forward. The driving sheets of rain made it impossible to see clearly, even with the windshield wipers on high, but Jeremy kept the accelerator down. A powerful set of claws scratched at Mason's window, making a bloodcurdling sound, until Jeremy dropped a gear and the truck sped away with a roaring burst of speed.

While Jeremy drove like a demon down the rain-soaked residential streets, his partner pulled out his cell phone. "I'm gonna try to get through to Dylan, if the storm hasn't wiped out the network."

It took several tries, but Mason finally gave a soft grunt of satisfaction.

"You have a problem on Lassiter Avenue," he growled into the wafer-thin phone. "I don't know what's going on, but Lycans are having their wolves... Hell, it's like they're being ripped out against their will and the goddamn things are feral. Jeremy and I have Jillian and Elise Drake, but you need to get on the scene before somebody gets killed."

Jillian could hear Dylan's furious reaction to the disturbing news, and then Mason said, "Just let us know when it's over. We'll be waiting for an explanation."

Shaking her head, Jillian was struggling to make sense out of everything that had happened when Elise's frail whisper reached her ears. *"Jilly."*

Twisting around, Jillian reached over the front seat and grabbed Elise's hand as her friend struggled to get out a broken, stammering string of apologies.

"Hey, it's okay," she murmured, trying to calm her down.

"No one's angry at you, Elise. You didn't do anything wrong. Everything's going to be fine."

"I need…I n-need to tell you what happened," Elise croaked, tears leaking from her eyes, leaving salty trails down her cheeks. "I have to t-tell you, Jilly."

"It can wait," she said gently, squeezing Elise's hand. "Right now, you need to rest and save your strength."

"But it was my f-father," she whispered, her mouth quivering.

"Oh, god," Jillian gasped, and at the same time Jeremy slammed on the brakes, jerking the truck to a screeching, jarring stop that nearly sent them skidding off the side of the rain-slick road.

"I could feel him in my h-head," Elise stammered, shaking like a leaf caught in the savage grasp of a storm. "Somehow, he made me change, and I c-could hear his voice telling me to k-kill you. And I think th-there was an-another one, but I couldn't tell who it was. It was only my father's voice that kept ordering me, t-telling me what to do. I couldn't— couldn't control it."

Finally, Elise's eyes slid closed, and she slumped against the back of the seat, overtaken with exhaustion.

"Son of a bitch," Jeremy snarled, his expression savage as he shoved open his door and jumped out of the truck.

"Where the hell are you going?" Mason demanded, rushing out the passenger's side as Jillian scrambled out of the driver's.

"Jeremy!" she screamed, terror sinking deep as she suddenly realized what he was doing, watching as he headed north, cutting across a field of tall grass that led back into the forest. He was going back to Shadow Peak, toward the northwest side of town that bordered Stefan Drake's property. Jillian rushed after him, but her bare feet slipped the moment she hit the rain-drenched grass and she fell on her hands and knees, sinking into the muddy soil. "Jeremy!" she screamed again.

Turning, Jeremy kept moving, walking backward as he yelled, "Get her back to the Alley, Mase, and keep her there!"

Strong arms suddenly banded her middle, pulling her to her feet. Jillian kicked and screamed, struggling to break free of Mason's hold, but he wouldn't budge.

"Dammit, Jeremy!" Mason shouted over her head, as the rain began coming down even harder, blurring the lines of Jeremy's body. His partner obviously knew, just as Jillian did, that Jeremy was heading back to Shadow Peak. After hearing Elise's confession, he was going after Drake for making an attempt on her life. "Wait for backup!" Mason snarled with fury. "That's an order!"

"Oh, god. You can't let him go!" she sobbed, hysterical, terrified that she was never going to see him again—that she was going to lose him. "What the hell is wrong with you? Go after him!" she cried, watching through rain and tears as Jeremy disappeared into the heavy line of trees. "He's going to get himself killed facing Drake on his own!"

"Jillian, calm down," Mason grunted, his chest heaving as he finally turned and carried her back to the truck. "Jeremy won't do anything stupid. He's too smart to—"

"He isn't thinking straight!" she seethed, wanting to scratch and claw at him, if only it would make him listen to reason. "You have to help him!"

"I'm going after him, as soon as I get you and Elise to the Alley," he barked, pushing her across the front seat of the truck as he climbed behind the wheel and immediately floored the gas pedal. She cast a swift glance at the passenger's side door, wondering… But knew she'd never catch up to Jeremy in time.

Pulling his phone back out, Mason tried to calm her down. "He won't be alone, Jillian. I'm going to call Dylan back and tell him to head to Drake's."

"By the time you drive us to the Alley, you'll be too late," she croaked, knowing there was only one hope—if she could just convince the Runner to trust her judgment. "And Dylan doesn't have the guts to stand up to Drake. You know that! You've got to call Eric, Mase. He'll help, I swear."

Mason slanted her a grim look, then cut his gaze back to the winding road. "You want me to call the son of the man Jeremy intends to kill for help?"

"Eric isn't like his father. Please, Mason," she whispered, clutching on to his arm with her muddy fingers, feeling as she were grasping at a lifeline. "Trust me. If you ask for his help, Eric will do the right thing. I know he will."

Mason worked his jaw, cursing something foul under his breath, then finally let out a harsh sigh. "You had better not be wrong," he muttered, handing her the phone. "Go ahead. Dial his goddamn number. But let me do the talking."

By the time Jeremy broke out of the forest at the edge of Stefan Drake's property, evening had fallen. The rain had finally eased to a light mist, but his clothes were soaked with water, as well as the blood that seeped from the shallow wounds Elise's claws had slashed across his arms and abdomen. And yet he didn't feel the pain from his injuries. All he felt was the hot, scalding burn of anger, his wolf prowling just beneath the surface of his skin—the savagery of the rumbling thunder the perfect complement to his murderous rage.

The second he'd heard Elise's whispered words, he'd known what he had to do.

Drake's house sat in silent darkness to his left, but there

was an eerie glow of light coming from the ancient barn at
the back of the property, off to his right. Lowering his head,
Jeremy sniffed at the air, catching what he wanted.

Drake.

The wind was on his side, and he sniffed at the air again.
His prey wasn't alone. He could just catch Cooper Sheffield's
foul stench, and wondered with a low snarl if Drake had felt
he needed his muscle for protection, now that his attack on
Jillian's life had failed.

Flexing his hands at his sides, his flesh burned as his
claws pricked the tips of his fingers. Blood trickled from
his hands, mixing with the rainwater on the soft grass beneath his feet, his gums burning as his fangs struggled to
break free. And yet, he resisted the shift, knowing he
needed to retain as much of his humanity as he could, before the seething darkness in him overshadowed the reason
of the man.

The wolf wanted blood—but the Bloodrunner wanted
justice.

Careful to stay downwind, Jeremy traveled the edge of the
property, until he came around the far side of the barn.
Sheffield's burgundy Avalanche had been left idling near the
barn's entrance, the metallic scent of the engine thick in the
evening air. They were obviously in a hurry…but Jeremy
had no intention of letting Drake escape. He could hear them
inside, their voices raised in anger. Moving with the stealth
skill of a hunter, he'd just reached for the heavy wooden door
when a sound off to his left had him spinning around, his
muscles tensed, ready to strike.

Jeremy blinked, unable to believe what he was seeing.
Eric Drake stood no more than five feet away, his hands lifted
in a gesture of peace, his clothes as rain-soaked as his own.
"What the hell are you doing here?" Jeremy snarled in a

stifled rasp, while lightning crackled across the sky and thunder rumbled like a monstrous bellow of rage.

Eric's gray eyes burned with a hard, steely purpose. "Your partner called me. He told me about Jillian and my sister. Then he asked for a favor."

It was on the tip of Jeremy's tongue to tell the Lycan there was no way in hell Mason would have asked him for help, when he suddenly realized just whose idea calling Eric must have been. "Jillian was wrong to involve you. I can handle this on my own."

"I'm sure you can." The Lycan took a step closer, his face set in an expression of pure, ruthless determination. "But the good news is that you won't have to."

"Just stay the hell out of my way," Jeremy grunted. Turning back to the door, he kicked it open, grinning with cold satisfaction when Drake and Sheffield spun around in startled surprise. They'd both been so engrossed in their argument, neither had noticed they had company.

"Well, imagine that," Jeremy remarked with deceptive calm, his voice soft as he stepped into the dank structure, aware of Eric following just behind him. "You two actually look surprised to see me."

The barn was completely open inside, with exposed beams, a rustic plank floor and an assortment of tables and chairs clustered together in groups. Jeremy guessed the building was used as a headquarters for Drake's "pure-blooded" movement, and it was almost as if he could smell the thick scent of hatred in the stale air, the taste rotten and sharp against his tongue.

Drake and Sheffield stood in the center of the floor, before a massive oak table littered with a variety of automatic handguns and rifles, reminding Jeremy of the healing bullet wound in his shoulder. He had no doubt, now, that the shots in the forest that day had come from the pack's security chief. Sheffield took a step forward, his expression carved with sneering malice, but Drake stayed his second-in-command with a touch on his arm. "It's all right, Cooper," he murmured, stepping around him. "We have nothing to fear. After all, he's here because he wishes to do the honorable thing and challenge me for daring to rid the world of that pathetic little mate of his. Isn't that right, Runner?"

"I'm challenging you, all right," Jeremy offered in a gritty rasp, allowing a hard smile to curl the edges of his mouth. "And I'm going to enjoy watching you die when I'm done with you."

"And I see you've brought my son along for help," the Elder drawled, throwing back his head with a faint, hoarse cackle. "How pathetically fitting, considering Eric never could choose the winning side. He's always been one to champion the underdog, like that worthless sister of his."

Jeremy could sense the cold burn of fury pouring through the Lycan, though Eric refused to rise to the bait. Instead, he crossed his arms over his broad chest, his attention focused on Sheffield, just daring the bastard to make a move, and Jeremy couldn't help but admire his restraint. He could only assume that Eric Drake had mastered the art of ignoring his psychotic father a long time ago.

Keeping his own attention focused on Drake, Jeremy allowed his claws to fully slip his skin, the razor-sharp weapons piercing through the tips of his fingers with a sinister hiss of sound. "Are you ready, Drake? Any last words before Eric does the honors and draws the sacred Challenge Circle?"

"I'm afraid you've come all this way for nothing," the Elder murmured, his pewter brows lifted high on his wrinkled brow. "I'd enjoy nothing more than tearing into you, Runner, but the League no longer allows the challenge of an Elder."

Jeremy stalked closer, enjoying the shadow of panic that darkened Drake's eyes with each step that he took. "Then forget the challenge," he suggested, the guttural sound of his voice more animal than human as his wolf struggled for control...for dominance. "Let's deal with this the old-fashioned way, without any rules and regulations. Just two enemies going at one another, hungry for the kill."

Drake's eyes went wide, his lip curling as he snarled, "You wouldn't dare kill me without the authority of a proper challenge fight!"

"See, that's where you're wrong." Jeremy gave him another slow, arrogant smile. "If my partner were here, he could tell you I have a bad reputation for being a rule breaker." He paused, letting his words sink in, while taking another step closer, then another, each movement countered by Drake until the Elder's thighs were plastered against the heavy edge of the table at his back. "So what's it gonna be? If you're too chicken to fight me like a man, I can only assume you're ready to die like an animal."

Drake's body vibrated with outrage, but there was a pale cast beneath his skin, and Jeremy could smell the acrid scent of the bastard's fear. "I would never lower myself to fight you. You're not even worth the effort, when I can just have you killed off instead." The thin line of his mouth twisted into a grotesque semblance of a smile, his eyes glowing with the maniacal burn of insanity. "And I'll send my rogues after your little bitch, too. You, they'll take down fast—but they'll do Jillian slowly. She deserves to suffer for allowing something as filthy as you to touch her," he snarled. "She deserves to die for daring to turn her back on the pack—for choosing a half-breed like you over her duty to her wolves!"

It only took a fraction of a second for Jeremy to have the monster's throat in his grip, then slam him down backward on the cluttered surface of the table with a jarring thud. Sheffield started to lunge forward, when Eric whipped a gun from the waistband of his jeans at the center of his lower back. He aimed the intimidating weapon point-blank between the Lycan's eyes, and Sheffield lifted his arms, while a screeching, furious roar poured from Drake's throat, his damp hands pulling ineffectually at Jeremy's wrists.

Smiling down into the Elder's terror-filled face, Jeremy slowly shook his head. "You've truly lost your mind, haven't you, Drake?"

"I've lost my humanity!" the Elder croaked. "And gladly! Unlike you and your sniveling friends, I've accepted the true nature of my beast. I've embraced the purity of what I am, of what the Silvercrest are *meant* to be. You and your Runners can't stop what I've set in motion. Not even the combined forces of hell can stop me now!"

Jeremy leaned closer, going nose-to-nose with the Elder. "That's what all the sick sons of bitches say, just before they take their last breath." His fingers tightened, nearly cutting off the Lycan's air, and in a soft, almost silent whisper, Jeremy said, "All I have to do is twist."

"My s-son would n-never let you do it," Drake stammered, spittle spraying from his thin lips as his face turned dark with a violent wash of color.

"Eric?" A rough laugh burst from Jeremy's chest. "You just used his little sister like a puppet on a string. Do you really think he cares what I do with you?"

"Elise got exactly what she deserved! I set her up today, knowing damn well she would go running off and tattle to her friend, convinced she was doing the right thing. It was so easy it was pathetic. And there's nothing you can do about it, because the League would never let you get away with killing me. Do it, and they'll demand your life for mine—and Jillian will be left at the mercy of those who will avenge me. No matter what you do, in the end, her blood will be on your hands, Runner. Jillian's blood will be on *your* hands!"

"On second thought," Jeremy growled, allowing his fangs to finally slip free, "I think I'll go ahead and rip your throat out, you psychotic piece of—"

"Burns!" Eric shouted, the Lycan's gun still aimed at Sheffield while he caught Jeremy's wild-eyed gaze, demanding he listen. "Don't do it!"

Jeremy's eyes narrowed with suspicion. "Whose side are you on, Eric?"

"I couldn't care less what happens to him," Eric grunted, jerking his chin toward his father, "but he's right. If you kill him in cold blood, the League will demand your execution. He isn't worth it."

"And maybe I don't give a shit," Jeremy growled, aware of his wolf's primal, visceral need for retribution overshadowing what he knew was right. "Maybe it's worth it," he panted, cutting his eyes back to Drake, "so long as I'm taking this bastard with me."

"And what about Jillian?" Eric demanded in a harsh shout, urging him to listen to reason. "She's going to need you now more than ever, Jeremy. Are you willing to leave her on her own? Are you willing to give up the chance for a life with her?"

He ground his teeth while the man in him struggled to regain control, but the beast was still seething, hungry for blood. "He deserves to die!" he snarled in a stifled roar.

"I know he does," Eric grated, "but *not* like this. That's what separates you from him. That's what makes you different, Burns. You're stronger than the animal, goddamn it. You're stronger than the need to kill."

Jeremy squeezed his eyes closed, his heart pounding, chest heaving as he fought a violent internal battle that would determine the rest of his life. Kill the bastard in cold blood…or let him go, saving his punishment for another day in order to have a life with the woman he loved.

And in the end, it was the purity—*the power*—of that love that tipped the balance. It was Jillian that brought him back from the edge.

Heaving a deep, shuddering sigh, Jeremy released his hold on Drake's throat and slowly eased away, his beast howling in outrage, while a burning spark of hope began to slowly ease the knots of fury twisting him up inside. With each backward step, he moved that little bit closer to the chance of having a life with Jillian—closer to the one thing he'd always wanted most in this godforsaken world.

"This isn't over," he rasped, taking another step away, followed by another, watching as the Elder sluggishly pushed himself up from the table. "I'll be waiting for you to make your move, and when you do, you're mine. I'll be the last wolf hunting you down, Drake—and in the end, you *are* going to pay for your crimes. Every single goddamn one of them."

Pulling the shreds of his dignity around him like a cloak, Drake straightened his shirt, then ran his hands through his hair. Jerking his chin toward Jeremy, he curled his lip and addressed his second-in-command. "Stop standing there and do your job, Cooper. I want this half-breed out of my presence."

Sheffield reached for him, but Jeremy cut the Lycan a hard smile and jerked his arm away. "Touch me just once, Sheffield, and it'll be the last thing you do."

"Burns, come on," Eric called out, already waiting by the door. "Let's get the hell out of here."

Nodding, Jeremy turned and began making his way toward the door, eager to get back to Jillian and hold her in his arms, assuring himself that she was okay…that she was safe and unharmed. He'd just reached the entrance when he caught

Eric's outraged expression from the corner of his eye, the Lycan's dark gray stare narrowing with fury as he started to shout out a warning. But Jeremy was already reacting. Knowing he had only seconds, he pivoted on the balls of his feet and whipped around, just in time to see a fully shifted Sheffield hurtling toward him. He tried to counter the attack at the same moment Eric fired off a shot, but the wolf was moving too quickly, its distended claws sinking into Jeremy's abdomen with a sickening burst of pain that threatened to consume him in a dark, smothering wave. The only thing that kept him on his feet was the knowledge that Jillian was waiting for him—that she needed him.

With the bastard's claws buried deep in his belly, Jeremy lifted his hands and quickly wrapped them around the wolf's thick neck, twisting until he heard a sharp crack of sound, snapping Sheffield's spinal column. "Nice try," he rasped, "but you lose."

The werewolf's heavy body sagged to the floor, a hoarse cry breaking out of Jeremy's throat as Sheffield's claws pulled free. Nausea rolled through him like a poison, while his blood poured from the deep wounds in a warm, wet spill that soaked his shirt and jeans. He staggered, light-headed, only to find Eric's arm wrapped around his side, holding him upright.

Glancing back at Drake, Jeremy shook his head with mock pity. "Is that best that you've got?" he taunted, lifting his brows.

Drake refused to remark, his sinister features rigid with fury. Only the dark tinge of rage cresting his cheekbones kept him from looking like a statue that'd been carved from granite, lifeless and cold.

"Come on, Burns," Eric muttered, shifting toward the door. "You have something a lot better than this waiting for you."

"Just take his truck," Jeremy grunted through clenched teeth when they were outside, fighting the rolling waves of agony ripping his insides to shreds. He closed his eyes, hoping like hell he could make it long enough to see Jillian before he lost consciousness. If he hadn't lost so much blood from the bullet wound just days before and from the run-in with the rogues before that, he probably would have had a fighting chance—but the past few weeks had been hell on his body. He knew the odds weren't in his favor, but he also knew he was a stubborn son of a bitch who wouldn't give up without a fight.

"Hold on, Burns," he heard Eric mutter through the roaring pain in his head, his shredded abdominal muscles screaming in protest as the Lycan got him into the truck's backseat. "Just hold on and I'll get you to Jillian."

He tried to say thanks, only his lips were too numb to form the words. He struggled, fighting it, but the darkness kept pulling him deeper, as if he were falling to the bottom of a steep, dark lake. He kicked and screamed and raged against the cold, stark burn of reality that told him he was dying. God-damn it, he wasn't going to let it happen. Not before he'd told her how he felt. Not before he'd had the chance to hold her in his arms and tell her he loved her. That he was sorry for being proud…sorry he hadn't fought for her all those years ago. That he never wanted to spend another second of his life without her.

Jeremy struggled…and seethed…and raged, but no matter how hard he fought against it, he just kept sinking deeper.

Chapter 16

Tossing restlessly atop a cool, comfortable bed, a light sheet tangled around his legs, Jeremy struggled to pull himself back to a lucid state of consciousness. His eyes felt gritty as he forced them open, his lids heavy…weighted. He braced himself for a sickening wave of pain that lingered at the edges of his memory, but it never came. Squinting, he stared into the shadowed room, wondering where he was.

"There you are," a deep voice rumbled at his side. "You've been out for a few hours. I was starting to wonder when you'd come around."

"Mason?" he croaked.

"Yeah, I'm here." A small lamp on the bedside table turned on, sending a warm wash of mellow gold through the room that didn't quite reach into the dusky corners. Jeremy instantly recognized the basement apartment in Mason's cabin.

He was lying on one of the twin beds, his partner sitting in a chair that had been placed near his bedside.

Licking his dry lips, he said, "What happened? Where's Jillian?" He winced at the scratchy sound of his voice, but as bad as he sounded, his body felt unusually good. No aches. No pains. Just this sluggish climb back from the depths of wherever he'd been…floating or sleeping or whatever the hell he'd been doing.

"Do you remember what happened with Sheffield?" Mason asked.

"Yeah. I remember breaking the bastard's neck, and then Eric shoving me into the backseat of a truck. But…it's all a blank after that." Again, he said, "Where's Jillian?"

Instead of answering the question, his partner gave him a lopsided smile. "That's one hell of a woman you've got there, Jeremy. I hope you know how lucky you are."

This time, his words grated with impatience. "Where the hell is she?"

Mason chuckled softly under his breath. "She's here, in the Alley. There's no need to worry. I just want to talk to you a minute before you go barging off after her."

Impatient to do just that, Jeremy tested his body by tightening his abs and pulling himself into a sitting position, amazed when he didn't experience so much as a twinge of discomfort. And suddenly, as the cobwebs cleared from his mind, he realized why. "She healed me," he stated, his flat monotone devoid of emotion, while inside he experienced a deep, piercing twinge of regret. She knew the truth now, about everything.

Jeremy knew it shouldn't bother him—but it did.

Dammit, he'd wanted her to believe in him, only…not like this. He'd wanted to earn her faith on his own, not because of what she learned in his head.

"Before you get maudlin on me," Mason drawled, "you might be interested to know that she kept herself out of your head, even though it about killed her to do it without the aid of your mind, considering how badly you were hurt."

He whipped his head to the side so quickly, he damn near gave himself whiplash. *"What?"*

Mason gave him a small, knowing smile, understanding his demons. "It's true. She did the healing without peeking into that thick head of yours, but she suffered because of it. The process took so much out of her, I thought she was going to collapse when it was finally over."

"Is she okay?" he rasped, his voice roughened by concern as he threw his legs over the side of the bed.

"Sayre was able to use her own power to boost Jillian's energy afterward, and it helped get her back to normal. But it was rough there for a while," Mason told him. "She looked like someone who'd had their life sucked right out of them, but I guess she poured everything she had into making sure you lived. And she even called Graham and demanded he come down here to see your injuries for himself, so that there could be no doubt you had killed Sheffield in self-defense."

"Was she…upset, when she saw me?" he asked, flicking a quick look at his partner.

Mason rolled his eyes, a low chuckle rumbling in his throat. "Upset doesn't even begin to cover it. I think my ears are still ringing from the lashing she gave me for allowing you to go off and almost get yourself killed."

Jeremy glanced toward the stairs, keenly aware of the urgent, driving need to get to her as quickly as possible. "Is she still here?" he asked thickly.

Standing, Mason said, "She left Sayre here and headed back to your cabin about fifteen minutes ago. I think she was going to try and get some more rest."

"I need some clothes," he grunted, anxious to get the hell out of there.

Mason shot him a hard grin and jerked his chin toward the foot of the bed. "You've got jeans and a T-shirt waiting for you right there."

"Thanks, man. For everything."

"No problem," Mason replied with a low laugh. "Just don't scare the hell out of me like that again. I think I lost ten years when I saw how bad he'd gotten you."

"Trust me, I have every intention of living a very long, very healthy life from this point on," Jeremy drawled, running his hand over the pink, puckered scars scattered across his abdomen, before pulling on the borrowed shirt and jeans. He'd just reached the bottom stair, when Mason said his name. Looking back over his shoulder, Jeremy asked, "Yeah?"

His partner's mouth twitched with humor. "I just wanted you to know that if you make Hennessey your best man instead of me, I'll kill you myself."

"Idiot," he snickered, while his shoulders shook with silent laughter. Then he set off up the stairs…taking them two at a time.

When he found her, she was taking her bath.

As Jeremy stood just outside the closed bathroom door, he clutched the handle in a death grip and rested his forehead against the door's cool wood grain, ruefully aware of his heart thundering like a drum in his chest. He was so hard he could barely see straight, so excited his breath jerked from his lungs in a harsh, erratic rhythm.

He couldn't believe that after all these years, it was finally going to happen—and he couldn't wait one single second more.

Jillian gasped the instant he swung the door open, her brown eyes shocked wide with surprise. She sat up so quickly that the bathwater sloshed over the edge of the tub, spilling out over the floor. "What are you doing out of bed?"

He tried to answer, but his throat wouldn't cooperate. Instead, he found himself grabbing her up out of the water, swallowing her soft shriek with his mouth as he set her sleek, wet body on the counter. He pressed between her legs, urging her knees wide with his hands, and against her mouth, he groaned, "Why did you do it, Jillian?"

He knew she would understand what he was asking, that he wanted...*needed* to know why she'd healed him the way that she had.

"Do you remember what I told you the night you came back, after the challenge fight?" she asked, her skin rosy and damp from the bathwater, so beautiful that she took his breath away. "About my destiny?"

Jeremy lifted his hands, cradling her precious face in his palms, staring into the warm depths of her eyes, feeling as if he could see his every emotion—his love and hope and the burning, white-hot glow of hunger—mirrored right there, gazing back at him. "I remember," he told her in a voice gritty with emotion. "You said that the pack was your destiny."

"I was wrong," she whispered, velvety brown eyes glistening with tears—and it was a kind of magic, the way her eyes revealed her soul. "*You're* my destiny. I stayed out of your head tonight because I want a future with you, Jeremy. One that isn't trapped in the past." She lifted her hand, stroking the cool tips of her fingers against the heat of his cheek in a way that felt as spiritual as it did sexual, the look in her eyes tender and soft, melting his heart. "I did it because I trust you, with everything that I am. But most of all, I did it because I love you."

In that moment, he was completely undone by her—by

every precious, exquisite detail, from her mind-drugging scent to the soft, silken feel of her body beneath his hands as he explored the feminine curve of her shoulder, the delicate line of her spine. But more than anything, he'd been undone by those three little words on her lips. Words he felt as if he'd waited a lifetime to hear.

There was so much he needed to say in return, so much he needed to explain, but first, he needed to make sure she understood exactly where they went from here. That he was in this for keeps…for forever. That he didn't want a night… but an endless eternity. "There isn't going to be any Mate Hunt—*ever*—because I'm going to be the *last* wolf hunting you down, Jillian. I'm not letting you run from me anymore."

"That's good, because I'm done running," Jillian whispered, while her head spun with a sweet, dizzying swirl of excitement. He watched her with a predatory expression of searing, savage sensuality, of barely restrained animal need, that made her painfully aware of every inch of her body, her skin tingling and warm. Stroking her fingertips across the sensual perfection of his mouth, his softly panting breath warm against her skin, she said, "I realized today that we could have lost everything without ever having given it a chance, and I can't live with that. I've been so afraid of losing you someday that I almost let you get away forever. I'm not going to let that happen, Jeremy. I can't. I need you too much."

He breathed deeply as their stare lengthened into a tangible, physical thing, the air between them swollen with lust and love, thick in her lungs, and he said, "You're trembling."

"I'm nervous," she admitted breathlessly.

He lifted one big, warm hand, and cradled her jaw. "You don't have to be afraid with me, Jillian."

"It's not that," she told him. "I just want you so badly. I feel as if I'm going to scream."

A low, husky chuckle rumbled in his chest. Lifting his other hand, he cupped her face in his palms once again, and in a ragged, groaning rush, he said, "God, I thought I had lost you tonight, sweetheart. Never again. I can't go through that again."

He held her tear-drenched stare, and she sensed that there was something more he wanted to tell her. "What? What is it?"

"Sayre came to see me today," he confessed in a quiet rasp.

"I know," she whispered, and she could sense his relief when she gave him a watery smile. "I'm so sorry, Jeremy. I should have told you myself, about the way of a witch and her heart, but I wasn't brave enough."

A rough sound burst from his throat, his green eyes glittering beneath the heavy weight of amber lashes. "I wish I could have made you understand how much you meant to me all those years ago. I wish I'd had the guts to tell you before how much I love you, because I do, Jillian. *I love you.* So much that it's terrified me for years, thinking we might never get this chance to make things right."

She gave a glad, shivery cry, and turned her face to press a tender kiss against the heat of his palm. Then, taking a deep breath for courage, she said, "Before we do this, there's something I need to tell you."

He caught a teardrop with his thumb, his own eyes damp as he asked, "What is it, angel?"

"I've never...that is, I mean..." She drew in another trembling breath, and forced the embarrassing words out. "I've never done this before."

"Done what?" he murmured, his glowing eyes blistering a greedy trail of possession over her face, her breasts, her belly...then lower.

"I'm still a virgin," she blurted out in a rush.

His gaze jerked instantly back to her face, green eyes wide with shock. "You're…what?" he asked thickly, his voice hoarse…strained.

"You heard me," she murmured, grinning at his stunned expression. "I only ever wanted you, Jeremy. No one else has ever touched me."

His cheekbones went dark with a hot rush of color, chest heaving as he drew in a deep, ragged gulp of air, before groaning a certain coarse four letter word.

When his powerful body began to tremble, she said, "Are you okay?"

"Of course I'm not okay," he said between his clenched teeth, running both hands back through his hair, the golden strands sifting between his long, tanned fingers. "How *the hell* am I going to control this? I have ten years' worth of hunger stored up, ready to unleash on you, and you—"

"Want the same thing," she cut in, *wanting* him to lose his control…to lose himself in their mating.

"How would you know what you want? You're a *virgin*," he groaned with a raspy sound of awe, the deep, velvet-rough timbre of his voice vibrating with emotion. If she hadn't already known she loved him, Jillian knew she would have tumbled at that sweet, shivery sound.

Hoping to soothe him, to put him at ease, she said, "I know you, Jeremy. I'm not afraid of you losing control. I don't have to get inside your head to know that I trust you, with my body and my heart. I'm sorry it took me so long, but if you're willing to give me the chance, I'll spend the rest of my life proving it to you."

"Proving it to me?" Jeremy stared down at the woman who owned his heart, his very soul, and prayed for the strength to make this *right*—to make this *good* for her. "Christ, Jillian. You don't need to prove anything to me, sweetheart."

A fresh wave of tears glistened in her eyes as she stared up at him, and he felt her love move through him like a wondrous, awe-inspiring miracle, nearly bringing him to his knees.

"Are you sure you're strong enough for this right now?" he asked, his concern obvious in the huskily spoken words, as well as his hunger.

"More than strong enough," she told him. "Sayre boosted my energy—and your touch doesn't weaken me. It makes me feel powerful, Jeremy. Makes me feel as if I could take on the world."

Wondering how he was going to hold himself together, he lifted her hands to his mouth and pressed a tender kiss to her delicate knuckles. "Then come to bed with me," he rasped in a dark, lust-thickened voice. "Let me show you how much you mean to me. Let me prove to you that I can't go on without you. I need you to breathe, Jillian. I need you to make me feel alive."

She wrapped her arms around his neck and gave him a shy smile. Sweeping her up into his arms, Jeremy carried her to his unmade bed, where he laid her out over the soft sheets, his throat tight with a deep, shattering wave of emotion at the sight of her lying in his bed. Finally, after all these years, *she was in his bed,* and he planned on keeping her there forever.

Half-terrified that he was moving too quickly for her, he struggled to keep the beast within him under tight control, but the sharp, cutting edge of craving was too much. And knowing she was all his—damn, he could barely take it. Too hungry to wait, his breath panting, pulse roaring in his ears, he tore off the borrowed shirt and moved over her, straddling her hips. Growling low in his throat, he cradled her breasts in his hands, so cool and soft and perfect, and then he was taking her into his mouth, desperate for every sweet, silken discovery. Her nipples, so pink and swollen, were exquisitely soft against the flat of his tongue, like ripe, succulent berries. Jeremy closed his mouth around one lush, delicate tip, suckling at its velvety thickness, a dark, primitive groan rumbling deep in his chest.

When he heard her cry out in passion, he lost it. Cursing the clinging denim of his jeans, Jeremy rolled to the side and fought them down his legs, then moved back over her, settling between her shyly parted thighs. A quick glance up at her face revealed eyes so dark, they looked midnight black beneath the shadowed veil of her lashes, her pale hair floating around her face, spread out across his pillow like a shimmering wave of summer sunshine. Her lips were parted, damp, her cheeks flushed with the rosy heat of desire.

A slow, wicked smile curled over his mouth, and Jeremy held her stare as he smoothed his hands up the petal-soft skin of her thighs, pressing them farther apart. Then he leaned forward and put his mouth on that most intimate, exquisite part of her.

She made a stunned sound in her throat, her white teeth sinking into the plump swell of her lower lip, and Jeremy kissed her deeper, the intoxicating taste of her rushing through his system with the scorching intensity of a flame, burning him alive. He opened her with his thumbs and lowered his gaze, while a harsh, erotic slide of words fell from his lips, the vision before him the most beautiful thing he'd ever seen. Moaning, he put his mouth to her again—and this time he kissed the damp, pink beauty of her sex hungrily, greedily…pushing his tongue into the silken depths of her body with a slow, rasping thrust.

"Jeremy," she sobbed, arching against him as he made

love to her with his mouth. His eyes stung from where she pulled his hair, but he didn't care. He loved her like this, so open and yielding before him. Her limbs trembled, restless with energy and need, her soft hands stroking him wherever she could reach, bathing his body with such a sweet, searing pleasure that his breath caught, his own need raging past the bounds of his control. He wanted to be everywhere at once. Wanted his mouth on her, his hands. Wanted his body buried deep inside her, their flesh sealed together, heart against heart. But most of all he wanted to give her pleasure. The most earth-shattering pleasure she'd ever known—and he wanted her to take it now.

Poised on the edge of something explosive, Jillian tangled her hands back in the cool silk of Jeremy's hair; his mouth hungry and hot and relentless between her thighs. One second she was climbing...and climbing, everything in her body pulling exquisitely tight, and then she was crashing over the edge, the orgasm melting through her in a shivering, incandescent rush of warm, liquid light, setting her on fire.

And just like the time in the forest, her power escaped in a violent burst of energy, shuddering through the room like a dizzying maelstrom. A picture fell off the far wall, the newspaper on his dresser scattering through the air in a flurry of pages. She didn't know how much time passed, how long she lay there trembling while the endless waves of ecstasy roared through her, but suddenly she was aware of drawing in deep, panting breaths of air, and Jeremy was whispering to her...his voice urgent and soft.

"You came so hard I thought you were going to pass out," he breathed against the tear-drenched corner of her eye, his powerful body shaking. "So beautiful," he murmured, smiling at her as she lifted the heavy weight of her lashes. "God, you should see your eyes, Jillian. They're like fire. You look like you're lit up inside."

She blinked at him lazily, her body boneless, muscles like candy that'd been left out in the summer sun. "I feel as if I'm melting."

"Mmm, you are," he moaned, reaching between her legs and slipping one thick finger into her. "Like sweet, sticky taffy, all honeyed and soft. I can't get enough of you."

His finger thrust deeper, hitting that tender sweet spot that set her ablaze, pushing her relentlessly toward another overwhelming burst of chaos before she'd even found her way back from the first one. Then he added a second finger, working them into her body, and she knew he was stretching her because she was small…and he wasn't.

"Jeremy," she gasped, her body buzzing, alive with another shocking current of pleasure. She was hot and slick and slippery, soaking his hand, years' worth of lust and hunger and craving rushing through her, unstoppable and overwhelming. "I can't think…"

"Good," he growled against the sensitive shell of her ear. "I don't want you thinking. I only want you feeling. I don't want anything in your head except what it feels like to have my hands on you, pushing you over the edge. What it feels like to have my body moving inside of yours, making you scream because it feels so damn good."

And then his strong, work-roughened hands were holding her face, and he was kissing her mouth in a tender, breathless, coaxing caress, pulling the emotion from her, until her cheeks were damp, her throat shaking, and at the same time she felt that hard, huge part of him pushing into her.

Jillian cried out in shock, arching beneath him. He held her down, anchoring her with his strength, and drove himself into her, heavy and strong, going deeper…deeper, working himself into her until she didn't think she could take any more of him. "Too much," she gasped, staring up at him in dazed amazement, shocked at the feel of him inside her, so thick and hot and deliciously hard.

A low, wicked rumble of laughter vibrated in his chest as he lowered his mouth back to hers. He nipped her bottom lip in an act that was as provocative as it was possessive, then licked away the sting, the heat between their bodies burning and damp. "Take all of me," he groaned, his eyes glowing golden as he held her stare, the smoky green completely eclipsed by the visceral sexuality of his beast. She shifted beneath him, spreading her legs wider, and he sank deeper into her, shuddering. "Jillian, I can feel it," he confessed in a dark, savage rasp. Threading their fingers together, his body a strong, beautiful shelter, he watched her through eyes that were bright with emotion. "All of it…"

He was struggling to explain, but she knew. He didn't have to say what he was feeling with words. She could see everything, every thought and emotion written on his beautiful face, carved into the intensity of his expression. The tendons in his neck were rigid with strain, the sharp points of his fangs glittering beneath the sensual curve of his upper lip.

He pressed his face into the hollow of her throat, his teeth scraping across her skin in a carnal act that only made her burn hotter, before returning to her lips, kissing her tongue-to-tongue. Taking her throaty cries into his mouth, he began moving over her, inside of her, the powerful muscles beneath his hot, slick skin flexing as he drove the pleasure up into her until it was impossible to breathe…to think…to hold it inside. All she could do was surrender to his body's relentless, breathtaking demand, and let the white-hot bliss sweep her away.

* * *

Grinding his jaw against the indescribable heaven of Jillian clenching around him in an endless, heart-stopping climax that once again sent chaos crashing through the room, Jeremy took her fragile wrists in his hands and pulled them over her head, stretching her out beneath him. He closed his eyes as sensations almost too good to bear poured through him, and struggled against the blistering need to come. He didn't want it to end too quickly. He wanted to drag it out, make it last forever, but it was too good. Good? Hell, it was blowing his goddamn mind.

He'd never lost himself in a woman—until now. Until this moment—until this woman who was everything to him. Always before, he'd held a part of himself back. He'd shared pieces of himself as he chose, but *never* his emotions. Sex had been a physical release, and though he could say with confidence that his past had left him damn good at it, nothing in his experience had prepared him for this—for being with Jillian. It left him feeling shaken and powerful all in the same breath; a constant, whirring explosion of ecstasy and hunger and tenderness.

With Jillian, everything slid into that perfect focus. He lost himself in his little witch, hyperaware of her slender body beneath his, so fragile and yet capable of so much strength. He opened his eyes to stare at her in wonder, the power she carried inside of her shimmering beneath her skin, lighting her up, her beauty so intense it almost hurt his eyes. He felt each breath she drew in, the way those breaths hitched when he pulled back and stroked back into her, thrusting his body harder, shafting her, stretching her deep inside. Felt the damp heat of her silken skin, his head hazy with the intoxicating scent of her flesh, her arousal, watching as the pleasure burned in her gaze like a hot, smoldering glow.

And most of all, he felt the love that burned inside of her. It rushed through him like a warm, gusting breeze, and his beast seethed with the need to stake its claim by sinking its teeth into her throat and making the bond that would join them forever. His gums burned from the heat of his fangs, his muscles cramping, needing to make that connection and cement the claim he was making on her body.

But not yet. Not this first time. This first time he wanted it to be about nothing but what burned between them, about the love that tied their hearts and lives and souls together for all eternity.

"I love you, Jillian," he gasped in a rough, shaken voice. He buried his face in the curve of her throat, his words hot against the silk of her skin. "I've always loved you. Always."

"I love you, too," she cried out softly, tangling her hands in his hair and pulling him to her, so that she could press kiss after kiss against his chin, his eyes, his throat.

He stiffened above her then, his body held hard and tight, buried deep inside of her, and Jillian felt the dark energy and restless power of him blast through her as he came, beautiful and raging. His eyes burned, the intensity of his stare holding her so that she couldn't look away. "Only you," he groaned, pressing his mouth to hers, spilling into her in a jaw-grinding climax that went on…and on…and on. "No one but you."

And as she followed him over, she knew that he meant every word.

With the soft warmth of sunlight on her face, Jillian opened her eyes to the sweetest feeling she'd ever known, as if everything bright and wonderful was hers for the taking, just waiting for her to stretch her arms and grab it. She pressed her fingertips to the bite marks in the side of her throat, evidence of the *blood bond* Jeremy had made with her during the beautiful, provocative, passion-drenched hours of the night, feeling so happy she didn't know how she held it all inside. Butterflies filled her stomach, her heart pounding a wild, wonderful cadence. She'd never imagined that making love could be so overwhelming and earth shattering, endlessly beautiful and intimate.

She longed to hold him in her arms, but remembered him pressing a lingering kiss to her lips when he'd climbed from bed, whispering for her to keep resting, explaining that Mason had called and he'd be back as soon as he could.

After borrowing his toothbrush, she washed her face, combed her hair with her fingers and slipped back into her clothes. She'd hung them up over the shower rod, so at least they were dry and warm, though she planned on sending him up to her house as soon as possible to get some of her clothes and makeup.

Opening the front door, she stepped out onto his front porch, squinting against the bright glare of sunshine, and found him standing beside his truck, his arm wrapped around Elise's shoulders. Elise had obviously borrowed some of Torrance's things, because the jeans were too short, as well as the sleeves of the thick cable-knit sweater she was wearing, her feet bare against the damp grass as she stood within Jeremy's embrace.

The wind picked up, surging around Jillian's body, and Jeremy lifted his gaze, his nostrils flaring as he scented her on the morning air. She smiled at him and waved, but her smile fell as she watched him frown and say something to Elise. The other woman nodded, turned and waved at Jillian, then strolled across the grass toward the Dillingers' cabin.

Wondering what was wrong, Jillian waited as he walked toward her, and suddenly she knew. She could see the shadow of worry in his eyes, but he had no reason to be alarmed. She trusted him, with all her heart. "Hey," she said softly, blushing at the thought of all the scintillating, intimate things they'd done to each other through the long, wonderful night.

He stared at her soft smile, and then an answering grin began to curl across his mouth. "You—"

"Didn't jump to the wrong conclusion when I saw you with Elise?" she finished for him. She gave a quiet laugh, tucking her hair behind her ear. "I love you. I believe in you. That means that I trust you, Jeremy."

He pulled her to him, crushing her against his chest. "I don't deserve you, Jillian," he whispered gruffly against her hair.

"I feel the same way about you," she admitted with a soft laugh, and turning her head as she returned his hug, she finally noticed that Eric's truck was parked down beside Mason's cabin. "Is Eric here?" she asked.

"Yeah, he showed up about twenty minutes ago to pick up Elise, since she wasn't in any shape to go home with him last night. We talked for a bit, and then he headed inside to see Mason. That's when Elise came outside to talk to me."

Jillian gave him a narrow look. "You didn't fight with him, did you?"

"Naw," he drawled, rolling his shoulder. "I wanted to hate him, but he's actually kind of okay. And it's hard to hold a grudge against a guy who helped save your life."

Her own shoulders shook with silent laughter. "I told you there was no reason for you to dislike him. We're just friends."

Looking sheepish, he said, "I know that *now.*"

"You know *everything* now," she whispered in a sultry drawl—and he stiffened against her, in more ways than one.

Shaking his head, his mouth curved in a wry smile. "Before I lose the small shred of control that's enabling me to stand here and act civilized, I wanted to tell you that Eric said everything's okay in town. I know you've probably been worried," he told her, running one palm down her spine in a soothing gesture. "But I want you to try and take it easy today. You've been through enough, Jillian. You need to give yourself a break."

Lowering her lashes, she murmured, "Then come back to bed with me."

His hand went still. "If I come back to bed with you, I'm going to make love to you," he warned in a soft growl.

She rolled her eyes, laughing. "Well, geez, that's what I was kinda hoping for."

He gave a rich, sexy chuckle, and they moved together to head back inside, when her father's Jeep pulled into the Alley, rolling to a slow stop in front of Jeremy's cabin. Unfolding his stocky body from the cab, Bill Murphy stepped around his front bumper, coming to a stop at the bottom of the porch steps.

"You okay?" he asked, giving her a pointed look of fatherly concern, his hands rubbing together in an unexpected show of nerves.

"I'm wonderful," Jillian said with a smile, and Jeremy hugged her closer to his side, pressing a soft kiss to the top of her head.

Her father watched the tender exchange, his gray eyes narrowed, and shoved his restless hands into his front pockets. "I've come to pick up Sayre from Dillinger's place, but figured I ought to use the time to go ahead and do what's right. I know you may hate me because of this, Jilly, but considering how things have worked out, there's something I need to tell you. The record needs to be set straight, and I like to think that I'm man enough to own up to my mistakes."

She nodded, her throat too tight for words.

"I let rumors poison my opinion," her father said in a gritty voice, "and so I lied to you, Jillian. I never saw Jeremy with that Danna girl all those years ago. Your mom, she'd seen you kissing him that day. We did what we thought was right at the time, and told you I'd seen him with her. It was a lie, honey. Far as I know, he hadn't been involved with anyone since you came home from school."

Jeremy stiffened beside her, and she knew the news had shocked him, since he'd always believed one of her friends had told her he'd been messing around with Danna. "Mother I would have been suspicious of," she said unsteadily, "but you knew I would believe it if it came from you."

"I'm sorry," he replied, his tone solemn with regret. "I thought I was doing the right thing at the time, saving you from heartbreak, but I made a mistake. I hope…I hope one day that you'll forgive me. I was only trying to do what I thought was right for you."

She nodded again, swallowing at the tears gathering in her throat, not knowing what to say. Finally, he gave a deep sigh. "I should be going now, but your mother and I would like to invite you both to dinner tonight."

At those gruff words, she felt the blood drain from her face. "Oh…uh, we can't pos—"

"We'd love to," Jeremy interrupted, giving her hip a slow, encouraging caress. "What time should we be there?"

"'Bout seven," her father called out, heading back to his Jeep. He stopped in front of the Dillingers' cabin, where Sayre stood waiting for him. She waved goodbye to them, climbed into the Jeep, and a moment later, they drove away, while Jillian shook her head in slow amazement. "Jeremy," she whispered, "you don't have to do this for me—"

"I have to do this for *us*," he told her, lifting her chin with the edge of his knuckles. "I want a family, Jillian. I want our kids to have two sets of grandparents who spoil them rotten."

"It isn't fair," she argued. "After everything that's happened, *they* should come to *you*."

"If you're worried about my pride, beautiful, don't be. I have you, and that's all that matters. Everything else pales in comparison. I want to make things right with your parents." Pulling her against his chest, he nuzzled her throat as he said, "Your dad finally did the right thing, but I'm glad you found faith in me without his confession."

Giving him a trembling smile, Jillian swiped at the tears glistening on her cheeks. "I'm so sorry, Jeremy. Will you ever forgive me for all the years we've wasted?"

"I've been in your heart," he whispered, holding her close; a beautiful look of love in his hazel eyes that dazzled her— that made her believe in miracles. "I know what you feel for me, Jillian. I know everything. And I love you more now than ever before, as impossible as that sounds, since I've been half mad for you for what feels like forever."

Then he kissed her, his hands slipping up her sides, and Jillian gave herself up to the wonder of having everything she wanted in the world right at her fingertips.

Chapter 17

Later that afternoon, everyone had gathered in the Dillingers'
kitchen, while Jeremy relayed the harrowing tale of Elise's
attack, and his subsequent confrontation with Stefan Drake.
Carla Reyes and Wyatt Pallaton had driven up from Covington with the Doucets, so the Runners were all there to hear the
accounting.

Even Dylan had come for the meeting, standing with his
back to the stove, a visible tension seeming to ride the rigid
lines of his lean body. Brody stood in brooding silence by the
bay window, his dark gaze fixed belligerently on the Elder,
while Cian lounged with his shoulder propped against the
archway leading into the living room. Everyone else sat in
chairs around the large breakfast table, its polished surface
littered with steaming cups of coffee and tea.

And though Jeremy had shared with them the information
he and Jillian had learned about Helen Drake, he'd admitted

only that it came from a "reliable source." Not that he didn't trust Dylan, but he'd told Pippa he wouldn't involve her and he intended to keep his word.

Now, as he finished his account, the room was so still...so quiet, you could hear the gurgle of water in the pipes buried deep within the walls of the cabin. It was into this heavy, thought-filled silence that Mason finally said, "You've done good, man."

"Yeah, right," Jeremy snorted, his tone thick with disgust. "I was sent back to Shadow Peak to hunt down the traitor. Last I checked, we still didn't have him, because I let him go."

"You did the right thing," Mason argued. "I'd rather have you both alive, than Drake dead and you facing your own execution. And you got us exactly what we needed. Hell, it's because of you that we're now certain Drake's the one we want, and we've got a clearer understanding of what we're dealing with."

"So we know Drake's behind the rogues, but do we still think he's responsible for the human kills?" Reyes asked, folding her hands around the warmth of her coffee mug, her brow furrowed beneath the pale fringe of her bangs.

"Directly...indirectly." Jeremy released a harsh sigh. "Who knows? At this point, nothing that bastard does could surprise me."

"If he isn't the one," Brody rumbled in a deep, scratchy baritone, "we said before that it could be one of his followers."

"Hell, one of his followers," Mason muttered, "or his accomplice."

A strange energy filled the room as everyone—with the exclusion of himself, Jillian and Torrance, who had already been told the news before the others had arrived—narrowed their eyes on his partner.

"His accomplice?" Wyatt grunted, the Runner's normally stoic expression creased in a scowl. "What the hell does that mean?"

"It means that I have some new information to share with you," Mason told them, his tone as grim as the dark look in his eyes. "Which brings us to the second reason for this meeting. I had a call from my father today."

"And what good news does Robert have to share with us this time?" Cian drawled, arching one raven brow in a cynical lift. It had been Robert Dillinger who told the Runners of an Elder's ability to teach another to dayshift. Until that time, they'd been unaware of the carefully guarded secret, and it was this discovery that had first pointed them toward Stefan Drake in their search for the traitor. Scanning the faces of his friends and colleagues, Jeremy realized that no one looked happy at the prospect of a new twist in an investigation that was already frustrating them at every turn.

"You're not going to like it," Mason warned them, rubbing at the back of his neck.

"Now why doesn't that surprise us?" Brody snorted.

Leaning back in his chair, Mason's golden-brown gaze moved from Runner to Runner as he began to explain. "After what happened in Shadow Peak yesterday, Graham asked my father for some help searching the library of ancient texts that belong to the League. Together, they poured over every volume, and found an archaic reference to an interesting legend."

"A legend?" Dylan repeated, the corners of his mouth pulled in a skeptical frown.

"I know it sounds crazy," Mason sighed, "but they just might be on to something. According to the archives, a Lycan from one of the European packs named Azakiel discovered a way to combine his 'inner power,' or whatever you want to call it, with another Elder. Together, they were strong enough to pull another's beast—one that he could then command to do as he chose. It was considered the ultimate dark art, enabling Azakiel to control his followers, forcing them to commit unspeakable crimes at his bidding, until the day they finally banded together and rebelled, murdering him for his cruelty."

"Happy story," Reyes murmured dryly, rubbing her hands up and down her arms as if to ward off a chill.

"Are you trying to tell us that Graham believes Drake learned about this dark art, and now there's another Elder who's helping him perform some kind of ancient hocus pocus?" Cian questioned, stroking his jaw.

"It makes sense that there was someone with him," Jillian murmured, and Jeremy knew she was thinking of Elise's whispered confession in the truck. "Elise told us that she felt another's presence in her mind, but couldn't identify them. Her father's voice was the only one controlling her, telling her what to do."

"Having one psychotic Elder bent on destruction was bad enough," Brody muttered, his scarred features hardened with worry. "If we're hunting two… Christ, we're going to be in some serious trouble."

"And why would anyone be willing to help Drake?" Wyatt snorted, leaning back in his chair. "The guy's a total asshole."

"Who knows." Jeremy sighed, wishing he'd been able to uncover the answers they still needed. "Maybe they're as evil as he is. Maybe they're insane. Or maybe he's got something on them and they don't have a choice."

Cian's brows lifted with interest. "You mean, like blackmail?"

"Maybe," he said, rolling his shoulder. "I don't think we can rule out anything yet. This could turn out to be—"

"This could turn out to be a crock," Dylan cut in, his words sharp with the biting edge of impatience. "I can't believe you're all actually buying in to this legend crap. What's next? Are we going to hold a séance? Buy silver bullets and hang garlic over our doors?"

"Garlic's to ward off vampires, not werewolves," Cian murmured. "But it doesn't work."

"My point," Dylan snarled, glaring at the grinning Irishman, "is that we need to ground ourselves in reality—*not* fantasy."

"Whether you believe the legend or not, Dylan, Drake *was* pulling the wolves out of those Lycans," Jillian whispered. "We know this puts you in a terrible position, but you're going to have to watch your back and be careful. The League *is* being affected by his corruption, which means your life is in danger as much as ours. No matter how you look at it, this is a sound threat."

"This is bullshit."

"Watch it," Jeremy growled.

Dylan worked his jaw, his chest rising and falling, hands clenched against the edge of the stove so tightly his knuckles had turned white. "Look, I know Drake's a psychotic son of a bitch who needs to be dealt with, but if you keep pointing fingers at the League, pretty soon there won't be anything left of us. I don't know how to explain what happened yesterday, but I *do* know that I'm not ready to see the entire structure that holds the Silvercrest together fall apart. Believe that Drake has this damn power if you want—but don't keep hurling accusations at the rest of us. If there *is* an accomplice, maybe he's found a way to use one of his minions. Hell, maybe it was Sheffield himself. I just don't think we should jump to conclusions until—"

"Until what?" Brody rasped, his personal dislike for the Elder evident in his aggressive tone. "Until we're all dead?"

"Until we know more!" Dylan shouted, his tenuous hold

on his temper fraying before their eyes in an uncharacteristic burst of fury. "We need facts. Not a goddamn bedtime story!"

"That's enough," Jeremy grunted, not liking where this conversation was headed. Dylan was their closest link to the League and they needed his cooperation—not his resentment. "We know you're under a lot of pressure, but you're either with us in this or you're not. Things are getting too complicated for there to be any middle ground or indecision."

Glaring at Jeremy, Dylan leaned back against the stove, his arms crossed over his chest. "Am I getting a slap on the wrist for not playing nice with the other kids?"

"We're not asking you to agree with us on everything," Mason murmured, his tone calm as he eyed his friend with a mixture of frustration and concern. "You're an Elder, not a Runner, which means that although we're friends, we stand on different sides of the fence. We understand that, and we've never asked you to do anything that would compromise your job. But we need to know that you're at least willing to work with us."

"You know I am, Mase." Dylan scrubbed his hands down his face, sounding as haggard as he looked. "But these are delicate times for the Silvercrest. We can't go making blind accusations without some solid proof to back them up. The pack would have your throats if you did. Too many of them are being pulled in by Drake's 'pure-blood' propaganda, looking up to him as if he's some kind of god."

"Solid proof?" Jeremy said roughly. "Exactly how much proof are you after? We have more than enough on Drake for you to make a formal accusation to the League. Hell, we have motive and a goddamn confession!"

"If I'm going to take this before the League," Dylan argued, "I need more than a runaway wife and hatred. More than the word of a Runner who threatened to kill the very Elder he's accusing. I need cold, hard facts. And you don't have any!"

"What about Elise?" Jillian offered.

"You know what he'd say." Dylan sighed. "Drake would just make Elise look like a fool, claiming her story was the paranoid ranting of an emotionally scarred young woman."

"Then nothing's going to be done," Jillian said in a low, shaken voice. "I can't believe he's going to get away with this, after what he did to her."

"He isn't going to get away with anything," Jeremy promised, squeezing her hand while slanting a sharp look of warning at Dylan to keep quiet. The Elder narrowed his eyes, his mouth pressed into a hard, flat line, and then he pushed away from the stove, stalking out of the room. A few seconds later, the front door slammed shut behind him.

"Well, that was fun," Cian muttered under his breath.

"I think now would be a good time to let our tempers cool," Mason stated quietly, "and give the information we've learned a chance to sink in. We can meet back here in the morning."

Weary nods of agreement went around the room, but before anyone could make a move to leave, Jeremy stood and said, "Hold up, guys. Just stay put for a minute."

With a wry smile curving his mouth, he shot a quick wink at Jillian before turning back to the roomful of curious faces. "Before we head out, I wanted to go ahead and let you all know that I'm going to be staying in Shadow Peak. Permanently."

Stunned silence met the outrageous announcement, until Jillian shook herself out of her stupor, saying, "Ooh, no, you're not."

"Ooh, yes, I am," Jeremy countered with a slow, deliciously warm smile. "Shadow Peak is where you belong, and wherever you are, that's where I'll be."

"Jeremy," she whispered, pressing her hand to her heart, its rhythm rapid and urgent beneath her palm. "What are you thinking? Anyone who knows you *knows* that you wouldn't be happy in town."

Pulling her to her feet, Jeremy lifted his hand and cupped her jaw, rubbing his thumb against her trembling lower lip. "I'll be happy wherever you are, honey. I'll still work with these jackasses," he snorted, cutting a cocky smirk at his fellow Runners—who were watching them with rapt fascination—before focusing that breathtaking hazel gaze back on her. "But I'll *live* with you."

"I know you don't want this," she said in a shivery rush, her eyes hot with the threat of tears. There was no way she was going to let him make that kind of sacrifice for her.

"Just because you own my heart," he admitted in a warm, sexy drawl, "doesn't mean you can tell me what I want, sweetheart. What I want more than anything is for you to be happy."

"But you're a Bloodrunner!"

His smile fell, replaced by a dark look of determination. "I'm a man," he said firmly, gripping her chin, demanding she hold his brilliant stare. "One who's tired of being put in a box. I'll always be a Bloodrunner, but I'll also be the Spirit Walker's mate." His expression shifted, the devilish, wicked grin playing softly at his mouth again, and then he was cradling her face in his warm, rough palms. "Trust me, baby. I know what I want."

"But I'm tired of being put in a box, too," she argued, grasping on to his muscled wrists. "If this is going to work, we compromise. Because while I may be the pack's Spirit

Walker, I'm *also* a Bloodrunner's mate. So we'll split our time between Shadow Peak *and* the Alley. And th-that's my final offer. Take it or leave it."

He held her gaze with a vivid intensity that stole her breath, and then he laughed—the rich, warm sound of happiness rumbling up from deep within his chest—and pulled her into his arms. She could feel the uneasy tension in the warm, cinnamon-scented kitchen begin to lessen, the Runners releasing quiet sighs of relief as Jeremy said, "Are you sure that's what you want?"

"Yes, that's exactly what I want," she told him, thinking that it didn't matter where they lived, so long as they were together. But she was awed by the depth of his love, stunned that he'd been willing to stay in Shadow Peak with her permanently, even though he hated it there, simply because he thought it would make her happy.

Sensing his sudden tension, Jillian watched as a shadow fell over the heat in his eyes, his grip tightening as he said, "Drake could demand you step down for this, Jillian."

"Let Drake do his worst," she murmured, smiling, having already come to a decision on that front. "Even if he has my title rescinded, I can still continue to help people. Being Spirit Walker isn't something they can take away from me so easily, and I'm not going to let fear of the League affect my decision. I've done enough of that. This is our life, Jeremy. Not theirs."

"I don't want you to regret this," he said in a low voice, searching her eyes.

"Jeremy, this is what I want," she asserted with a soft laugh, feeling as if her smile, her happiness, were blooming up from the depths of her soul. "As a matter of fact, I already talked to Graham about it yesterday, when he was here, and told him to set up a meeting. Tomorrow I'll go before the League and declare my intention to live wherever you are."

His eyes went wide. "You already told him?"

Jillian snuffled a giggle under her breath at his stunned expression, and threw her arms around his neck. "Sure did."

"Christ, you're incredible," he rumbled in a deep sexy rasp, running his hands down her back in a touch that spoke of possession and tenderness, as well as hunger and need. "And I love you so damn much."

"I bet I love you more," she teased.

"Hmm... Not possible," Jeremy growled, already lowering his lips to hers. He'd just found the heat of her mouth, when Cian's laughing voice suddenly drawled, "I'm happy as hell you two sorted that all out, but you need to take this somewhere private before I get jealous."

A short bark of laughter jerked from his throat, but Jillian made a strangled sound of mortification, obviously having forgotten their audience, and buried her face against his chest. Knowing she was embarrassed, Jeremy winked at his grinning friends, swept her up into his arms, and headed for the door, while she hid her face in the curve of his shoulder, her skin warm with what he suspected was a killer blush.

"Good luck at dinner tonight," Mason called out, just before they disappeared into the living room.

"Thanks," he drawled, his tone dry. "I'll take all the luck I can get."

A moment later, he was carrying her through the front door and out into the lavender twilight. Jeremy took a deep, refreshing breath, enjoying the spray of rain that had mellowed to a fine, thin mist, while Jillian made a muffled protest about being carried. Grinning to himself, he hugged her closer to his chest. "I know you're not weak, and I know you're a tough little thing, but... just let me hold you," he murmured. "I still haven't gotten over the fear that I'd never be able to do this again."

"You'll always be able to hold me," she whispered, and his body tensed at the erotic feel of her lips moving against his skin. "Because I'll always be with you, Jeremy."

It was harder than he'd thought it would be, swallowing the lump of emotion that settled into his throat at the sweetness of her words. When they reached his front door, he carefully set her on her feet, the top of her head not even coming to his chin, and fished his keys out of his back pocket.

Once the door was open, Jeremy ushered her inside, shutting the door behind him with his foot, ruefully aware that he was as nervous as a teenager on his first date, if not more. He gathered her close, gave a soft, wanting kiss to the corner of her mouth, then buried his nose in the silken fall of her hair, breathing in her warm, sweet scent. Taking her face in his hands, he smoothed his thumbs over her delicate skin as he said, "There's something I want to ask you."

She shivered, her eyes going big and wide.

Dropping to his knees, Jeremy clutched her narrow hips and pressed his face into the giving softness of her belly, then reached into his front pocket. Catching her left hand, he pulled it to his mouth, pressing his lips against the fragile skin, then turned it over and laid a glittering sapphire and diamond ring in her palm.

"Ohmygod," she gasped, and tears overflowed her eyes, the rich, velvety brown shimmering and bright, like sunshine.

"This was my grandmother's," he told her, holding her glistening stare. "I wanted to give this to you a long time ago, but things went wrong. If you let me, Jillian, I promise I'll spend the rest of my life making them go right."

"Jeremy," she whispered, and a fine, delicate vibration tremored through her, her lips parted for the excited rush of her breath.

"I love you, Jillian Louise Murphy," he said huskily. "For

always and forever. Will you be my wife? Grow old with me? Let me cherish you for the rest of our lives?"

Her mouth trembled, dewy and soft and too tempting to resist, and then she gave him a blinding, breathtaking smile. "Yes! God, yes. A million yeses!"

"Thank god," he groaned, smiling as he pulled her to the floor with him, his heart so full it felt as if it would burst from his chest. Jeremy slipped the ring on her finger, then sealed the poignant act by taking her mouth in a searing, head spinning kiss as he laid her across the floor. Then he took it again, as he covered her with his body…and again as he thrust inside of her…

Then again…and again…and again.

* * * * *

Look for LAST WOLF WATCHING
by Rhyannon Byrd—the exciting conclusion
in the BLOODRUNNERS miniseries
from Silhouette Nocturne.

Follow Michaela and Brody on their fierce journey
to find the truth and face the demons from the past,
as they reach the heart of the battle between
the Runners and the rogues.

Here is a sneak preview of book three,
LAST WOLF WATCHING.

Michaela squinted, struggling to see through the impenetrable darkness. Everyone looked toward the Elders, but she knew Brody Carter still watched her. Michaela could feel the power of his gaze. Its heat. Its strength. And something that felt strangely like anger, though he had no reason to have any emotion toward her. Strangers from different worlds, brought together beneath the heavy silver moon on a night made for hell itself. That was their only connection.

The second she finished that thought, she knew it was a lie. But she couldn't deal with it now. Not tonight. Not when her whole world balanced on the edge of destruction.

Willing her backbone to keep her upright, Michaela Doucet focused on the towering blaze of a roaring bonfire that rose from the far side of the clearing, its orange flames burning with maniacal zeal against the inky black curtain of the night. Many of the Lycans had already shifted into their preternatural shapes, their fur-covered bodies standing like monstrous shadows at the edges of the forest as they waited with restless expectancy for her brother.

Her nineteen-year-old brother, Max had been attacked by a rogue werewolf—a Lycan who preyed upon humans for food. Max had been bitten in the attack, which meant he was no longer human, but a breed of creature that existed between the two worlds of man and beast, much like the Bloodrunners themselves.

The Elders parted, and two hulking shapes emerged from the trees. In their wolf forms, the Lycans stood over seven feet tall, their legs bent at an odd angle as they stalked forward. They each held a thick chain that had been wound around their inside wrists, the twin lengths leading back into the shadows. The Lycans had taken no more than a few steps when they jerked on the chains, and her brother appeared.

Bound like an animal.

Biting at her trembling lower lip, she glanced left, then right, surprised to see that others had joined her. Now the Bloodrunners and their family and friends stood as a united force against the Silvercrest pack, which had yet to accept the fact that something sinister was eating away at its foundation—something that would rip down the protective walls that separated their world from the humans'. It occurred to Michaela that loyalties were being announced tonight—a separation made between those who would stand with the Runners in their fight against the rogues and those who blindly supported the pack's refusal to face reality. But all she could focus on was her brother. Max looked so hurt...so terrified.

"Leave him alone," she screamed, her soft-soled, black satin slip-ons struggling for purchase in the damp earth as she rushed toward Max, only to find herself lifted off the ground when a hard, heavily muscled arm clamped around her waist from behind, pulling her clear off her feet. "Dammit, let me down!" she snarled, unable to take her eyes off her brother as the golden-eyed Lycan kicked him.

Mindless with heartache and rage, Michaela clawed at the arm holding her, kicking her heels against whatever part of her captor's legs she could reach. "Stop it," a deep, husky voice grunted in her ear. "You're not helping him by losing it. I give you my word he'll survive the ceremony, but you have to keep it together."

"Nooooo!" she screamed, too hysterical to listen to reason. "You're monsters! All of you! Look what you've done to him! How dare you! *How dare you!*"

The arm tightened with a powerful flex of muscle, cinching her waist. Her breath sucked in on a sharp, wailing gasp.

"Shut up before you get both yourself and your brother killed. I will *not* let that happen. Do you understand me?" her captor growled, shaking her so hard that her teeth clicked together. "Do you understand me, Doucet?"

"Dammit," she cried, stricken as she watched one of the guards grab Max by his hair. Around them Lycans huffed and growled as they watched the spectacle, while others outright howled for the show to begin.

"That's enough!" the voice seethed in her ear. "They'll tear you apart before you even reach him, and I'll be damned if I'm going to stand here and watch you die."

Suddenly, through the haze of fear and agony and outrage in her mind, she finally recognized who'd caught her. *Brody.*

He held her in his arms, her body locked against his powerful form, her back to the burning heat of his chest. A low, keening sound of anguish tore through her, and her head dropped forward as hoarse sobs of pain ripped from her throat. "Let me go. I have to help him. *Please,*" she begged brokenly, knowing only that she needed to get to Max. "Let me go, Brody."

He muttered something against her hair, his breath warm against her scalp, and Michaela could have sworn it was a single word.... But she must have heard wrong. She was too upset. Too furious. Too terrified. She must be out of her mind.

Because it sounded as if he'd quietly snarled the word *never.*

Silhouette

nocturne™

THE FINAL INSTALLMENT OF THE BLOODRUNNERS TRILOGY

Last Wolf Watching

Runner Brody Carter has found his match in
Michaela Doucet, a human with unusual psychic powers.
When Michaela's brother is threatened, Brody becomes
her protector, and suddenly not only has to protect her
from her enemies but also from himself....

LOOK FOR
LAST WOLF WATCHING
BY
RHYANNON BYRD

Available May 2008 wherever you buy books.

Dramatic and Sensual Tales of Paranormal Romance

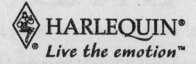

HARLEQUIN® *Romance*®

Western Weddings

Jason Welborn was convinced that his business
partner's daughter, Jenny, had come to claim her share
in the business. But Jenny seemed determined to win
him over, and the more he tried to push her away, the
more feisty Jenny's response. Slowly but surely she
was starting to get under Jason's skin....

Look for

Coming Home to the Cattleman

by

JUDY CHRISTENBERRY

Available May wherever you buy books.

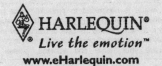

HARLEQUIN®
Live the emotion™
www.eHarlequin.com

HRI7511

REQUEST YOUR FREE BOOKS!

2 FREE NOVELS PLUS 2 FREE GIFTS!

Silhouette®

nocturne™

Dramatic and Sensual Tales of Paranormal Romance.

YES! Please send me 2 FREE Silhouette® Nocturne™ novels and my 2 FREE gifts (gifts are worth about $10). After receiving them, if I don't wish to receive any more books, I can return the shipping statement marked "cancel." If I don't cancel, I will receive 4 brand-new novels every other month and be billed just $4.47 per book in the U.S. or $4.99 per book in Canada, plus 25¢ shipping and handling per book plus applicable taxes, if any*. That's a savings of about 15% off the cover price! I understand that accepting the 2 free books and gifts places me under no obligation to buy anything. I can always return a shipment and cancel at any time. Even if I never buy another book from Silhouette, the two free books and gifts are mine to keep forever.

238 SDN ELS4 338 SDN ELXG

Name	(PLEASE PRINT)

Address	Apt. #

City	State/Prov.	Zip/Postal Code

Signature (if under 18, a parent or guardian must sign)

Mail to the **Silhouette Reader Service:**
IN U.S.A.: P.O. Box 1867, Buffalo, NY 14240-1867
IN CANADA: P.O. Box 609, Fort Erie, Ontario L2A 5X3

Not valid to current subscribers of Silhouette Nocturne books.

Want to try two free books from another line?
Call 1-800-873-8635 or visit www.morefreebooks.com.

* Terms and prices subject to change without notice. N.Y. residents add applicable sales tax. Canadian residents will be charged applicable provinaal taxes and GST. This offer is limited to one order per household. All orders subject to approval. Credit or debit balances in a customer's account(s) may be offset by any other outstanding balance owed by or to the customer. Please allow 4 to 6 weeks for delivery. Offer available while quantities last.

Your Privacy: Silhouette is committed to protecting your privacy. Our Privacy Policy is available online at www.eHarlequin.com or upon request from the Reader Service. From time to time we make our lists of customers available to reputable third parties who may have a product or service of interest to you. If you would prefer we not share your name and address, please check here. ☐

SN08

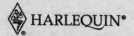

HARLEQUIN®

American ★ Romance®

Three Boys and a Baby

When Ella Garvey's eight-year-old twins and
their best friend, Dillon, discover an abandoned
baby girl, they fear she will be put in jail—
or worse! They decide to take matters into their
own hands and run away. Luckily the outlaws are
found quickly…and Ella finds a second chance
at love—with Dillon's dad, Jackson.

LOOK FOR
Three Boys and a Baby
BY
LAURA MARIE ALTOM

Available May
wherever you buy books.

LOVE, HOME & HAPPINESS

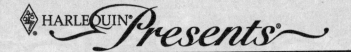

Don't forget Harlequin Presents EXTRA
now brings you a powerful new collection
every month featuring four books!

Be sure not to miss any of the titles in

In the Greek Tycoon's Bed,

available May 13:

THE GREEK'S
FORBIDDEN BRIDE
by Cathy Williams

THE GREEK TYCOON'S
UNEXPECTED WIFE
by Annie West

THE GREEK TYCOON'S
VIRGIN MISTRESS
by Chantelle Shaw

THE GIANNAKIS BRIDE
by Catherine Spencer

Silhouette

nocturne™

COMING NEXT MONTH

#39 LAST WOLF WATCHING • Rhyannon Byrd
Bloodrunners

Brody Carter never acted on impulse—until he had to protect Michaela Doucet. A fiery psychic, the Cajun made his beast crazed, and drew his hunger. Now, as they join forces to hunt down a threat to their pack, can Brody finally let go of his own demons?

#40 SCIONS: INSURRECTION • Patrice Michelle
Scions

Investigating the mafia has NYPD detective Kaitlyn McKinney knee-deep in a supernatural war. Her only ally: Landon Rourke, a werewolf who has no love for the vampires in his city. But the secret he holds is the darkest of them all—setting everyone's tempers and passions flaring.

SNCNM0408